'53

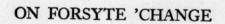

ON FORSYTE 'CHANGE

On Forsyte 'Change

by
John Galsworthy

1930
Charles Scribner's Sons
New York

TO
H. VINCENT MARROT

CONTENTS

FOREWORD

TO

"ON FORSYTE 'CHANGE"

BEFORE a long suffering public and still more long suffering critics, I lay this volume of apocryphal Forsyte tales, pleading the two excuses: That it is hard to part suddenly and finally from those with whom one has lived so long; and, that these footnotes do really, I think, help to fill in and round out the chronicles of the Forsyte family.

They have all been written since 'Swan Song' was finished, but in place they come between the Saga and the Comedy, for without the Saga they would not be understood, and they are over before the Comedy begins.

In the hope of forgiveness I send them forth.

JOHN GALSWORTHY.

THE BUCKLES OF SUPERIOR DOSSET
1821–1863

THE BUCKLES OF SUPERIOR DOSSET

IN the year 1821 'Superior Dosset' Forsyte came to Town
—if not precisely on a milk-white pony. According to
the testimony of Aunt Ann, noted for precision, to young
Jolyon on holiday from Eton, the migration from Bosport
was in fact tribal and effected in two post-shays and the
Highflyer coach.

"It was after our dear mother's death, and our father—
that is your grandfather, Jo dear,—was very taciturn on the
journey; he was never a man who showed his feelings. I
had your Aunt Susan in arms, and your Uncle Timothy—
two years old, such an interesting child, in the first post-
shay with your grandfather. And your dear father, he was
so dependable and very like you—he must have been fifteen
then, just your age—he had your Aunts Juley and Hester
with him and your Uncle Nicholas, who was four, in the
second post-shay; and your Uncle James and Swithin and
Roger were on the coach. I am afraid Swithin was very
naughty with his pea-shooter on the journey. We started
early in the morning, and we all went for the night to your
Great-Uncle Edgar's at Primrose Hill. I remember he still
wore knee-breeches and a very large bunch of seals. Of
course, *we* were all in black. Your grandfather wore black
for two years after our dear mother's death; he felt it very
much, though he never said anything."

"What was he like, Auntie?"

"Strongly-built, my dear, with a high colour. In those
days they drank a great deal of wine, especially Madeira."

"But what was he?"

"He began as a mason, dear."

"A Freemason?"

"Not at first. A stonemason. You see, *his* father was a farmer, and he apprenticed your grandfather to a stonemason, so that he should learn all about building. I think it was a very wise decision, because in those days there were such opportunities for builders, so your grandfather soon made his way. He was becoming quite a warm man when we came to London." And Aunt Ann's shrewd eyes appraised her nephew.

He had risen, and was standing, slender in his first tail-coat, against the mantelpiece, looking downward at his boots. Elegant the dear boy looked, but a little embarrassed, as if his nerves had received a shock. Of course, he was at Eton among the nobility. And she said with decision:

"We should never be ashamed of our origin, dear Jo. The Forsytes are very good country stock, and have always been men of their word, and that is the great thing. And our dear mother was a lady in every respect. Her name was Pierce—a Devonshire family—and she was the daughter of a solicitor at Bosport who was very respected. He died bankrupt because his partner ran away with some funds, and all his fortune went to make up the loss. She had a sweet face and was most particular how we spoke and behaved. This is her miniature."

Young Jolyon moved over and saw an oval face with fair hair parted in the middle and drawn in curves across the forehead, dark grey eyes looking up at him from rather deep beneath the brows, a chin with a delicate point, and shoulders shrouded in lace.

"Your grandfather was devoted to her in his way. For years after we first came to London he worked all day long, and at night I used to see him sitting up in his little study with his plans and his estimates—he couldn't bear to go to

bed. And then he took to horse exercise. It was such a mercy."

Young Jolyon looked up. His brow had cleared, as if his grandfather had at last done something creditable.

"Of course, on the farm, when he was a boy, he used to ride. And when he took to it again, he went riding every day until his gout got too bad."

"Oh! had he gout, too, Aunt Ann?"

"Yes, dear, gout was much more prevalent then than it is now. In same ways your grandfather was rather like your Uncle Swithin, only much shorter. He was fond of a horse, and quite a judge of wine."

Young Jolyon caressed his waistcoat, as if smothering emotion at these marks of gentility, subtle enough to see that his Aunt was watching him for signs of snobbery.

"Where did you live, Auntie?"

"Well, at first, dear, we took a house on Primose Hill close to your Great-Uncle Edgar. We lived there many years till we moved into a house of our own that your grandfather built, in St. John's Wood; and there we lived till his death in 1850, when we came here, of course, with your Uncle Timothy."

"What sort of houses did my grandfather build, Auntie?"

"I don't know that I ever saw any, dear, except the one we lived in. But I believe they were always very good value. At first I think they were mostly out Fulham way, and some were at Brighton, but later they were in St. John's Wood. That was then the coming part of London. He was not at all what is called a Jerry-builder. He had a funny nickname among his cronies—'Superior Dosset'."

"Why?"

"Well, for one thing he never liked being called a Dorsetshire man, he always said he was born just over the border in Devonshire, though the parish was in Dorset and the

Church, but he always looked down on Dorsetshire people
—he used to say they were a cocky lot—he had funny ex-
pressions; and that made them tease him. He was quite a
character. Some people, of course, might have called him
perverse."

"And how did he dress, Auntie?"

Aunt Ann replaced the miniature with her long thin
fingers, and from the little drawer took forth another.

"That is your grandfather, my dear—painted in 1820,
just before our dear mother's death."

Young Jolyon saw a florid face, clean-shaven, with eyebrows running a little up and bumps above them, a wide
rather fleshy mouth, a straight broad nose, a broad cleft chin;
light eyes that seemed to hold a jape under their thick lids;
brown hair brushed back from a well-formed forehead, a
neck swathed in a white stock, a blue coat short-waisted and
with tails, a double waistcoat light-coloured, a bunch of seals
on a black ribbon—no lower half to him at all.

"Did he wear trousers?"

"Yes, dear, generally buff, I think, till after our mother's
death. But in the evening he wore knee-breeches, and his
shoes had buckles. I still have them. Some day I shall give
them to you, because after your dear father you will be the
head of the family, just as my father was in his day."

"Oh! was my grandfather the eldest too?"

"Yes, like his father before him; the name Jolyon goes
with that. You must never forget that, dear Jo. It is a great
responsibility."

"I'd rather have the buckles without the responsibility,
Auntie."

His Aunt lowered her spectacles till they were below the
aquilinity of her nose. So, she could see her nephew better,
and her thin fingers with three rings and pointed nails inter-

laced slowly, as if tatting some slow conclusion. Dear Jo! Was he being taught to take things lightly? Eton—it was nice, of course, and very distinguished, but perhaps a little dangerous! And her eyes chased him down from the wave of fair hair on his forehead to the straps confining his trousers to his boots. Was he not becoming a little foppish?

"Your grandfather, dear, always took his position seriously. I could tell you a story——"

"Hooray!"

Aunt Ann frowned. Yes! It *would* do him good to hear.

"It was in the year when your dear father and his friend Nick Treffry had just set up for themselves in tea. That would be about six years after we came to London. Your grandfather had done very well with his building, so that he had been able to give all the boys a good education; your Uncle Nicholas especially was such a promising little chap, and your Uncle James was just in his articles—he was admitted a solicitor afterwards on his twenty-first birthday, and that is the earliest possible. But in spite of all the expense we were to him, your grandfather had put by quite a lot of money; though we were still living on Primrose Hill and so we saw a great deal of your Uncle Edgar; and, indeed, your grandfather had invested some of his money in your uncle's business——"

"What was that, Auntie?"

"Jute, dear. Your grandfather was not a partner with him, but he was interested. Uncle Edgar was not at all like your grandfather; he was a very amiable man, but rather weak, and I am afraid he paid too much attention to other people's advice. Anyway he was tempted to gamble for what I think is called 'the rise.' And very foolishly he did not consult your grandfather. So, of course, when your grandfather heard of it, he was in a regular stew. You see I took a little of our dear mother's place, and I can remember him saying: 'What on earth is the chap about—weak-kneed beggar—gambling for a rise! Mark my words, Ann, he'll be in Queer Street in no time!'"

Aunt Ann paused, recalling that far scene. The stocky figure of her father bent forward over the mahogany of the old dining table now in the room below, his broad, short-fingered hand suddenly clenching, the flush of blood below his eyes, screwed up in the visioning of Queer Street.

"And was he, Auntie?"

"Yes, dear. It was that dreadful year when everything went down suddenly, especially jute. Poor Uncle Edgar was so amiable that he never seemed to realise that other people could be hard and greedy."

"Was he ruined, Auntie?"

"I was going to tell you. As I said, your grandfather was not in partnership with Uncle Edgar, and as soon as he heard what Uncle had done, he sold his investment and saved his bacon, as he would have called it. And then jute went down instead of up, and Uncle Edgar was threatened with bankruptcy. Your grandfather went through a dreadful time making up his mind whether to help him or not. You see, he knew it would mean years of set-back for him in his building business, and for all of us great economy, and going without things that we were accustomed to. And he felt your uncle's conduct in not consulting him very much —he used to say bitter things about him. It all came to a head one evening when your Uncle Edgar cried—he was not a strong character. I can see him now: he had large red bandana handkerchiefs, and he sat there with his face all buried in one. Your grandfather was walking up and down talking about his expecting him to pull the chestnuts out of the fire for him, and he wasn't going to, not he. I thought he would have had a fit. And then, suddenly, he stopped and looked a long time at Uncle Edgar. 'Edgar,' he said, 'you're a poor fish. But I'm the head of the family, and I'm not going to see the name dishonoured. Here, get out, and to-morrow I'll see you through.' "

"And did he, Auntie?"

"Yes, Jo. It was a terrible sacrifice. But I think we were all glad; we were fond of Uncle Edgar, and it would have made such a scandal to have him go bankrupt, especially as he had not been quite straight. We never saw very much of him after, but he died better off than ever, entirely owing to your grandfather. So you see, dear, it doesn't do to take responsibility lightly." Her nephew had ceased to look at her, as if he had suddenly perceived why he had been told the story.

"I should have thought it did, Auntie, if he died better off than ever."

Aunt Ann smiled. Really, the dear boy was very naughty!

"Jo," she said, grave again, "I can tell you another story of your grandfather."

"Oh! do, Auntie!"

"This was in the thirties, very hard years for everybody; and your grandfather was building some houses in Brighton. He was always a man who cut his coat to fit his cloth; but he used to tell me that if he made five per cent on his money with those houses, it would be all he could hope for. I remember it all very clearly because just then I was *so* hoping he would do well, I had a special reason." Aunt Ann paused, seeing again her special reason in pegtop trousers looking down at her all braided and crinolined on the sofa; hearing again his voice, so manly, saying: 'Dear Ann, may I speak to your father?' hearing again her own answer: 'Please wait, dear Edward, Papa is so preoccupied just now. But if, as I hope, things go well—next year I shall, I trust, be able to leave him and the dear children.'

"What special reason, Auntie?"

"Oh! never mind that, dear. As I was saying, your grandfather was extremely anxious because those houses meant turning the corner of all his difficulties. It was a dreadful year, and I am sorry to say there was a great deal of chicanery."

"What is chicanery?"

"Chicanery, dear, means trying to get the better of your neighbour at all costs."

"Did grandfather get the better of anyone?"

Aunt Ann looked at her nephew sharply.

"No," she said, "they got the better of him, Jo."

"Oh! Go on, Auntie. How interesting! I do want to hear."

"Well, one day your grandfather came home from Brighton in a dreadful taking. It was a long time before I could quieten him down to tell me what had happened. It seems that three of those houses wouldn't dry. The first houses were all right, so of course your grandfather never suspected anything. But the man who supplied the building material had taken advantage to mix some of it with sea water instead of fresh. I could never make out what he gained by it, or whether he had done it out of ignorance, but your grandfather was convinced that he was a rascal. 'They won't dry, they won't dry,' he kept on saying. I think if he had died that moment those words would have been printed on his heart. You see, it meant ruination to his reputation as a builder. And then it seems somebody showed him a way by which he could make the houses seem dry although in wet weather they never really would be. That night I heard him, long after I went to bed, walking about in his room next door; but in the morning I heard him mutter: 'No, I'm jiggered if I will!' He had made up his mind, after a dreadful struggle, not to be party to any trick."

"And what happened then, Auntie?"

"Well, he just took those three houses down and built them afresh—it cost him thousands."

"Didn't he make the man who used the sea water pay?"

"He tried to, Jo; but the man went bankrupt. It aged your grandfather very much. We *all* felt it dreadfully."

Aunt Ann was silent, lost in memory of how she had felt it. Edward! . . . Her nephew's voice recalled her.

"Grandfather didn't go bankrupt himself, did he, Auntie?"

"No, Jo; but very nearly. Perhaps it was all for the best. It made him very respected, and in after years he was always glad that he had been so above-board."

She looked up startled; young Jolyon was examining her face in a peculiar manner.

"I expect *you* had a sad time, Auntie."

Aunt Ann's lips firmed themselves against the suspicion of being pitied.

"So you see, dear," she said, "your grandfather had good principles, and that is the great thing."

"Did he go to Church, and that?"

"Not very much. He was brought up to be a Wesleyan, so he never quite approved of Church. He used to say the service was full of fallals. Of course, *we* all liked Church much better than Chapel, and he never interfered with our going."

"I expect he was glad not to go at all, really."

Aunt Ann covered her mouth with a little paper fan.

"You mustn't be flippant, dear."

"Oh! no, Auntie; I meant it."

"Well, Jo, I don't think I should call your grandfather a very religious man after our dear mother's death. He always grudged that so much."

"Did my father get on well with him?"

"Not very. Your father was so much our mother's boy."

"I see."

"Yes, dear, your grandfather was always so occupied that he hadn't much time for us children. I think he was perhaps fonder of me than of any of us."

"I expect that was because you were so good, Auntie."

"Hssh! Jo. You mustn't make fun of me. I was the only one old enough to talk to when our mother died."

"I thought you said my father was my age."

"Yes but in those days people did not talk to children as they do now."

Young Jolyon did not reply, but he tilted his chin slightly. Children!

"How much money did he leave, Auntie, after all that?"

"Thirty thousand pounds, dear, divided equally amongst the ten of us——he was very just."

Young Jolyon took out his watch; it was an old one of his father's, and he liked to take it out.

"I must go now, Auntie; I'm meeting a man at Madame Tussaud's. Oh! might I have those buckles?"

Aunt Ann's eyes lingered on him; he was her favourite, though to admit it was not in her character.

"Are you to be trusted with them, dear?"

"Of course I am."

"They're an heirloom, Jo. Don't you think we'd better wait till you're older?"

"Oh! Auntie, as if I wasn't——!"

Aunt Ann's fingers rummaged in the little drawer.

"Well, on condition that you take the greatest care of

them. And you mustn't ever wear them, until you go to Court."

"Do they wear buckles at Court?"

"I believe so, dear. I have never been. Here they are."

From folds of tissue paper she took them out—of old blackish paste set in silver. Very discreetly, on the bit of black velvet to which they were attached, the two buckles gleamed.

Young Jolyon took them in his hand. Into which of his pockets would they go without spoiling a man's figure?

"I like them, Auntie."

"Yes, dear, they are genuine old paste. Have you somewhere safe to keep them?"

"Oh! yes, I've got lots of drawers." He placed the buckles in his tail coat pocket, and bent over to kiss his Aunt.

"You won't sit on them, Jo?"

"We never sit on our tails, Auntie."

His Aunt's eyes followed him wistfully to the door, where he turned to wave his hand. Dear Jo! He *was* growing up! Such a pleasure to see him always. He would be quite a distinguished-looking man some day, like his dear father, only with more advantages. But had she done right to give him the buckles? Was he not too young to realise the responsibility? She closed the little drawer whence she had taken them, and before her eyes there passed the pageant of old days—days of her childhood and her womanhood with no youth in between. Days of her own responsibility— mother to all the family from the age of twenty on! Just that one abortive courtship—'a lick and a promise,' Swithin would call it—snuffed out by sea water and her father's reputation. Did she regret it? No! How could she? If her father had not been honest about those houses—a man of his word—then, why then she could not have given his buckles to dear Jo, as symbols of headship and integrity. Edward! Well, he had married very happily after all. She had not grudged him the pleasure; his wife had soon had twins. Perhaps it was all for the best: they were always very good to her, her brothers and sisters that she had been a mother to, and it was such a pleasure to see their dear little children growing up. Why, Soamey would be coming in directly on his way back from the Zoo; it was his eighth birthday and she had his present ready; a box of bricks, so that he could build himself a house—like his grandfather, only not—not with sea water . . . Ah! . . . Um! . . . Just a little nap, perhaps, before the dear little chap came— perhaps a little—um—ah!——

The thin lips, so generally compressed, puffed slightly in their breathing above that square chin resting on her cameo. The delicious surge of slumber swayed over the brain under the corkscrewed curls; the lips opened once and a word came forth: "Bub—Buckles."

SANDS OF TIME
1821–1863

SANDS OF TIME

IN the Spring of 1860, on the afternoon of the last day before his son went to Eton, old Jolyon hung up his top hat on a wooden antler in the hall at Stanhope Gate and went into the dining-room. Young Jolyon, who had hung up his top hat on a lower wooden antler, followed, and so soon as his father was seated in his large leather chair, perched himself on the arm thereof. Whether from the Egyptian mummies they had just been seeing in the British Museum, or merely because the boy's venture to a new school, and a Public school at that, loomed heavy before them, they were both feeling old, for between the ages of fifty-four and thirteen there is not, on occasions like this, a great gulf set. And that physical juxtaposition, which, until he first went to school at the age of ten, had been constant between young Jolyon and his sire, was resumed almost unconsciously under the boy's foreboding that to-morrow he would be a man. He leaned back until his head was tucked down on his father's shoulder. To old Jolyon moments like this, getting rarer with the years, were precious as any that life afforded him—an immense comfort that the boy was such an affectionate chap.

"Well, Jo," he said, "what did you think of the mummies?"

"Horrible things, Dad."

"Um—yes. Still, if we hadn't got 'em, somebody else would. They say they're worth a lot of money. Queer thing, Jo, to think there are descendants of those mummies still living, perhaps. Well, you'll be able to say you've seen them; I don't suppose many other boys have. You'll like Eton, I expect." This he said because he was afraid his boy would not. He didn't know much about it, but it was a great big place to send a little chap to. The pressure of the boy's cheek against the hollow between chest and arm was increased; and he heard the treble voice, somewhat muffled, murmur:

"Tell me about *your* school, Dad."

"My school, Jo? It was no great shakes. I went to school at Epsom—used to go by coach up to London all the way from Bosport, and then down by post-shay—no railways then, you know. Put in charge of the guard, great big red-faced chap with a horn. Travel all night—ten miles an hour—and change horses every hour—like clockwork."

"Did you go outside, Dad?"

"Yes—there I was, a little shaver wedged up between the coachman and a passenger; cold work—shawls there were in those days, over your eyes. My mother used to give me a mutton pie and a flask of cherry brandy. Good sort, the old coachman, hoarse as a crow and round as a barrel; and see him drive—take a fly off the leader's ear with his whip."

"Were there many boys?"

"No; a small school, about thirty. But I left school at fifteen."

"Why?"

"My mother died when your Aunt Susan was born, so we left Bosport and came up to London, and I was put to business."

"What was your mother like, Dad?"

"My mother?" Old Jolyon was silent, tracing back in thought through crowded memories.

"I was fond of her, Jo. Eldest boy, you know; they say I took after her. Don't know about that; she was a pretty woman, refined face. Nick Treffry would tell you she was the prettiest woman in the town—good woman, too—very good to me. I felt her death very much."

A little more pressure of the head in the hollow of his arm. All that he felt for the boy and that, he hoped and believed, the boy felt for him, he had felt for his own mother all that time ago. Only forty-one when she had died bearing her tenth child. Tenth! In those days they made nothing of that sort of thing till the pitcher went once too often to the well. Ah! Losing her had been a bitter business.

Young Jolyon got off the arm of the chair, as if he were sensing his father's abstraction.

"I think I'd better go and pack, Dad."

"All right, my boy! I shall have a cigar."

When the boy had gone—graceful little chap!—old Jolyon went to the Chinese tea chest where his cigars reposed, and took one out. He listened to it, clipped its end, lighted and placed it in his mouth. Drawing at the cigar, he took it out of his mouth again, held it away from him between two rather tapering-nailed fingers, and savoured with his nostrils the bluish smoke. Not a bad weed, but all the better for being smoked! Returning to his chair, he leaned back and crossed his legs. A long time since he'd thought of his mother. He could see her face still; yes, could just see it, the clear look up of her eyes from far back under the brows, the rather pointed chin; and he could hear her voice—pleasant, soft, refined. Which of them took after her? Ann, a bit; Hester, yes; Susan, a little; Nicholas, perhaps, except that the fellow was so sharp; he himself, they said—he didn't know, but he'd like to think it; she had been a gentle creature. And, suddenly, it was as if her hand were passed over his forehead again, brushing his hair up as she had liked to see it. Ah! How well he could remember still, coming into his father's house at Bosport after the long cold coach drive back from school—coming in and seeing his father standing stocky in the hallway, with his legs a little apart and his head bowed, as if somebody had just hit him over it—standing there and not even noticing him, till he said: "I've come, Father."

"What! You, Jo?" His face was very red, his eyelids puffed so that his eyes were hardly visible. He had made a queer motion with both hands and jerked his head towards the stairs.

"Go up," he had said. "Your mother's very bad. Go up, my boy; and whatever you do, don't cry."

He had gone up with a sort of sinking fear in his heart. His sister Ann had met him at the door—a good-looking upstanding young woman, then; yes, and a mother to them all, afterwards—had sacrificed herself to bringing up the young ones. Ah! a good woman, Ann!

"Come in, Jo," she had said; "Mother would like to see you. But, Jo—oh! Jo!" And he had seen two tears roll down her cheeks. The sight had impressed him terribly; Ann never cried. In the big four-poster his mother lay, white as the sheets, all but the brown ringlets of her hair— the light dim, and a strange woman—a nurse—sitting over by the window with a white bundle on her lap! He had gone up to the bed. He could see her face now—without a line in it, all smoothed out, like wax! He hadn't made a sound, had just stood looking; but her eyes had opened, and had turned a little, without movement of the face, to gaze full at him. And then her lips had moved, and whispered: "There's Jo, there's my darling boy!" And never in his life before or since had he had so great a struggle to keep himself from crying out, from flinging himself down. But all he had said was: "Mother!" Her lips had moved again.

"Kiss me, my boy." And he had bent and kissed her forehead, so smooth, so cold. And then he had sunk on his knees; and stayed there gazing at her closed eyes till Ann had come and led him away. And up in the attic that he shared with James and Swithin, he had lain on his bed, face down, and sobbed and sobbed. She had died that morning, not speaking any more, so Ann had told him. After forty years he could feel again the cold and empty aching of those days, the awful silent choking when in the old churchyard they put her away from him for ever. The stone had been raised over her only the day before they left for London. He had gone and stood there reading:

IN MEMORY OF
ANN,
The Beloved Wife of
Jolyon Forsyte
Born Feb. 1, 1780; Died April 16, 1821

A bright May day and no one in that crowded graveyard but himself.

Old Jolyon shifted in his chair; his cigar was out, his cheeks above those grizzling whiskers—indispensable to the sixties—had coloured suddenly, his eyes looked angrily from deep beneath his frowning brows, for he was suddenly in the grip of another memory—bitter, wrathful and ashamed— of only ten years back.

That was on a Spring day too, in 1851, the year after they had buried their father up at Highgate, thirty years after their mother's death. That had put it into his mind, and he had gone down to Bosport for the first time since, travelling by train, in a Scotch cap. He had hardly known the place, so changed and spread. Having found the old parish church, he had made his way to the corner of the graveyard where she had been buried, and had stood aghast, rubbing his eyes. That corner was no longer there! The trees, the graves, all were gone. In place, a wall cut diagonally across, and beyond it ran the railway line. What in the name of God had they done with his mother's grave? Frowning, he had searched, quartering the graveyard like a dog. At least, they had placed it somewhere else. But no—not a sign. And there had risen in him a revengeful anger shot through with a shame which heightened the passion in his blood. The Goths, the Vandals, the ruffians! His mother—her bones scattered—her name defaced—her rest annulled! A stinking railway track across her grave. What right—! Clasping the railing of a tomb his hands had trembled, and sweat had broken out on his flushed forehead. If there were any law that he could put in motion, he would put it! If there were anyone he could punish, by Heaven he would punish him! And then, that shame, so foreign to his nature, came sweeping in on him again. What had his father been about—what had they all been about that not one of them had come down in all those years to see that all was well with her! Too busy making money—like the age itself, laying that sacrilegious railway track, scattering with its progress the decency of death! And he had bowed his head down on his trembling hands. His mother! And he had not defended her, who had lain defenceless! But what had the parson been about not to give notice of what they were going to do? He raised his head again, and stared around him. Over on the far side was someone weeding paths. He moved forward and accosted him.

"How long is it since they put that railway here?"

The old chap had paused, leaning on his spud.

"Ten year and more."

"What did they do with the graves in that corner?"

"Ah! I never did 'old with that."

"What did they do with them? I asked you."

"Why—just dug 'em up."

"And the coffins?"

"I dunno. Ax parson. They was old graves—an 'undred years or more, mostly."

"They were not—one was my mother's. 1821."

"Ah! I mind—there was a newish stone."

"What did they do with it?"

The old chap had gazed up at him, then, as if suddenly aware of the abnormal on the path before him:

"I b'lieve they couldn't trace the owner—ax parson 'e may know."

"How long has he been here?"

"Four year come Michaelmas. Old parson's dead, but present parson 'e may 'ave some informashun."

Like some beast deprived of his kill old Jolyon stood. Dead! That ruffian dead!

"Don't you know what they did with the coffins—with the bones?"

"Couldn' say—buried somewhere again, I suppose—maybe the doctors got some—couldn' say. As I tell you, Vicar 'e may know."

And spitting on his hands he turned again to weeding.

The Vicar? He had been no good, had known nothing, or so he had said—no one had known! Liars—yes, liars— he didn't believe a word of what they said. They hadn't wanted to trace the owner, for fear of having a stopper put on them! Gone, dispersed—all but the entry of the burial! Over the ground where she had lain that railway sprawled, trains roared. And he, by one of those trains, had been forced to go back to that London which had enmeshed his heart and soul so that, as it were, he had betrayed her who had borne him! But who would have thought of such a thing? Sacred ground! Was nothing proof against the tide of Progress—not even the dead committed to the earth?

He reached for a match, but his cigar tasted bitter and he pitched it away. He hadn't told Jo, he shouldn't tell Jo—not a thing for a boy to hear. A boy would never understand how life got hold of you when you once began to make your way. How one thing brought another till the past went out of your head, and interests multiplied in an ever-swelling tide lapping over sentiment and memory, and the green things of youth. A boy would never comprehend how Progress marched inexorably on, transforming the quiet places of the earth. And yet, perhaps the boy ought to know—might be a lesson to him. No! He shouldn't tell him—it would hurt to let him know that one had let one's own mother—! He took up *The Times*. Ah! What a difference! He could remember *The Times* when he first came up to London—tiny print, such as they couldn't read nowadays. *The Times*—one double sheet with the Parliamentary debates, and a few advertisements of places wanted, and people wanting them. And look at it now, a great crackling flourishing affair with print twice the size!

The door creaked. What was that? Oh, yes—tea coming in! His wife was upstairs, unwell; and they had brought it to him here.

"Send some up to your mistress," he said, "and tell Master Jo."

Stirring his tea—his own firm's best Soochong—he read about the health of Lord Palmerston and of how that precious mountebank of a chap—the French Emperor—was expected to visit the Queen. And then the boy came in.

"Ah! Here you are, Jo! Tea's getting strong."

And, as the little chap drank, old Jolyon looked at him.

To-morrow he was going to that great place where they turned out Prime Ministers and bishops and that, where they taught manners—at least he hoped so—and how to despise trade. H'm! Would the boy learn to despise his own father? And suddenly there welled up in old Jolyon all his primeval honesty, and that peculiar independence which made him respected among men, and a little feared.

"You asked just now about your grandmother, Jo. I didn't tell you how, when I went down thirty years after her death, I found that her grave had been dug up to make room for a railway. There wasn't a trace of it to be found, and nobody could or would tell me anything about it."

The boy held his teaspoon above his cup, and gazed; how innocent and untouched he looked; then suddenly his face went pinker and he said:

"What a shame, Dad!"

"Yes; some ruffian of a parson allowed it, and never let us know. But it was my fault, Jo; I ought to have been seeing to her grave all along."

And again the boy said nothing, eating his cake, and looking at his father. And old Jolyon thought: 'Well, I've told him.'

Suddenly the boy piped up:

"That's what they did with the mummies, Dad."

The mummies! What mummies? Oh! Those things they had been seeing at the British Museum. And old Jolyon was silent, staring back over the sands of time. Odd! how it hadn't occurred to him. Odd! Yet the boy had noticed it! Um! Now, what did that signify? And in old Jolyon there stirred some dim perception of mental movement between his generation and his son's. Two and two made four. And he hadn't seen it! Queer! But in Egypt they said it was all sand: Perhaps things came up of their own accord. And then——though there might be, as he had said, descendants living, they were not sons or grandsons. Still! The boy had seen the bearing of it and he hadn't. He said abruptly:

"Finished your packing, Jo?"

"Yes, Dad, only do you think I could take my white mice?"

"Well, my boy, I don't know——perhaps they're a bit young for Eton. The place thinks a lot of itself, you know."

"Yes, Dad."

Old Jolyon's heart turned over within him. Bless the little chap! What he was in for!

"Did you have white mice, Dad?"

Old Jolyon shook his head.

"No, Jo; we weren't as civilised as all that in my young day."

"I wonder if those mummies had them," said young Jolyon.

HESTER'S LITTLE TOUR
1845

HESTER'S LITTLE TOUR

THOSE who frequented Forsyte 'Change at Timothy's on the Bayswater Road, and were accustomed to the sight of Aunt Hester sitting in her chair to the left of the fireplace with a book on her lap which she seemed almost too quiescent to be reading, must often have wondered: What, if any, adventures or emotional disturbances had ever come the way of that still figure? Had she ever loved, and if so —whom? Was she ever ill, and if so—where? To whom had she ever confided—what? Not that she imparted to the observer the impression of a sphinx. That would hardly have been nice. And yet, curiously enough, of the three sisters who dwelled at Timothy's, it was Aunt Hester who exhaled, in spite of all her quietism, an atmosphere of—one would almost say free thought, but for fear of going too far. Better, perhaps, say that she conveyed a feeling of having abandoned, out of love of a quiet life, more desires, thoughts, hopes and dislikes, than either of her sisters had ever been capable of entertaining. People felt, in fact, not that Aunt Hester owned a past, but that all her life she had been renouncing a past which she might very well have had. And they felt, too, that she knew it, and found it somehow not tragic, but comic, as if she were always saying to herself: 'To be like this when you're so unlike this—droll, isn't it?' When the Freudian doctrine of complexes and inhibitions came in, younger members of the family, such as Violet, given to pastels, Christopher, inclining to the stage, and Maud Dartie, nothing if not daring, would speculate on what had happened to Aunt Hester before she was as she was. And theory was divided between the assumption that she had been dropped on her head when she was three, or chased by a black man when she was thirteen. In a word, it was widely felt that there were strange potentialities in Aunt Hester, which she had deliberately not developed. The doctrine of 'balance redressed' which had contrived out of a family containing so many 'characters' a sort of reserve or sinking fund in Hester and Timothy, seemed to offer a sound biological explanation, and it was only when she died in 1907 and left to Francie Forsyte her china, that there came to at least one member of the family knowledge that Aunt Hester had once 'tried herself out' before for good and all she resigned a past. For in a Lowestoft teapot Francie found a little sheaf of yellowed leaves of paper, which seemingly Aunt Hester had been too passive to destroy, before she entered a passivity even more profound; leaves deeply buried beneath a pot-pourri of very old cloves, and the dust of rose petals, together with three boot buttons which appeared to have been dropped in at moments when Aunt Hester couldn't be bothered to put them in any other place. The leaves had been detached as if pulled out of a diary, and this alone gave food for thought, in its implication that Aunt Hester must at one time have manifested energy, or there would have been no diary to pull them out of. That they came into the hands of Francie was perhaps fortunate, for no other Forsyte could have relished them adequately. Indeed she so relished them that she even fancied Aunt Hester had wished them to survive as a sort of protest against her unspent life; and presently she dressed them up anonymously in the form of a story which she sent to the 'Argonaut,' who did not accept it. In her version the names were altered, but are here restored to their pristine purity. It was entitled: 'Hester's Little Tour, being Leaves from a Very Early Victorian Diary found in a Lowestoft teapot,' and it began abruptly:

"Wednesday morning early. How entrancing it was last night to stand in the moonlight with that beautiful Rhine flowing by my feet, and to fancy that it wandered past castles and cities, only to lose itself at last in the great blue sea! How the moonbeams glistened on the water! To think that under this moon the Loreley lured men to destruction, and the robber barons issued from their fastnesses on their forays, with the soft moonlight gleaming on their armour! But was I, indeed, thinking of all this? No, I had but one thought: Would he come? Would he really come? And what would they say at home if they could see me standing there with the hood drawn over my face, waiting for my lover? Lover! Oh, the dear word! If only, I thought, I do not forget all my German, so that I can understand what he says to me in his dear voice, and not weary him by having to talk English! You must not think, my diary, that I did not know how immodest it was of me to have come out. Yes, I knew that, but I did not care. I did not care. Why should I? My heart tells me that I am in love with him. My heart tells me that he loves me. And then he came, he came almost before I knew he was there, wrapped in that flowing cloak which Swithin would laugh at, but which looks so martial on him, he is so upright. How terribly my heart beat when without a word he took me in his arms, wrapping his cloak right round me so that we seemed one person. Ah! it was divine; and strange how I had no fears or misgivings. I never once thought of home while I was standing there in his embrace. A nightingale was singing; so romantic, so beautiful, I shall never forget. Rolandseck, dear Rolandseck! . . . When I was back in my room, fortunately quite unobserved, I felt cold and sick at the thought that we were leaving on the morrow for Bonn. Would that not be too far for him to come, for he has his military duties. But if I can believe his words, or rather his lips, he will not fail. At six o'clock, he said, under the linden trees in the Platz at Bonn. Oh, my diary, where is your Hester going? When I was in his embrace last night I felt I could give up the world for him; and of course he is of very good family. But, lying in my bed, everything seemed so difficult and to need such an effort, for indeed I think it would give our dear father a fit to think of me in Germany married, or perhaps not married —for I do not even know if he has a wife already—to an Army officer. And soldiers are proverbially fickle; they love and ride away. And then what would become of me? But the delight I felt when he put his arms round me—can there be anything in the world more beautiful than love? And I have so often laughed at it; but indeed I do not know myself any more, nor where my sense of humour has gone. To think that only three weeks ago we were in the packet crossing to Calais—it seems a century; and all the towns and people I have seen are faded as if I had dreamed them; and just these last few days seem real. Or perhaps this is the dream and I shall wake up and find that I have never met him. Fancy! If we had not gone into the Pump rooms that night at Ems, I never should have met him. Those divine valses we danced together—how elegantly he dances! It was love at first sight, and I have behaved most immodestly, but that does not seem to me to matter at all. Yet sometimes I wonder what he thinks of me when I am not with him. After all, I am thirty years old, not just a young girl as perhaps he believes, for he says I look so young. His *Englisches Mädchen*—he calls me! Oh me! How difficult is life! I am surprised to find that all the deportment and good conduct I have been taught seem to count for nothing when I am with him. I am really naughty, for it makes me smile to think what John and Eleanor would feel and say if they only knew where

their 'dear demure Hester' had been last night, and how all
she is thinking about now is how to get away from them
again to-night and meet him under the lime trees in the Platz
at Bonn. It is nearly seven by my watch; I must close you
now, my diary, and get ready for the chaise. . . .

"Wednesday evening. Oh! dear, how many stories I have
told! First I said I had a headache after the jolting in the
chaise, and was going to lie down and sleep, so as to be fresh
for dinner. And then I listened till I heard John and Eleanor
in their room, unpacking; and out I stole. He was there already—all impatience, and his boots all dusty; for he had
ridden all the way and was going to ride back for his inspec-
tion in the morning. Ah! what a beautiful hour; but not so
beautiful as last night because there were people about, and,
though the linden trees were thick and lovely, they didn't
hide us as I would have liked. Yes, I would—I am quite
abandoned! To-night—dare I write it even in you, my
diary?—he says he will come to my window. When I chose
to be on the ground floor, did I think of that? Yes, I will be
honest, I did; so that's that! I shall never smile again at
people in love. It is too sweet, and too upsetting. It makes
you do what you would never dream of doing, and feel quite
proud of it, so long as nobody knows. And then, when I was
coming in, I met John and told him I had been pining for air
to cure my headache, and so I had gone for a walk. And I
quite enjoyed seeing dear John so deceived! Yes, and I said
I should be all right to-morrow if I went to bed *early after
dinner*. Poor John, he is very trustful, and has such nice
eyes. Eleanor is very fortunate, I think. It is all so smooth
for them! Ah me! It is so different and difficult for us.
It is too cruel that he is not English. Bernhard—the name is
beautiful and very strong—just what a name should be;
only, I like it better without the 'h.' He is six feet tall and

twenty-eight years old, and he thinks I am twenty-four; and I have not told him that I am not. When he touches me nothing matters, not even the truth. I feel it is fortunate that we can only speak to each other in a broken way; it seems to excuse me for deceiving him about my age. Yet, after all—thirty and twenty-eight—there is not much difference; and he is so big and strong and manly, I feel humble enough with him to be the younger. There is something so romantic about this beautiful Rhineland that I do not feel as I should feel in England; in England I could never act as I am acting now, indeed no—I should be ashamed of having such violent, such delicious feelings. I am writing in bed, for fear dear Eleanor should come and find me up, after I had said that I was going to bed at once. But I think I can venture soon now to get up and lock my door, and then I shall don my mauve négligé; it goes with my hair, and I shall keep my hair down. I know how daring that is, but sometimes I feel as daring as a tigress defending her young; and then, all suddenly, it is as if my heart would creep out at the soles of my feet, to think that I have a sweetheart coming to my window. 'Romeo, Romeo, wherefore art thou Romeo?' Oh! Why is he not English? It would all be so much easier. For then he could woo me openly. If anybody knew he was coming to-night, could I ever hold up my head again? And yet, if I were sure no one would ever know, I should feel like a bird, free and happy, rejoicing that its mate was coming to it in the moonlight. Only birds do not come to their mates in the moonlight. How silly I am! But oh! if he should be seen! I will not think of that; I will not. Be brave, my heart! He says I am 'so schön'—such a pretty word. But I know I am not really. I have not the pink cheeks, the corn-coloured hair, the coral lips of these German maidens. I am dark, and thinner. Perhaps that is why he admires me. Oh! how my heart is beating! I must put you away now, my diary. What—ah! what will have come to me when I write in you again! . . .

"Friday afternoon. I am distraught. I cannot tell what to do, I cannot tell. All to-day my mind has been going this way and that, ever since I had his dear letter. I have made it all out with the help of the dictionary. His regiment is marching to-morrow to Frankfort, and he begs me to come to him there. He says we will be married, and he will make me 'ever happy.' But until he goes he is so busy that he cannot come again. I know it is my besetting weakness not to be able to act for myself; Ann is always at me about it. I wonder what she would say if she knew that if I could act now I should go to him and disregard the consequences. It is not that I am afraid of the consequences, but it is so difficult to act all by myself; there are so many things I must do if I am to go. Ah! if only someone could do them for me. It is not my soul, but my body that lags and lags. I wish I were like Ann, who always does at once what she feels to be right. Is it that I am ashamed of what has happened? No, not to myself. How can I be ashamed of obeying the dictates of my heart and his? But I cannot face having to explain to John and Eleanor. They would be so horrified, and how could I make them understand? And then there is the arranging for my journey and selling my necklace, for I have not enough money. He would send me money if he knew, but I could not ask him. Oh dear! it is all so difficult. Yesterday I was intoxicated on the memory of our night, it still makes me burn; but to-day my courage and my energy is all run out of me. Our night! Never, never could I write of it, even in you, my diary. It was too wonderful, and terrifying, and sweet. Did I care then what I was doing, do I care now what I did? A thousand times no! If he were here at this moment it should be again as it was. I think I must be wanton by nature, for I am proud of it to myself. But to the world—and then John and Eleanor! After all their kindness in taking me this tour, how can I leave them without a word? And if I do not, how can I ever tell them what I have done—what we have done! I should die of shame! But if I cannot make up my mind to leave them without a word, and do all those other things that are necessary, I must go on with them to Cologne, and back to London, and never see him again. Soon he will not remember me. I shall be just a night of love. Perhaps one of many nights, for what do I know of him but that I love him, and that he seems to me brave and beautiful? If I look up I can see him there leaning above me in the moonlight. O God! I was wicked, but I was happy. There is the bell for supper. Yes! I am distracted. Perhaps in the night I shall gain courage to act, because I shall want him so! . . .

"Sunday, Cologne. All has moved on as it seemed without me, and my body has come here with John and Eleanor. I have just written to him. I have told him that if he really loves me, he will come to England to claim me; but I know he will not come. I feel it is the end. I am not a fool. John and Eleanor think I have a touch of the sun; it was very hot in the chaise. It is a touch of the moon I have. The moon! I, Hester, who always laughed—! Ah me! I have a lump of lead in my chest. Eleanor came to my room early yesterday morning and insisted on helping me to pack; she is so kind; we started at eight o'clock and drove all day. Now we shall go to the Cathedral and to-morrow travel by train, and in four days we shall be home. John said to-night: 'Well, I think it has been a very enjoyable little tour.' He is a dear nice fellow, but quite blind! When I go home I shall kiss them all and say: 'Oh, such a lovely tour!' As I sit here

in my bedroom writing, I seem to see myself with malice:
Dear prim proper little Hester! Ugh! I have not cried at
all, but an' I would——! To-morrow morning we shall travel
on and on and on away from him. All my mind and will
feel paralysed, my heart only is alive and sore; I know that
if it came over again I should act just the same. And my nature will always be like this; always want love and freedom,
always be free in thought but not in deed. . . .

"Saturday. I have not written in you for days, my diary.
What was the use? Yesterday we crossed in the packet and
came up to London. I laughed when I saw our house, but I
was not amused. It looked so pokey, and like other houses.
Oh! Rolandseck! and the moonlight on the river! There
was no letter from him. I have been a fool; I know it now.
My pride is hurt, and I am sore—sore. Ann looked at me so
hard, I could not help smiling bitterly. Poor Ann! And
Juley gushed about my looking pale. She is a fool. I feel
much older than them both. And now I shall go on day
after day doing exactly what we have always done; but I
shall never feel the same again, for I have been where they
have not. I have had my little tour . . ."

In her capacity of editress Francie had added: "This is
surely a curious little sidelight on the nature of our Victorian
foremothers."

"F. F."

TIMOTHY'S NARROW SQUEAK
1851

TIMOTHY'S NARROW SQUEAK

IN 1920 Soames Forsyte on the death of his uncle Timothy, proved that will which but for the law against accumulations would in course of time have produced such astounding results. He had been at pains to explain to Timothy how, owing to that law, what Timothy intended would not come about; but Timothy had merely stared at him very hard and said: "Rubbage! Make it so!" And Soames had made it. In any case the legal limit of accumulation would be reached, and that was as near to what the old chap wanted as could be. When, as executor, he came to the examination of the papers left behind by Timothy, he had fresh confirmation of his uncle's lifelong passion for safety. Practically nothing had been destroyed. Seventy years and more of receipted bills, and cheque books with the paid-out cheque forms carefully returned to them in order of date, were found, and—since Timothy had been spoon-fed and incapable of paying a bill since before the War—burned out of hand. There was a mass of papers referring to the publishing business, which he had abandoned for Consols in 1879, and which had died, very fortunately for Soames, a natural death not long after. All these were committed to the fire. But then—a far more serious matter—there were whole drawers full of private letters and odds and ends not only Timothy's, but of the three sisters who had made house with him since their father's death in 1850. And with that conscientiousness, which ever distinguished him in an unconscientious world, Soames had decided to go through them first and destroy them afterwards. It was no mean task. He sneezed his way through it doggedly, reading the spidery calligraphy of the Victorian era, in bundle after dirty bundle of yellowed letters; cheered slightly now and then, among the mass of sententious gossip, by little streaks of side light on this member of his family or on that. The fifteenth evening of his persual, for he had had the lot conveyed by motor lorry down to Mapledurham, he came on the letter which forms the starting point of this narration. It was enclosed in a yellowed envelope bearing the address, "Miss Hatty Beechers"; was in Timothy's handwriting; bore the date, "May the twenty-seventh 1851," and had obviously never been posted. Hatty Beecher! Why that had been the maiden name of Hatty Chessman, the lively, elderly, somewhat raddled widow and friend of the family in his youth. He remembered her death in the Spring of 1899. She had left his Aunts Juley and Hester five hundred pounds apiece.

Soames began to read the letter with an ashamed curiosity, though it was nearly seventy years old and everybody dead; he continued to read it with a sort of emotion, as of one coming on blood in the tissue of a mummy.

"MY DEAR HATTY" (it began),

"I hope it will not surprise you to receive from me" ('obviously she never did,' thought Soames) "this missive which has caused me much anxiety, for I am not one of those lighthearted gentry who take the gravest steps in life without due consideration. Only the conviction that my best interests, indeed my happiness, and, I trust, your happiness, are involved, have caused me to write this letter. I have not, I hope, obtruded my attentions upon you, but you will not I equally hope have failed to notice that the charms of your person and your character have made a great impression upon me and that I seek your company with an ever growing ardour. I cannot, then, think that it will be in the nature of a shock to you when, with all the gravity born of long consideration and many heart searchings, I ask for the honour of your hand. If I am so fortunate as to meet with your approval as a suitor, it will be my earnest endeavour to provide for you a happy and prosperous home, to surround you with every attention, and to make you a good husband. As you know, I think, I am thirty-one years old, and my business is increasing, I am indeed slowly, I am happy to say, becoming a warm man; so that in material matters you will have all the comfort and indeed luxury with which I feel you should be surrounded. In the words of, I think, the Marquis of Montrose:

> 'He either fears his fate too much
> Or his deserts are small
> Who dares not put it to the touch
> To win or lose it all.'

"As I say, I have not taken this step lightly, and if, my dear Hatty, it pleases you to crown my aspirations with success, I think you may rely on me to make you happy. I shall be on tenterhooks until I have your reply which I hope will not be delayed beyond the morrow. I express to you my devoted admiration and am, my dear Hatty.

"Your faithful and attached Suitor,

"TIMOTHY FORSYTE."

With a faint grin Soames dropped the yellowed letter—six years older than himself—on his knee, and sat brooding. Poor old Timothy! And he had never sent it. Why not? Never 'put it to the touch' after all. If he remembered Hatty Chessman the old boy had been well out of it. Bit of a dasher Hatty Chessman in her time, from all that he had heard!

Still! There was the letter! Irrefutable evidence that

Timothy had been human once upon a time. 1851?—the year of the Great Exhibition! Yes, they had been in the Bayswater Road by then, Timothy and the girls, Ann, Juley, Hester! Fancy a thing like that letter coming out of the blue at this time of day! What had Hatty done that he didn't send the letter? Or what had Timothy done? Eaten something that disagreed with him—he shouldn't wonder, had a scare of some sort. The envelope had just Hatty's name but no address; was she then staying with them at the time or what—she had been a great friend, he knew, of Juley and of Hester! He put the letter back into its yellowed envelope with Timothy's cypher in an oval medallion on the flap, dropped it into a tray, and went on with his task of conning over his uncle's remains.

Hallo! What were these?

Three thin red notebooks held together by a bit of dingy rainbow-coloured ribbon tied in a bow. Whose writing? Aunt Ann's undoubtedly, more upright, more distinct than any other in the family. A diary, by George, and pretty old! Yes, begun when they went to 'the Nook,' "November 1850," and going on to "1855," the year that old Aunt Juley married Septimus Small. It would be old-fashioned twaddle! But suddenly Soames' eye lighted again on the yellowed letter in the tray and taking up the second volume of the diary he turned its pages till he came to April 1851.

"April 3. We are all agog about the Great Exhibition that is to be opened in Hyde Park. James says he doesn't know, but he thinks it will be a failure. They are making a great to-do and the Park does not look itself at all. It has quite upset dear Timothy. He is afraid that it will attract many rogues and foreigners and that our house will be burgled. He has become very distrait and never talks to us about his business, but we think from what

James said on Sunday that he must be in doubt whether or not to publish a new edition of the rhymes of Dr. Watts. They are very improving, but James says that Timothy does not know whether anyone will want to read them at this time of day." 'H'm!' thought Soames: ' "How doth the little busy bee!" If Timothy had really baulked at republishing that dreadful stuff, he must have regretted it all his life!' His eyes scanned on over the thin precise pages till he came to this:

"May 3. Hatty Beecher ('Ah! here it was!') came on April 30th to spend a month with us. She is a fine figure of a girl and has become quite buxom. We all went to the opening of the Exhibition. It was such a crowd, and the dear little Queen was so becomingly dressed. It was an occasion I shall never forget. How the people cheered! Timothy attended us, he seems quite taken with Hatty, he can hardly look at her. I hope she is really nice. Hester and Juley are already full of her praises. They all went to walk in the Park to-day, and look at the crowd going into the Exhibition, though there was a windy drizzle; but as our dear father used to say it was only 'pride of the morning,' for it soon cleared, and the sun shone . . .

"May 7. We all went to the opera. Dear Jolyon sent us his box—he put it so drolly. 'Take care Timothy doesn't lose his heart to Taglioni, she wouldn't make him a good wife.' I must say it is really wonderful how she supports herself on one toe, but Timothy seemed quite preoccupied. He was staring at Hatty's back all through the ballet. Mario was ravishing. I have never heard singing so like an angel's. We had great difficulty coming away. It rained and our crinolines got wet, the stupid coachman took some-one else for Timothy and we missed our turn and had to walk outside the portico. But Hatty was in such spirits that it did not seem to matter. She is such a rattle. I wonder whether it is quite wise for dear Timothy to see so much of her. I am sure she is very well intentioned, but I feel her evening dresses are lower than is quite nice. I have given her my Brussels fichu.

"May 13. To-day we went to the Zoo. Hatty had never seen it. In some ways she is quite provincial, but she picks things up very fast. Dear Timothy came all the way from his office to meet us. I fear it was Hatty's beaux yeux rather than the animals which brought him. I confess that the Zoo does not give me much pleasure, it is very common; and the monkeys are so human, and not at all nice in their habits. Hatty insisted on mounting the elephant, and of course Timothy was obliged to be her squire of dames, but I am sure he did not really enjoy it, and, indeed, he looked so grave bobbing behind her in the howdah that I could not help smiling, and Hester laughed so that I thought she would burst her bonnet strings. I was obliged to check her, for fear dear Timothy should see. I am glad we arrived too late to see the lions fed. The seal was very droll . . .

"May 17. James came to tea. He told us that Swithin has bought a new pair of greys, very spirited, and that he doesn't know what will happen. He advised Hatty not to venture if Swithin asks her to go driving. But Hatty said: 'I should adore it.' She certainly has a great deal of courage, indeed she is inclined to be rash. I was not sorry that Timothy should have the opportunity of seeing that she is so venturesome, for I feel more and more that he is attracted by her. I do not remember when he has behaved quite as he has this last fortnight. And though in some ways she is attractive, I do not really think she would make him a good wife. I cannot disguise from myself, too, that it would cause a great disturbance in all our lives; but I tell myself constantly that I ought not to be selfish, and if it were for dear Timothy's good, I hope I should not 'care a brass farden' as Nicholas would put it in his droll way. The girls are very fond of her and they do not see the little things that I see, and which make me uneasy. I must hope for the best. I spoke to my dear Jolyon about it yesterday, he is the head of the family now that our dear father is gone, and he has good judgment. He said I was not to worry, Timothy would never 'come up to the scratch.' I thought it such a peculiar expression.

"May 20. A Mr. Chessman has been to call. He came with Swithin. Juley thought he was elegantly dressed, but for my part, I do not care for these large shepherd's plaid checks which seem to be all the rage now for gentlemen. Hester and Hatty came in while we were still at tea, and Mr. Chessman was very attentive to Hatty. I hope I am not being unjust to her when I say that she made eyes at him in a way that I thought very forward. I was quite glad dear Timothy was not there. At least, to be honest, I am not sure that it would not have been for the best if he could have seen her. Swithin says that Mr. Chessman has to do with stocks and shares and is very clever in his profession. I must say that he seems to me much better suited to Hatty than Timothy could ever be. So perhaps it is providential that he came. Swithin has asked her and Hester to make four at the Royal Toxophilite Society's Meeting on Saturday. He pooh-poohed James about the new horses and said that he was an old woman. I shall not tell James, it would only put him about. In the evening after dinner I read Cowper aloud to the girls and Timothy. I chose his celebrated poem, 'The Task,' which begins with that daring line 'I sing the sofa.' I did not read very long because Timothy seemed so sleepy: he works too hard all day in his stuffy office. I must say Hatty did not behave at all nicely. She made faces behind my back, which I could see perfectly well in the mirror; but of course, I took no notice, because she is our guest. For myself I find Cowper very sonorous and improving, though to be quite honest I prefer 'John Gilpin' to any of his more serious poems . . .

"May 23. We have had quite a to-do, and I am not at all sure where my duty lies. This morning after Timothy had gone to the office I went to his study to dust the books which he bought with dear James when we came to live here. They each bought a complete little library, containing Humbolt's Cosmos, Hudibras and all the best works of the past; and who should I find there but Hatty, sitting in Timothy's own armchair, reading a book which I at once recognised as one of the little calf-bound volumes of Lord Byron. She was so absorbed that she did not see me till I was close to her. I received quite a shock when I apprehended that the book was that dreadful 'Don Juan' that one has heard so much about. She did not even try to hide it but said in a flippant way: 'Who'd have thought Timothy would have this book!' I am afraid I forgot myself, and spoke sharply.

" 'I think, my dear Hatty,' I said, 'it is hardly genteel to come into a gentleman's room and sit in his own armchair and read a book like that. I am surprised at you.' She took me up quite rudely.

" 'Why? Have you read it?'

" 'Of course I have not read it,' I replied.

" 'Then,' she said, pertly, 'what do you know about it?'

" 'It is common knowledge,' I answered, 'that it is not a book for ladies.'

"She tossed her head with a very high colour; but I continued to stand there looking at her, and she got up and put the book back whence she had taken it. It was in my mind to improve the occasion, but I remembered in time that she has no mother, and is our guest, so I only said: 'You know, dear Hatty, Timothy does not like his books touched.' She laughed and said flippantly: 'No, they don't look as if they were meant to be read.' I could have shaken her, but I controlled myself. After all she is young and high-spirited, and I daresay it is rather quiet for her in our little house. She flung out of the room, and I have not seen her since. I cannot make up my mind whether to tell Timothy or not. I feel sure that he is seriously *épris*. He looks at her so much when he thinks nobody sees him, and he has been biting his fingers, and has not answered any question for some days; indeed, he does not seem to hear us when we speak to him. I should tell him at once if I only knew how he would take it; but men are so funny and I am not quite sure that it might not inflame his feelings rather than allay them. I feel more and more, however, that Hatty would not prove the ideal mate for him. He needs a more womanly woman, and especially one who would not laugh at him. I think I must just wait and see, as our dear father used to say so often . . .

"May 25. Swithin sent his brougham this evening for Hester and Hatty and they dined with him to meet Mr. Chessman and Mr. and Mrs. Traquair. Timothy looked very blue; all the evening he sat as glum as glum; and I noticed that when the girls came back in the highest spirits he was in such a fluster that he gave Hatty his own negus by mistake. When she was going to bed she left her shawl on the back of her chair, and when Timothy took it up to restore it to her, I saw him put it to his nose. I very much fear that it is not the highest side of him that she appeals to. This makes it very difficult for me to say anything. I have a feeling that Mr. Chessman is providential. I questioned Hester closely about him and from what she says he and Hatty get on together like a house on fire. I do not suppose from what Swithin told us that he is so warm a man as dear Timothy, who has always been of a saving disposition and is doing so very well now with his primers, and I am sure he cannot be so safe a man, but to do Hatty justice I do not think she is of a mercenary turn of mind. It is very agitating, and I can only pray that all will turn out for the best . . .

"May 28. Timothy sent a message to me this morning that he was going to Brighton for some sea air and would not be back for a fortnight. *You cannot imagine what a relief it was to me* for, after what happened last night, I was dreading having to do my duty. I cannot but think he knows what I had to tell him and that it is all over for the best. He took a cab and caught the early train without saying good-bye or indeed seeing any of us. I must put it all down as clearly as I can.

"Yesterday evening Mr. and Mrs. Traquair called for Hatty to take her to dine and to their box at the opera afterwards. We four had a cosy little dinner at home just to ourselves, the first time since Hatty came. Cook had made some mincepies specially, and the pulled-bread was more delicious than I ever remember it. Timothy got up a bottle of the special brown sherry, and he filled our glasses himself; then he held his up and screwed up his eyes and said: 'Well, here's to home and beauty!' He looked quite waggish. But he was very distrait afterwards and went off to his study. I confess that I felt quite nervous, for I have never known him propose a toast or screw up his eyes like that; and knowing what I did I could not help fearing that he was making up his mind to a proposal. Juley and I played bézique for some time, and I got more and more anxious, and when the negus came I took Timothy's glass down to the study. He was sitting at his desk with a pen in his mouth and his eyes fixed on the ceiling; and I noticed that he had been tearing up paper. It was all strewn about, and when I ventured to pick up some pieces and put them into the wastepaper basket I saw the word 'Hatty' on one of them. He was quite cross at being interrupted. 'What's the matter with you, Ann?' he said: 'I'm busy.' And then he went off again into a brown study. I did not know what to do for the best. So I went away and sat in the drawing-room waiting for him to come up. The girls had gone to bed, and I took my tatting into the window, it was such a warm night. I confess that I prayed to God while I was sitting there. Timothy has always been my baby since our dear mother died when Susan was born, and it was dreadful to me to think that he might be taking a step that would lead to his unhappiness. I could not see what he could be writing and tearing up to Hatty except a proposal of marriage. His forehead had been flushed, and his eyes looked quite glassy. It seemed a very long time that I sat there. The Bayswater Road was quite quiet, and the lights of the Exhibition in the Park were so pretty, and there were stars in the sky, I always think they are wonderful, so bright and so far off. I could not tatt properly for thinking of dear Timothy. And still he did not come up, though it grew very late. I knew that he must be sitting up to let Hatty in; and that probably he would then give her the letter he had been writing. I was in despair till I thought: When she comes I will go down myself and open the door to her, and perhaps Timothy will let me talk to him before he puts the 'fat in the fire' as James would say. My nerves became all fiddlestrings, so at last I took up the works of Mr. Cowper, and tried to calm myself. The carriages and cabs were coming now bringing back people from the theatres and the Exhibition, and I knew I had not long to wait. I was just reading those clever little verses on 'The high price of fish' when I saw a hansom cab stopping at our door. I must say it gave me quite a shock, and I rubbed my eyes, because I had made sure that the Traquairs would bring Hatty back in their carriage. A man got out first in an opera cloak and hat, and then I saw him quite plainly assisting Hatty to alight. He placed her on the ground and lifted her hand to his lips, and I could see her look at him so archly. He got back into the cab and drove away. It was Mr. Chessman. At first I was so paralysed at the thought that she had driven all the way with him from the opera, *alone in the cab*, that I could not move. Then I wondered whether Timothy also had seen what I had seen. In my disturbance I ran down stairs into the hall. The door of his room was shut and there was the bell ringing. He did not come out, so then I knew that he must have seen. I am afraid I did a very unladylike thing, for I stood outside his door and listened. From my own feelings I could tell what a shock it must have been to him to know that the lady to whom he was about to offer his hand had driven alone at night with a comparative stranger in one of those new cabs which are so private. I could hear a noise, indeed, as if someone were breathing very hard—it was a dreadful moment; then, afraid that he might do something violent, I ran to the front door and opened it. There was Hatty, as cool as a cucumber. I am thankful now that I said nothing to her, but she must have seen from my face that I knew everything. 'Well,' she said, pertly, 'here we are again! Such a treat, dear Papa! Good-night, Miss Forsyte!' and ran upstairs. My heart bled for Timothy. I listened again at his door, and could hear

him walking up and down just like an animal in the Zoo.
He went on for quite a long time, for though he does not
show them, he has always had very deep feelings. You cannot imagine what a relief it was when suddenly I heard him
begin to whistle Pop goes the weasel!' I knew, then, that
the worst was over; and, though he was still walking up and
down, I stole upstairs as quietly as a mouse. I am sure I
was right in thinking that discretion was the better part of
valour. Timothy cannot bear anyone to see him affected in
any way, it puts him into a perfect fantod. When I got to
my room I fell on my knees, and thanked God for this providential escape; though, when I think of Hatty in that cab, I
feel that the ways of Providence are indeed inscrutable. It
is a great relief to me to think that by now Timothy must be
on the Pier at Brighton with the good sea air, and all the
distractions . . .

"June 1. Hatty left us to-day. I should be sorry to say
that I think her 'fast,' I am sure she really has a good
heart, but I confess that I feel her influence on Juley and
Hester has been unsettling—she is of course much younger
than they, and the young people of to-day, seem to have
no deportment, and very little sense of duty or indeed of
manners. I really find it difficult to forgive her for the
flippant thing she said at the last minute: 'Tell Timothy
that I'm sorry if I astonished his weak nerves.' And she
whisked off before I could even answer . . .

"June 6. Timothy is still in Brighton. Hester had a
letter from him yesterday in which he said that he had
walked up to the Devil's Punchbowl and that it had done
his liver good. He has seen the performing fleas too, and the
aquarium. Swithin has been down, he says, driving his
new greys—he—Timothy—does not think much of them;
but, of course, he is not the judge of a horse that Swithin

is. He made no allusion to Hatty in his letter, so I hope the wound is beginning to heal. Jolyon came in this afternoon when the girls were out, and told me of a picture he had bought 'Dutch fishing boats at Sunset'——he has such good judgment. He was so genial that I opened my heart to him about Timothy and Hatty. He twinkled and said:

" 'H'm! Timothy had a narrow squeak.' It was so well put, I think . . .

"June 11. Everybody says the Exhibition is a great success, in spite of all the foreigners that it has attracted. Prince Albert has become quite popular. Hester had a letter from Hatty this morning. Fancy! She has received an offer of marriage from Mr. Chessman. It is such a relief, because quite apart from dear Timothy, it has always been on my conscience that it was from our house that she behaved as she did. And now that Timothy comes home to-morrow everything is for the best, if only this news does not reopen his wound . . ."

Soames let the little red volume drop and took up the yellowed letter. He balanced it in his hand, feeling its thin and slightly greasy texture. So that was that! He cackled faintly. The quaint old things! But suddenly his veins tingled with a flush of loyalty. Nobody should laugh at them except himself! No, by Jove! And, taking the little volumes and the letter, he pitched them one by one into the wood fire.

AUNT JULEY'S COURTSHIP

1855

AUNT JULEY'S COURTSHIP

THE Crimean war and the marriage of Septimus Small
with Miss Julia Forsyte, which both occupied part of
the year 1855, were linked by a water picnic arranged for
the entertainment of that 'hero,' Major Small, a younger
brother of Septimus, who had been wounded in the leg.
What bound Septimus himself to the Forsyte family was
indubitably architecture, for he was a member of the firm
of Dewbridge, Small and Keyman, who specialised in the
domestic Gothic, which at that period was subjugating the
taste of the British Islands. Roger Forsyte, in the course
of his profession—the collection of house property—had
many dealings with this firm which had designed for him
a row of houses on a site he had picked up in Kensington,
then somewhat out of the world; and to Septimus Small's
riverside villa at Twickenham Roger sometimes repaired
on Sundays to consummate his plans over cigars and claret
cup. After his marriage in 1853 he would be accompanied
by Mrs. Roger, and they would take her on the river,
paddling with a rather deep-sea stroke, in long whiskers,
ducks, and shallow wide-brimmed straw hats, while pretty
little Mrs. Roger held the tiller and covered the boat's
stern and other matters with her crinoline. In the severe
winter of 1854 Septimus, a man of weak constitution, inadvertently contracted bronchitis. He emerged with the
long full beard and the cough which subsequently secured
for him the cognomen 'Cough Lozenge' from the young
Rogers, who all made their appearance between the years
of '53 and '62—George, inventor of the nickname, having
'56 to his vintage. There can be no doubt that it was this
cough and long beard which won the heart of Julia, then

barely 'Aunt Juley,' since only young Jolyon, young Roger, young Nicholas, Ernest, and St. John Hayman had been born, and were still mostly in the cradle. When, years later, she heard that dear Septimus went about being called 'Cough Lozenge' in the family, she nearly had a fit.

In 1855, at the age of forty, she had a certain pink and pouting charm; but would have denied with vigour Roger's frequent remark to Mrs. Roger: "Juley's setting her cap at Sep." The idea! *Her* cap, indeed, when it was entirely for *his* good, and his least cough set her trembling with a sort of delighted pity! He did so want someone to look after him and see that he took care at night, and to trim his beard, that was so manly and so sensible, covering his chest. To her the notion that anyone so interesting-looking, almost handsome, should be a 'confirmed bachelor,' as Roger put it, was painful. Her sister Susan, too, seven years younger than herself, and already for three years wedded to John Hayman, was always telling her how John admired her in this dress or in that, and had once gone so far as to imply that he admired her in nothing—so daring of Susan—not quite nice!

When, then, in July of 1855 she was invited to come with Roger and his wife to this water picnic, she was all of a flutter and gave much thought to her costume. She came out finally in pink with green ribbons in her bonnet, and a perfectly new crinoline. Roger, living then in Bayswater, warming a house that he intended to sell shortly at a reasonable profit—not till 'sixty-nine did he anchor himself permanently in Prince's Gate—called for her with his carriage of a new-fangled shape named 'Victoria' (always so unusual, Roger—eccentric, some people called it). On the way down to Twickenham he had to sit back to the horses on a narrow little seat that came out from below the high box, and was propped up with an iron stand; and he was so cross that it was quite a relief to them all three when they arrived, and dear Mr. Small met them at the gate, looking most manly in a puggaree and white trousers—'ducks,' Roger called them, he was so droll. In his hand, too, he had a bunch of picotees, and held them to her nose with quite an air. "These are for you, Miss Julia," he said. Tucked into her fichu they went beautifully with her dress, and were so fragrant; it would have been perfect if Roger had not closed his left eye quickly two or three times. As if——! Then they all went into the house to meet Major Small and have light refreshment before going on the river.

'Parsons' Villa' (Aunt Juley subsequently changed the name to Sunninglea) had not been built by Dewbridge, Small and Keyman; it was in fact Georgian, on two floors, with French windows from the drawing-room on to the lawn, the river close below, and a little island opposite. In the drawing-room were four persons, making eight in all for the picnic: Major Small, a fine, full-bearded figure of a man, with a stiff leg, in a tussore suit; Hatty Chessman, always the life and soul of any party, and— "Who do you think, my dear?"—Augustus Perry; almost famous for those delightful books with music and rhymes in them, and his recitals at parties. It was he who made up that 'Round' which became so popular:

> "A boat, a boat unto the ferry,
>   And we'll go over and be merry,
>   And laugh and quaff and sing Down-derry."

And he had witty variations for the last line, such as: "And laugh and quaff and drink brown sherry," or: "And laugh and quaff—Augustus Perry."

Seated on a chintz-covered chair with a glass of sherry

cobbler in her hand, and a bowl of lavender close to her
nose, Julia could not help looking at Mrs. Augustus Perry
and wondering a little if she liked being the wife of anyone
so popular, so sought after as Gus Perry, who played the
guitar, too. She was hoping so much that she herself
would not be in a boat with Roger—he was such a tease,
especially if their dear host were in the same boat. And
she hoped he was noticing how brightly she was talking
with Major Small; and indeed it was an honour to be talking to him, for after all it was he who had the stiff leg,
and was the hero; but all the time she contrived to watch
their dear host and to note that he looked a little anxious.
Then they all went down across the lawn to the two boats,
so graceful, with striped cushions and brown varnish. It
was a moment, not knowing in which boat she was to be,
with Augustus Perry cracking so many jokes. But her arm
was taken gently, firmly, above the elbow by Mr. Septimus,
and she was stepping into a boat, and sitting down quite
quickly beside her sister-in-law on the stern seat.

"My dear," she said, "I hope I am not required to steer.
It's such a responsibility."

"Oh! I will steer, dear Juley," replied her sister-in-law.

Crinoline by crinoline they sat, and—so gratifying—who
should step into the boat but dear Mr. Septimus himself,
and Augustus Perry. She could not help smiling when
that droll Gus said:

"I shall take my coat off, Sep."

And Mr. Septimus always courtly, asked:

"Do you mind, ladies?" Indeed, they didn't!

So both took their coats off, and placed the oars in the
rowlocks. And then the boat glided out. It *was* delightful! Julia felt, somehow, that not only herself, but dear
little Mary beside her, who was looking so pretty, was glad

that dear Roger (even though he was her husband) was not in their boat. How beautifully they rowed, almost together; Augustus Perry—his face was so round, without whiskers or anything—kept popping it out from behind Mr. Septimus's back, to make such amusing remarks. And then he 'caught a crab' on purpose! How they did laugh; he looked so droll! So first they went up the stream, and then they came down the stream, with the water all green and the swans all white—and landed on the little island opposite 'Parsons' Villa,' where they found the picnic baskets —fancy! It *was* all beautifully planned, and so romantic under the willow trees, with rugs for them to sit on, and Augustus Perry's guitar, quite like a picture by Watteau.

The lunch was exquisite: lobster salad, pigeon pie, tipsy cake, raspberries, and champagne: with plates and spoons, forks and napkins, and a dear little water rat looking on. She had never enjoyed anything so much, and she was really quite relieved when Major Small flirted outrageously with Hatty Chessman, and gave them no more anxiety. To be waited on by their dear host was such a privilege, and Roger and Gus Perry were so droll; altogether it was enchanting. When they had all finished lunch and the gentlemen were smoking their cigars, they sang some delightful 'rounds': 'A boat, a boat,' 'Three blind mice,' 'White sand and grey sand.' Mr. Septimus's voice was so manly—deep and hollow, almost like an organ. Then they played hide-and-seek. Each in turn was allowed five minutes to hide from the others—such a clever idea, so thoughtful. She herself hid among some willow bushes, and who do you think found her? Mr. Septimus: he was so surprised! When they had all hidden it was time for tea, and such a to-do boiling the kettle. Roger, indeed—it was just like him—suggested that they should leave the kettle and go

over and have tea in the house; but that would have destroyed all the romance. And when at last the kettle did
boil, it would have been a delicious cup, only the water
was smoky. But nobody minded, because, of course, it was
a picnic. Then came the moment when the other six got
into one boat and rowed away. It seemed quite providential. So she and their dear host helped the servants to
pack everything in the other boat to take over to the house.
While they were doing that, she noticed that he coughed
three times.

"I am sure," she said, "dear Mr. Septimus, it's too damp
for you on the river so late. It was past six." How good he
was about it!

"Let us sit on the lawn, then, Miss Julia," he said, "and
wait for the others to come back."

So they sat under the cedar tree where it was beautifully
cool, and quite private, for the branches came down very
low. She had quite a fluttery feeling, sitting there all alone
with him for the first time. But he was so considerate,
talking about Southey. Did she like his poetry? He himself preferred Milton.

"I must confess, Mr. Septimus," she said, "that I have
not read 'Paradise Regained,' but Milton is certainly a very
beautiful poet—so sonorous."

"And what do you think of Wordsworth, Miss Julia?"

"Oh! I love Mr. Wordsworth! I always feel he must
have had such a beautiful character."

As she said this she could not help wondering if he would
ask her whether she read Byron. If he did, she should be
daring and say: 'Yes, indeed!' She did not want to have
secrets from him, and she had been so impressed by 'Childe
Harold,' and 'The Giaour.' Of course Lord Byron had
not had good principles, but she was sure dear Mr. Septimus

would never suspect her of reading anything that was not nice. There was 'Don Juan' in Timothy's study—several volumes. Hester had read them and been horrified. And when he did not ask her she felt quite disappointed; it would have drawn them closer together, she was sure. But she could feel that he was shy about it; because he asked her instead whether she liked the novels of Charles Dickens.

"Of course," she said, "he is very clever, but I do think he writes about such very peculiar, such very common characters; and there is so much about drinking in 'The Pickwick Papers,' though most people, I know, like them very much. Do you admire 'The Pickwick Papers,' Mr. Septimus?"

"No, Miss Julia; it seems to me a very extravagant book."

Time went so quickly under the cedar, and it would have been quite perfect if the midges had not bitten her dreadfully through her stockings; for, of course, she could not scratch, or even say "La!" She did so wonder whether they were biting him, too. The longer they sat there the more she felt that he did not take enough care of himself, with no scarf on, in the evening air; he did so need someone to look after him. And so the midges bit, and she smiled, and the boat came back, with Augustus Perry singing to his guitar. What an agreeable rattle he was, was he not? And how romantic always—music on the water!

Then it all came to an end, and she drove home alone with dear little Mary in the Victoria, Roger refusing to sit back to the horses on 'that knife-board' any more, and going off with Hatty Chessman in her brougham. Such a relief! It had been such a—such a holy afternoon, and she did so want not to be teased about it. . . .

On the Bayswater Road that night she sat a long time at her window thinking of Septimus's beard, and whether she would dare to come to calling him 'Sep,' and whether he would ever ask her to let him go and see her eldest brother, dear Jolyon—now that their father was dead. . . .

And then came their correspondence; that *was* a delightful experience. His letters sometimes contained a sprig of lavender—his favourite scent; they were beautifully written, because he was an architect, and full of high principle, so refined. Now and then, indeed, she would feel as if he might be too refined, because she had often read the Marriage Service and—thought about what it meant, as who indeed would not? In her own letters she tried hard not to be just gossipy, but like Maria Edgeworth. All that time she was knitting him a scarf. It had to be quite a secret, and done in her bedroom, because if Timothy saw it he would be sure to say: "Is that for me?" And perhaps would add: "I don't want a great thing like that." And if she said: "No, it's not for you," he would be quite upset and want to know whom it was for; which would never do.

In August they went (Ann and Hester, herself and Timothy) to Brighton for the sea air, and in a letter she happened to mention it to Septimus—always Septimus in her thoughts. Imagine her surprise, then, when on the third day she saw him sitting on the pier. It gave her such a colour. Timothy stopped short at once.

"Why! That's Sep Small! I'm off!" It showed how little he understood, or he would never have left her like that alone with him. But what an adorable hour that was, hanging over the pier by his side. He knew such a lot about marine things—he pressed seaweed, and could not bear nigger-minstrels. He told her, too, that the sea air was good for his cough, and she was sure he had noticed her hat, for he said in such a far-away voice: "I dote on these pork-pie hats you see about, Miss Julia, and the veils are so sensible!" And there was hers floating almost against his cheek. It was all so friendly and delightful; and she did long to ask him to come back with her to lunch at their hotel so that she could get out his scarf and say: "I have a little surprise for you, dear Mr. Septimus," and clasp it round his neck; but she felt it would make a 'how-de-do'! It would be too dreadful if Timothy showed anything by his manner; and sometimes he showed such a lot, especially if he were kept waiting for meals. For, of course, neither he nor dear Ann, nor even Hester, knew anything about her feelings for dear 'Sep'; so on the whole it would be better not. And then—so providential!—*he* asked if he might escort her back to her hotel, and what *could* she say except that she would be flattered! He looked so tall and aristocratic walking beside her, with his full beard, and a puggaree round his hat, and his white, green-lined umbrella. She hoped, indeed, that people might be thinking: 'What a distinguished couple!' Many hopes flitted in her mind while they strolled along the front, and watched the common people eating winkles, and smelled the tarry boats. And something tender welled up in her so that she could not help stopping to call his attention to the sea, so blue with little white waves.

"I *do* love Nature," she said.

"Ah! Miss Julia," he answered—she always remembered his words—"the beauties of Nature are indeed only exceeded by those of—Tut!—I have a fly in my eye!"

"Dear Mr. Septimus, let me take it out with the corner of my handkerchief."

And he let her. It took quite a long time; he was so brave, keeping his eye open; and when at last she got it out, very black and tiny, they both looked at it together; it seemed to her to draw them quite close, as if they were looking into each other's souls. Such a wonderful moment! And then—her heart beat fast—he had taken her hand. Her knees felt weak; she looked up into his face, so thin and high-minded and anxious, with a little streak where the eye had watered; and something of adoration crept up among her pinkness and her pouts, into her light grey eyes. He lifted her hand slowly till it reached his beard, and stooped his lips to it. Fancy! On the esplanade! All went soft and sweet within her; her lips trembled, and two large tears rolled out of her eyes.

"Miss Julia," he said, "Julia—may I hope?"

"Dear Septimus," she answered, "indeed, you *may*."

And through a mist she saw his puggaree float out in the delicious breeze, and under one end of it a common man stop eating winkles, to stare up at her, as if he had seen a rainbow.

NICHOLAS–REX
1864

NICHOLAS–REX

IN the late seventies someone made the remark: "Nicholas Forsyte—cleverest man in London." And with this dictum those who observed him in his business and public capacity were frequently in agreement. It is in the hinterland of his existence that one must look for qualifications of the statement. Wherever he functioned Nicholas was certainly cock of the walk—indeed he looked a little like a cock, very natty, with a high forehead and his hair brushed off it in a comb, erect, and with quick movements of his head and neck. His colouring too was fresh and sanguine and his hair almost chestnut before it went grey. When he rose at a meeting and opened with one of his dry witticisms people sat forward, and seldom took their ears off him till he resumed his seat. He was almost notorious for his power of making an opponent look foolish, and than that no greater asset is in the balance sheet of a public man. For Nicholas was a public man in the minor sense suitable to a Forsyte. He never aspired to extravagances of power or position—never for instance went into Parliament. He confined himself to obtaining the practical, if not the nominal, control of any concern in which he held interests; and he had a certain tempered public spirit which led him almost insensibly to grasp the helm of two utility corporations, the one concerned with tramways, and the other with canals, although his holdings in them were not considerable. As a judge of an investment he was perhaps unique, so much so that his five brothers felt it almost a relief when one of his investments went wrong. He could be sharp and he could be genial, and no one ever knew beforehand which he was going to be; and this in itself was a source of sovereignty. One might say with a reasonable amount of certainty that he had never had a friend. Many men had tried it on with him, but he had always nipped them off sooner or later and generally sooner. He was perhaps constitutionally unable to associate with people on terms of equality. On the other hand his integrity was admirable, for he owed integrity to himself, and one could always follow him with a feeling that one would not be let down. Without knowing anything at all about him one would have taken him, perhaps, for one of those extremely high-class doctors who do not move out of their own houses, and that only at a good many guineas. With all this he had not much health, or rather just the health of a Forsyte, which kept him alive until he was ninety-one, and might better be termed vitality.

Without being exactly close in money matters he was the most guarded of the clan, partly no doubt because he had more children and partly because of a certain austerity which had little patience with fashion and fallals, and believed almost pitilessly in work being good for the human being. And this brings one to his hinterland which began, one may suggest, with his marriage in 1848. Whether in marrying at all he did justice to the truest instincts of supremacy will ever remain a question; but the fact is he was a man who had to be married and married somewhat young, given Queen Victoria and his own constitution. That he undoubtedly married money,—and long before the Married Woman's Property Act, so that he was able to make the most judicious use of it, and Mrs. Nicholas to make none at all—must not be regarded as proof of a cold-blooded selection. On the contrary he was an ardent wooer, in pegtop trousers, of a very pretty girl, the daughter of a county-town banker with whom finance had thrown him into contact. Limited by her mother and possibly by her crinoline, the young lady had kept Nicholas at a respectable distance until after a ceremony observed with every circumstance including a really witty speech from her bridegroom. She had been the more surprised afterwards.

To this surprise must be attributed the inception of that "fronde" which smouldered for so many decades behind the façade of his sovereignty.

We will not pause here to enquire whether the manners of the twentieth century would have saved Nicholas, or rather Mrs. Nicholas, from receiving the feeling that she was married. The fact remains that she received it. As, one by one, she produced little Nicholases the feeling if anything increased. When she had produced six in fourteen years, she flatly refused to produce any more. From a woman not quite thirty-five this seemed to Nicholas, who had by then a considerable fortune, wholly unreasonable—the more so as it was the first definite limit set to his prerogative. And to this fettering of his complete freedom must be attributed much of that nervous irritability which he undoubtedly developed. But who, seeing Mrs. Nicholas, would have dreamed that she was in any way responsible for the moods of her lord and master. The fact is that no one except Nicholas ever did see Mrs. Nicholas—'Fanny' as she was called, because her real name was Elizabeth. Her manner in public was almost the opposite of her manner in private. She is described somewhere as entering a room behind Nicholas "with an air of frightened jollity." How true! She did. And why? Because he would aim at her wittily caustic shafts which she had never learned to parry. And she would smile and smile with that frightened look in her eyes, and generally be so glad to get home before he had aimed one. But when she was home, and there was no one but herself to hear him, that frightened look would disappear. And in a hundred womanly ways (without perhaps deliberately meaning to) she avenged it. Not before the children, no—mainly in the privacy of the common bedroom, supremely in the privacy of the common bed. There she would reduce Nicholas from sovereignty to supplication. She did it not because he was repellent to her—he was never that—but almost as it were on principle, because she had, after all, a soul of her own, and there were no other means of asserting it. In all the manifest ways of life he was the perfect autocrat, paying the piper—incidentally not altogether without what had been her money—and calling the tune. Who can blame her, then, for reminding him that he was mortal, and that she was mortal too. We have here in miniature, indeed, a somewhat perfect illustration of monarchy and the attempt of subjects at its limitation.

This continual strife to limit Nicholas was of course but vaguely suspected on "Forsyte 'Change" and cannot therefore be recorded with any precision; but, in spite of all the instinctive camouflage lavished on the matter, there did come into the family consciousness news of a phase of it worth commemorating for the light it throws on the change in British institutions and the imperfection of human judgments. It began with a letter from Mrs. Nicholas dated: "June the twenty-fourth 1864: The Chine Hotel, Bournemouth" which ran thus:

"MY DEAR HUSBAND,—
    "I have long wished to take a step which I fear will cause you some anxiety and cannot fail to have roused your dis-

Nicholas-Rex

approval. I came to this nice hotel yesterday in this very charming spot with the intention of remaining here for some weeks. The sea air is delicious, and there are several quite nice people in the hotel. Please send me some of my money. Indeed, I think it would be nice if in future you paid me a regular allowance, out of the money that my dear father left me. Give my love to the dear children.

"Your affectionate wife,

"FANNY."

When Nicholas received this letter he was already in a state of considerable confusion—not to say anxiety—and he read it with a stupor unbecoming to the cleverest man in London. That a wife should have gone off by herself without giving notice had taken him—as he would not have expressed to anybody else—"flat aback." That, on the top of it, she should ask him to send her money and make her a regular allowance seemed to him outrageous. He went to bed and passed a wretched night. What was the woman about? The more he did not sleep the more he was inclined to think that he had never heard of such a thing. Next day he wrote in reply:

"MY DEAR FANNY,—

"I have received your letter. Your going off like that gave me a pretty surprise. If you choose to take things into your own hands, you must incur the consequences. I shall certainly not send you any money; and the best thing you can do is to come back home at once. As to a regular allowance what on earth do you want it for? I give you everything you can reasonably require. I suppose you have been listening to some clap-trap about married women's property. The sooner you rid your mind of any of these new-fangled notions the better it will be for both of us, and for the children.

"Now for goodness sake come to your senses, and come home.

"Your affectionate husband,
"NICHOLAS FORSYTE."

He went to a Board meeting irritably convinced that he had clinched the matter and that she would be home to-morrow. She was not, and the day after he received a second letter.

"MY DEAR HUSBAND,—

"I am sorry that you do not see the reasonableness of my conduct and of my requests. I shall therefore continue to stay on here. There is a very nice solicitor in the hotel, and he advises me that you will be liable for any debts I may have to incur, which I think, is quite reasonable. Of course, I did not tell him that I was speaking of myself. I hope your indigestion is better. Give my love to the dear children.

"Your affectionate wife,
"FANNY."

Nicholas put the letter down with the remark: "Well, for obstinacy give me a woman!" What on earth had come to her! Debts, indeed! Fiddlesticks! He was none the less "in a regular stew." To have his attention on important matters disturbed in this way was scandalous. Why! if it went on he would have to go down and bring her back! And it did go on. He answered the letter after waiting another day to see if she would come to her senses.

"MY DEAR WIFE,—

"Will you please understand that I expect you to come back, otherwise I shall be compelled to come down and fetch you. I am surprised and grieved at your conduct, especially at this moment when I have important business on hand. Now don't be silly, but come home like a good girl.

"Your affectionate husband,
                    "NICHOLAS FORSYTE."

To this letter he received no answer. Three days passed during which he experienced every kind of mental and some physical discomfort. He even began to have dark thoughts about the nice solicitor. Fanny was only thirty-seven, and with a woman you never knew. At last, thoroughly alarmed, he cried off from a meeting of the Central Canal Corporation, and went down to Bournemouth. At the hotel they told him that Mrs. Forsyte had left two days before. No! They had no address. The callous indifference to his feelings disclosed by this conduct upset Nicholas completely. That he should have to confront an almost grinning hotel manager and betray the fact that his own wife was acting independently was—was monstrous! He did not even ask if she had paid her bill; but his knowledge of hotels—he was on the Board of one—told him that she had, or they would have presented him with it. Where was she getting money from—throwing away her jewellery he shouldn't be surprised. He returned to London—there was nothing else to do. The next day he received a letter from her to say that she had moved on to Weymouth, but it was not as nice as she expected and she should not stay. She did not say where she was going. 'H'm!' thought Nicholas: 'Playing cat and mouse with me, is she?' And he went sullenly into the City.

Now a man may make the best resolutions about his wife, such as: "I'll have nothing more to do with her," or: "If she thinks she can tire me out she's very much mistaken."

But when, like Nicholas, he has given her six children—three of them at home; when, like Nicholas, he has a reputation for always having had his own way, and for being an irreproachable householder, it was exceptionally galling not even to be able to say with truth that he knew where his wife was, to have to avoid Forsyte 'Change as if it were the devil—as perhaps it was—and to sneak about his own house feeling that his children and his servants knew all about everything. He began to suffer severely from that kind of dyspepsia which arises from the thwarting of one's will, one's instincts, and one's self-esteem. He often thought: 'If she could see me, she wouldn't go on behaving like this.'

At the end of a fortnight he received from her a letter dated from an hotel at Cheltenham which, though it seemed to show a certain softening, mentioned a nice doctor who had given her some very kind advice—Doctors, indeed, as if he didn't know them!—and ended with the words: "I trust that you are now prepared, my dear husband, to make me a fixed and regular allowance, of course out of my own money. I think—do you not agree?—that £500 a year is the least amount that would be proper. I feel that if I had that I could come home again. In the meantime I have parted with my emerald pendant. Give my love to the dear children. Your affectionate wife, Fanny."

Parted with her emerald pendant! The thing had cost him ninety pounds, and he supposed she had got thirty or forty for it. The sheer folly of women had never seemed to him so patent. Five hundred a year, indeed, to throw away in fallals! But a cloud had undoubtedly been lifted from his brain by this letter. Here was at least a definite situation. If he promised her a fixed five hundred a year she would come home. It all came of agitators putting

ideas into women's heads, a mischievous lot! But the boys
would be back from school in another week or two; and it
would look extremely odd if their mother were not there
to go to the seaside with them.

An organ-grinder playing his confounded organ, had said
to him only yesterday: "No, Guv'nor, I knows the valley
of peace an' quietness—I don't move on under 'arf-a-
crown." The impudence of the ruffian had tickled Nicholas
and he had given him the half-crown. Fanny was behaving just like that. And who knew when she wouldn't be
off again to get out of him the rest of the thousand a year
he'd received with her. No, on the whole, he didn't think
she'd be as unreasonable as that; but he continued to combat his desire for peace and quietness at so considerable a
price. All the time he had a dim feeling that it wasn't
really the money she was after. She had never seemed to
know or care much about money, in fact he had often had
occasion to reproach her with indifference to its value.
What exactly she had in her head he hesitated to char-
acterize by a word which kept creeping nastily into his mind
—independence. Fanny independent! Why she'd be in
the workhouse to-morrow! Nicholas, indeed, was not unlike most people: he could not understand the need in others
for that without which he himself would have been wholly
miserable. What would be his own position if he made her
independent—he would be subject to her whims and fancies
and women's nonsense of all sorts! And then—this was a
bright moment—the solution occurred to him: Make her a
fixed and regular allowance, and stop it when he wanted
to! Everything seemed suddenly clear, he wondered he
hadn't thought of that before; and by the evening post he
wrote off to say that he had reconsidered the matter and was
prepared to pay her a regular allowance of a hundred and

twenty-five pounds a quarter, and he would send the carriage to meet the five o'clock train the day after to-morrow.

To say that he was surprised on receiving not Fanny, but another letter—saying that she had meant of course that the five hundred a year should be settled on her, with the word settled underlined—would be a gross under-statement. He would never have believed that Fanny of all women could be so sordid. He continued in this mood of surprised disgust for fully an hour seated in his study which specially faced north so that his head should never be heated by the intrusion of the sun. He was determined to do no such thing, and yet extremely conscious that he could not go on much longer in this wifeless condition. She had been away now for seventeen days, and every day his head was getting heavier and less clear. He would have to put an end to it somehow. While he sat thus, turning and turning the wheels of indecision, he was conscious of a whirring noise gradually becoming articulate—that confounded barrel organ, again, grinding out the popular song of the moment: "Up in a balloon boys, up in a balloon."

A flood of angry colour invaded Nicholas's clean-shaven face, running almost up into the grizzled cock's-comb rising from his forehead. He went to the window and threw it wide open. There was the ruffian grinding away and grinning at him. For a moment words failed Nicholas and then a flash of caustic humour redeemed him from his sober self. The fellow's impudence was really laughable! He grinned back and closed the window. If he'd been the organ grinder it was just what he would have done himself. The begger seemed to recognize that Greek had met Greek, for, after playing 'Champagne Charlie,' he wheeled his organ away.

Nicholas-Rex 79

But in Nicholas the little incident had changed the current of thought, or rather had swung the blood a little more to his head, so that now it seemed to him worth while to get Fanny back even on her own terms. His speech for the General Meeting of the "United Tramways Association" was due on Friday, and in the present heavy state of his head, due to this persistent wifelessness, he would be making a mess of it.

Five hundred a year—what was it after all—settled or not! He would go to James this very minute and get it over; then, with the settlement in his pocket, he would pop down himself to-morrow and bring her back. Calling a hansom, he uttered the word "Poultry" and got in. It was a long drive from Ladbroke Grove, and while he sat, behind the scuttling horse, erect, dapper, and shaken by the cobblestones of the London of those days, he thought of how he should put it to his brother James, in answer to the question the fellow would be sure to ask: "What d'you want to do that for?" And he decided merely to say: "What business is that of yours?" James was always a bit of an old woman, and it was best to be sharp with him.

With a certain dismay therefore he heard James say instead:

"I thought you'd be having to do that—they say Fanny's on the high horse."

"*Who* says?" barked Nicholas.

James ploughed through one of his ultra-Crimean whiskers: "Oh! They—Timothy and the girls."

"What business have they to gabble about what they know nothing of?"

James cleared his throat.

"Well," he said, "I don't know, they never tell me anything."

"What!" snapped Nicholas. "Why, you sit there and talk scandal by the hour together. Well, I've no time to waste. Draw this settlement and make yourself and old Bustard the trustees. I want it all ship-shape by eleven o'clock to-morrow. You can put in enough of my Great Western Stock to provide five hundred a year."

Cheltenham—there was something appropriate about the Stock; and to himself he thought: 'Railways—I don't trust them; they'll be inventing something else before long.'

He left James somewhat agitated over the hurry his brother was in. The fellow however came up to the scratch, and with the settlement all signed and sealed, Nicholas caught the afternoon train to Cheltenham. He spent the hours of travel in coining caustic remonstrances against being treated in the way he had been, but when he arrived and found her having tea in the hotel drawing-room looking quite fresh and young, he decided to postpone them, and all he said was: "Well, Fanny, you look quite bobbish."

And she answered: "What a long time, dear Nicholas! How are the dear children?"

"I've been bad with my head," said Nicholas, "the children are all right. I've brought you this," and he placed the settlement on the tea-table, "it's all right—you won't understand a word of it."

"I'm sure, dear Nicholas, that you've done it beautifully."

And while she read it, wrinkling her brows, Nicholas watched her, and thought:

'She's a better-looking woman than I remembered.'

Throughout the evening he was quite cheerful, not to say witty. It all seemed, indeed, a little like the days of their honeymoon at Brighton.

Not until nearly midnight, did he turn on his elbow and say rather suddenly:

"What on earth made you do it?"

"Oh, dear Nicholas," replied her voice, close to his own, "I did so want a nice quiet rest."

"Rest? What d'you want a rest from—you've got no work?"

She smiled.

"And now," she said, "I shall be able to go and have one whenever I feel I want it."

"The deuce you will!"

"How nice it will be, too, never having to ask you for money. It does so annoy you sometimes."

And Nicholas thought: 'Well, I *have* been and gone and done it. Women!' Turning still more on his elbow, he regarded her lying on her back with that queer little smile on her lips as if she were saying to herself: 'Dear Nicholas, the cleverest man in London!'

So was Nicholas, in common with other Kings, limited by his Constitution.

A SAD AFFAIR
1867

A SAD AFFAIR

IN 1866, at the age of nineteen, young Jolyon Forsyte left Eton and went up to Cambridge, in the semi-whiskered condition of those days. An amiable youth of fair scholastic and athletic attainments, and more susceptible to emotions, æsthetic and otherwise, than most young barbarians, he went up a little intoxicated on the novels of Whyte-Melville. From continually reading about whiskered dandies, garbed to perfection and imperturbably stoical in the trying circumstances of debt and discomfiture, he had come to the conviction that to be whiskered and unmoved by Fortune was quite the ultimate hope of existence. There was something not altogether ignoble at the back of his creed. He passed imperceptibly into a fashionable set, and applied himself to the study of whist. All the heroes of Whyte-Melville played whist admirably; all rode horses to distraction. Young Jolyon joined the Drag, and began to canter over to Newmarket, conveniently situated for Cambridge undergraduates. Like many youths before and after him, he had gone into residence with little or no idea of the value of money; and in the main this 'sad affair' must be traced to the fact that while he had no idea of the value of money, and, in proportion to his standards, not much money, his sire, Old Jolyon, had much idea of the value of money, and still more money. The hundred pounds placed to his credit for his first term seemed to young Jolyon an important sum, and he had very soon none of it left. This surprised him, but was of no great significance, because all Whyte-Melville's dandies were in debt; indeed, half their merit consisted in an imperturbable indifference to mere financial liability. Young Jolyon proceeded, therefore, to get into debt. It was easy, and 'the thing.' At the end of his first term he had spent just double his allowance. He was not vicious nor particularly extravagant—but what, after all, was money? Besides, to live on the edge of Fortune was the only way to show that one could rise above it. Not that he deliberately hired horses, bought clothes, boots, wine and tobacco, for that purpose; still, there was in a sense a principle involved. This is made plain, because it was exactly what was not plain to Old Jolyon later on. He, as a young man, with not half his son's allowance, had never been in debt, had paid his way, and made it. But then he had not had the advantages of Eton, Cambridge, and the novels of Whyte-Melville. He had simply gone into Tea.

Young Jolyon going up for his second term, with another hundred pounds from an unconscious sire, at once perceived that if he paid his debts, or any appreciable portion of them, he would have no money for the term's expenses. He therefore applied his means to the more immediate ends of existence—College fees, 'wines,' whist, riding, and so forth—and left his debts to grow.

At the end of his first year he was fully three hundred pounds to the bad, and beginning to be reflective. Unhappily, however, he went up for his second year with longer whiskers and a more perfect capacity for enjoyment than ever. He had the best fellows in the world for friends, life was sweet, Schools still far off. He was liked and he liked being liked; he had, in fact, a habit of existence eminently unsuited to the drawing-in of horns.

Now his set were very pleasant young men from Eton and Harrow and Winchester, some of whom had more worldly knowledge than young Jolyon, and some of whom had more money, but none of whom had more sense of responsibility. It was in the rooms of 'Cuffs' Charwell (the name was pronounced Cherrell) who was taking Divinity Schools, and was afterwards the Bishop, that whist was first abandoned for baccarat, under the auspices of 'Donny' Covercourt. That young scion of the Shropshire Covercourts had discovered this exhilarating pastime, indissolubly connected with the figure Nine, at a French watering-place during the Long Vacation, and when he returned to Cambridge was brimming over with it, in his admirably impassive manner. Now, young Jolyon was not by rights a gambler; that is to say, he was self-conscious about the thing, never properly carried away. Moreover, in spite of Whyte-Melville, he was by this time indubitably nervous about his monetary position—on all accounts, therefore, inclined to lose rather than to win. But when such cronies as 'Cuffs' Cherrell, 'Feathers' Totteridge, Guy Winlow, and 'Donny' himself—best fellows in the world —were bent on baccarat, who could be a 'worm' and wriggle away?

On the fourth evening his turn came to take the 'bank.' What with paying off his most pestiferous creditors and his College fees, so unfeelingly exacted in advance, he had just fifteen pounds left—the term being a fortnight spent. He was called on to take a 'bank' of one hundred. With a sinking heart and a marbled countenance, therefore, he sat down at the head of the green board. This was his best chance, so far, of living up to his whiskers—come what would, he must not fail the shades of 'Digby Grand,' 'Daisy Waters,' and the 'Honble. Crasher'!

He lost from the first moment; with one or two momentary flickers of fortune in his favour, his descent to Avernus was one of the steadiest ever made. He sat through it with his heart kept in by very straight lips. He rose languidly at the end of half an hour with the 'bank' broken, and, wanly smiling, signed his I.O.U.'s, including one to 'Donny' Covercourt for a cool eighty. Restoring himself with mulled claret, he resumed his seat at the board, but, for the rest of the evening, neither won nor lost. He went across the Quad to his own rooms with a queasy feeling——he was seeing his father's face. For this was his first unpayable debt of honour, so different from mere debts to tradesmen. And, sitting on his narrow bed in his six-foot by fifteen bedroom, he wrestled for the means of payment. Paid somehow it must be! Would his Bank let him overdraw to the amount? He could see the stolid faces behind that confounded counter. Not they! And if they didn't! That brute Davids? Or——the Dad? Which was worse? Oh, the Dad was worse! For, suddenly, young Jolyon was perceiving that from the beginning he had lived up here a life that his father would not understand. With a sort of horror he visualized his effort to explain it to that high-domed forehead, and the straight glance that came from so deep behind. No! Davids was the ticket! After all, 'Daisy Waters,' 'Digby Grand,' the 'Honble. Crasher,' and the rest of the elect——had they jibbed at money-lenders? Not so! Did 'Feathers,' did 'Donny'? What else were money-lenders for but lending money? Trying to cheer himself with that thought, he fell asleep from sheer unhappiness.

Next morning, at his Bank, very tight lips assured him that an overdraft without security was not in the day's work. Young Jolyon arched his eyebrows, ran fingers through a best whisker, drawled the words: "It's of no consequence!" and went away, stiffening his fallen crest. In front of him he saw again his father's face, and he couldn't stand it. He sought the rooms of 'Feathers' Totteridge. The engaging youth had just had his 'tosh' and was seated over devilled kidneys, in his dressing-gown.

Young Jolyon said:

"Feathers, old cock, give me a note to that brute Davids!"

Feathers stared. "What ho, friend!" he said. "Plucked? He'll skin you, Jo."

"Can't be helped," said young Jolyon, glumly.

He went away armed with the note, and in the afternoon sought the abode of Mr. Rufus Davids. The Hebraic benefactor read the note, and bent on young Jolyon the glance of criticism.

"How mutth do you want, Mithter Forthyte?" he said.

"One hundred and fifty."

"That will cotht you two hundred thicth month from now. I give good termth."

Good terms! Young Jolyon checked the opening of his lips. One didn't chaffer.

"I like to know my cuthtomerth, you know, Mithter Forthyte. I athk a little bird or two. Come in to-morrow."

"You can take me or leave me," said young Jolyon.

"Thatth all right, Mithter Forthyte. To-morrow afternoon."

Young Jolyon nodded, and went out.

It hadn't been so bad, after all; and, cantering over to Newmarket, he almost forgot how 'Post equitem sedet atra cura.'

In the afternoon of the following day he received one hundred and fifty pounds for his autograph, and seeking out 'Donny' and the others who held his I.O.U.'s, discharged the lot. Not without a sense of virtue did he sit down to an evening collation in his rooms. He was eating cold wild duck, when his door was knocked on.

"Come in!" he shouted. And, there—in overcoat, top hat in hand—his father stood. . . .

Sitting in the City offices of those great tea-men, 'Forsyte and Treffry,' old Jolyon had been handed, with the country post, a communication marked: 'Confidential.'

"Great Cury,

"DEAR SIR,—   "Cambridge.

"In accordance with your desire that we should advise you of anything unusual, expressed to us when you opened your son's account a year ago, we beg to notify you that Mr. Jolyon Forsyte, Junr., made application to us to-day for an overdraft of one hundred pounds. We did not feel justified in granting this without your permission, but shall be happy to act in accordance with your decision in this matter.

"We are, dear Sir, with the compliments of the season,
"Your faithful servants,
"BROTHERTON AND DARNETT."

Old Jolyon had sat some time regarding this missive with grave and troubled eyes. He had then placed it in the breast pocket of his frock coat, and taking out a little comb, had passed it through his grey Dundreary's and moustachios.

"I am going down to Cambridge, Timming. Get me a cab."

In the cab and in the train, and again in the cab from the station at Cambridge, he had brooded, restless and unhappy. Why had the boy not come to *him?* What had he been doing to require an overdraft like that? He had a good allowance. He had never said anything about being pressed for money. This way and that way he turned it in his mind, and whichever way he turned it, the conclusion was that it showed weakness—weakness to want the money; above all, weakness not to have come to his father first. Of all things, Old Jolyon disliked weakness. And so there he stood, tall and grey-headed, in the doorway.

"I've come down, Jo. I've had a letter I don't like."

Through young Jolyon raced the thought: 'Davids!' and his heart sank into his velvet slippers. He said, however, drawling:

"Charmed to see you, Sir. You haven't had dinner? Can you eat wild duck? This claret's pretty good."

Taking his father's hat and coat, he placed him with his back to the fire, plied the bellows, and bawled down the stairway for forks and another wild duck. And while he bawled he felt as if he could be sick, for he had a great love for his father, and this was why he was afraid of him. And old Jolyon, who had a great love for his son, was not sorry to stand and warm his legs and wait.

They ate the wild duck, drank the claret, talking of the weather, and small matters. They finished, and Young Jolyon said:

"Take that 'froust,' Dad;" and his heart tried to creep from him into the floor.

Old Jolyon clipped a cigar, handed another to his son, and sat down in the old leather chair on one side of the fire; young Jolyon sat in another old leather chair on the other side, and they smoked in silence, till old Jolyon took the letter from his pocket and handed it across.

"What's the meaning of it, Jo? Why didn't you come to me?"

Young Jolyon read the letter with feelings of relief,

dismay, and anger with his Bank. Why on earth had they written? He felt his whiskers, and said:

"Oh! That!"

Old Jolyon sat looking at him with a sharp deep gravity.

"I suppose it means that you're in debt?" he said, at last.

Young Jolyon shrugged: "Oh! well, naturally. I mean, one must———"

"Must what?"

"Live like other fellows, Dad."

"Other fellows? Haven't you at least the average allowance?"

Young Jolyon had. "But that's just it," he said eagerly. "I'm not in an average set."

"Then why did you get into such a set, Jo?"

"I don't know, Sir. School and one thing and another. It's an awfully good set."

"H'm!" said old Jolyon, deeply. "Would this hundred pounds have cleared you?"

"Cleared me! Oh! well—yes, of what matters."

"What matters?" repeated old Jolyon. "Doesn't every debt matter?"

"Of course, Dad; but everybody up here owes money to tradesmen. I mean, they expect it."

Old Jolyon's eyes narrowed and sharpened.

"Tradesmen? What matters are not tradesmen? What then? A woman?" The word came out hushed and sharp.

Young Jolyon shook his head. "Oh! No."

Old Jolyon's attitude relaxed a little, as if with some intimate relief. He flipped the ash off his cigar.

"Have you been gambling, then, Jo?"

Struggling to keep his face calm and his eyes on his father's, young Jolyon answered:

"A little."

"Gambling!" Something of distress and consternation in the sound young Jolyon couldn't bear, and hastened on:

"Well, Dad, I don't mean to go on with it. But Newmarket, you know, and——and——one doesn't like to be a prig."

"Prig? For not gambling? I don't understand. A gambler!"

And, again, at that note in his voice, young Jolyon cried:

"I really don't care for it, Dad; I mean I'm just as happy without."

"Then why do you do it? It's weak. I don't like weakness, Jo."

Young Jolyon's face hardened. The Dad would never understand. To be a swell—superior to Fate! Hopeless to explain! He said lamely:

"All the best chaps——"

Old Jolyon averted his eyes. For at least two minutes he sat staring at the fire.

"I've never gambled, or owed money," he said at last, with no pride in the tone of his voice, but with deep conviction. "I must know your position, Jo. What is it? Speak the truth. How much do you owe, and to whom?"

Young Jolyon had once been discovered cribbing. This was worse. It was as little possible as it had been then to explain that everybody did it. He said sullenly:

"I suppose—somewhere about three hundred, to tradesmen."

Old Jolyon's glance went through and through him.

"And that doesn't matter? What else?"

"I did owe about a hundred to fellows, but I've paid them."

"That's what you wanted the overdraft for, then?"

"Debts of honour—yes."

"Debts of honour," repeated old Jolyon. "And where did you get the hundred from?"

"I borrowed it."

"When?"

"To-day."

"Who from?"

"A man called Davids."

"Money-lender?"

Young Jolyon bowed his head.

"And you preferred to go to a money-lender than to come to me?"

Young Jolyon's lips quivered; he pitched his cigar into the fire, not strong enough to bear it.

"I—I—knew you'd—you'd hate it so, Dad."

"I hate this more, Jo."

To both of them it seemed the worst moment they had ever been through, and it lasted a long time. Then old Jolyon said:

"What did you sign?"

"I borrowed a hundred and fifty, and promised to pay two hundred in six months."

"And how were you going to get that?"

"I don't know."

Old Jolyon, too, pitched his cigar into the fire, and passed his hand over his forehead.

Impulsively young Jolyon rose, and, oblivious of his whiskers, sat down on the arm of his father's chair, precisely as if he were not a swell. There were tears in his eyes.

"I'm truly sorry, Dad; only, you don't understand." Old Jolyon shook his head.

"No, I don't understand, Jo. That's the way to ruin."

"They were debts of honour, Dad."

"All debts are debts of honour. But that's not the point. It seems to me you can't face things. I know you're an affectionate chap, but that won't help you."

Young Jolyon got up.

"I *can* face things," he said: "I——! Oh! You can't realise."

Scattering the logs with his slippered foot, he stared into the glow. His eyes felt burned, his inside all churned up; and while the 'swell' within him drawled: 'A fuss about money'; all his love for his father was raw and quivering. He heard old Jolyon say:

"I'll go now, Jo. Have a list of your debts for me to-morrow. I shall pay them myself. We'll go to that money-lender chap together."

Young Jolyon heard him getting up, heard him with his coat and hat, heard him open the door; and, twisting round, cried:

"Oh! Dad!"

"Good-night, Jo!" He was gone.

Young Jolyon stood a long time by the dying fire. His father did not, could not know what a fellow had to do, how behave to——to be superior to fortune. He was old-fashioned! But, besides loving him, young Jolyon admired his father, admired him physically and mentally—as much —yes, more than the Honble. Crasher or Digby Grand. And he was miserable.

He sat up late, making a list of his debts as well as any-one could who had the habit of tearing up his bills. Re-pressed emotion tossed his slumbers, and when he woke the thought of the joint visit to Mr. Davids made him feel unwell.

Old Jolyon came at ten o'clock, looking almost haggard. He took the list from his son.

"Are these all, Jo?"

"So far as I can remember."

"Send any others in to me. Which of your friends are the gamblers?"

Young Jolyon coloured.

"You must excuse me, Dad."

Old Jolyon looked at him.

"Very well!" he said. "We'll go to this money-lender now."

They walked forth. By God's mercy no one had bounced in on his way to Newmarket. Young Jolyon caught sight of 'Donny' Covercourt on the far side of the quadrangle and returned him no greeting. Quite silent, side by side, father and son passed out into the street. Except for old Jolyon's remark:

"There's no end to these Colleges, it seems," they did not speak until they reached the office of Mr. Davids, above a billiard room.

Old Jolyon ascended, stumping the stairs with his umbrella; young Jolyon followed with his head down. He was bitterly ashamed; it is probable that old Jolyon was even more so.

The money-lender was in his inner office, just visible through the half-open doorway. Old Jolyon pushed the door with his umbrella.

Mr. Davids rose, apparently surprised, and stood looking round his nose in an ingratiating manner.

"This is my father," said young Jolyon, gazing deeply at his boots.

"Mr. Davids, I think?" began old Jolyon.

"Yeth, Thir. What may I have the pleasure——"

"You were good enough yesterday to advance my son the sum of a hundred and fifty pounds, for which he signed a promissory note for an extortionate amount. Kindly give me that note, and take this cheque in satisfaction."

Mr. Davids washed his hands.

"For what amount ith your cheque, Thir?"

Old Jolyon took a cheque from his pocket and unfolded it.

"For your money, and one day's interest at ten per cent."

Mr. Davids threw up his well-washed hands.

"Oh! No, Mithter Forthyte; no! Thath not bithneth. Give me a cheque for the amount of the promithory note, and you can have it. I'm not ancthious to be paid—not at all."

Old Jolyon clapped his hat on his head.

"You will accept my cheque!" he said, and thrust it under the money-lender's eyes.

Mr. Davids examined it, and said:

"You take me for a fool, it theemth."

"I take you for a knave," said old Jolyon. "Sixty-six per cent, forsooth!"

Mr. Davids recoiled in sheer surprise.

"I took a great rithk to lend your thon that money."

"You took no risk whatever. One day's interest at ten per cent is ninepence three-farthings; I've made it tenpence. Be so good as to give me that note."

Mr. Davids shook his head.

"Very well," said old Jolyon. "I've made some inquiries about you. I go straight from here to the Vice-Chancellor."

Mr. Davids again began to wash his hands.

"And thuppothe," he said, "I go to your thon's College and tell them that I lend him thith money?"

"Do!" said old Jolyon; "do! Come, Jo!" He turned and walked to the door, followed by his agonised but unmoved son.

"Thtop!" said Mr. Davids. "I don't want to make no trouble."

Old Jolyon's eyes twinkled under his drawn brows.

"Oh!" he said, without turning, "you don't! Make haste, then. I give you two minutes," and he took out his watch.

Young Jolyon stood looking dazedly at the familiar golden object. Behind him he could hear Mr. Davids making haste.

"Here it ith, Mithter Forthyte, here it ith!"

Old Jolyon turned.

"Is that your signature, Jo?"

"Yes," said young Jolyon, dully.

"Take it, then, and tear it up."

Young Jolyon took, and tore it savagely.

"Here's your cheque," said old Jolyon.

Mr. Davids grasped the cheque, changing his feet rapidly.

"Ith not bithneth, really ith not bithneth," he repeated.

"The deuce it isn't," said old Jolyon; "you may thank your stars I don't go to the Vice-Chancellor, into the bargain. Good-bye to you!" He stumped his umbrella and walked out.

Young Jolyon followed, sheepishly.

"Where's the station, Jo?"

Young Jolyon led the way, and they walked on, more silent than ever.

At last old Jolyon said:

"This has been a sad affair. It's your not coming to me, Jo, that hurt."

Young Jolyon's answer was strangled in his throat.

"And don't gamble, my boy. It's weak-minded. Well, here we are!"

They turned into the station. Old Jolyon bought *The Times*. They stood together, silent on the platform, till the London train came in; then young Jolyon put his hand through his father's arm, and squeezed it. Old Jolyon nodded: *25820*

"I shan't allude to this again, Jo. But there's just one thing: If you must be a swell, remember that you're a gentleman too. Good-bye, my boy!" He laid his hand on his son's shoulder, turned quickly and got in.

Young Jolyon stood with bared head, watching the train go out. He then walked, as well as he knew how, back to College.

Indeed, yes! A sad affair!

REVOLT AT ROGER'S

1870

REVOLT AT ROGER'S

WHEN the house of Roger Forsyte in Prince's Gate was burgled in the autumn of 1870, Smith was undoubtedly drunk and made no serious attempt to rebut the accusation. A broad man of extremely genial disposition, he had in the few months of his butlerdom in Roger's new house endeared himself to the young Rogers, and even Roger was wont to speak of him as 'an amiable chap.' To be drunk without anyone's knowing, is a tort; to be discovered drunk, a misdemeanour; to be drunk when burglary is committed under one's nose, a crime, if not a felony. This, at least, was Roger's view, and he acted on it by immediate dismissal. His spoons had gone and Smith must go, too.

"If you hadn't been drunk," he said, "you'd have heard the ruffians. Call yourself a butler—you're a disgrace."

"Yes, Sir," said Smith, humbly, "a glass has always been my weakness, but I never thought it'd come to this."

"Well, it has," said Roger, "and so have you. Off you go this very day, and don't come to me for a character."

In mitigation of Roger's harshness it will be remembered that in those days there was no such practice as insurance against burglary. Indeed, it was Roger (always original) who started the habit, and he had to go to Lloyd's to get it done.

"It's the most barefaced thing I ever knew," he added. The plate-basket, indeed, with all the spoons, forks, saltcellars and pepper-pots of Roger's menage, had been rived practically from under the nose of the intoxicated Smith snoring on the turn-up bedstead in his own pantry. He had still been asleep, indeed, with a glass and empty whisky bottle by his bedside, when the page-boy entered in the morning.

Smith having withdrawn to his pantry, with his tail between his legs, Roger repaired to his bedroom, where in the four-poster his wife still lay thinking about less than usual, and put the matter in a few forcible words.

"Oh! Roger, what a pity! Such an amiable man. The children will be very upset."

"Fiddlesticks!" said Roger. "I must go out and see the police. But they're no good. Precious little chance of getting anything back."

Mrs. Roger remained lying, flat as ever. She had been married to him seventeen years, and if she now had a life of her own, no one knew where she kept it.

Smith, on the other hand, upright in his shirt-sleeves, had an expression on his broad and amiable face as though he had mislaid his trousers. To him thus standing the pantry door was flung open, and in the doorway stood Miss Francie. Francie Forsyte was then aged twelve, a dark-haired child with thin legs always outgrowing their integuments. Her Celtic-grey eyes shone ominously.

"You're not to go, Smith. I won't have it. You couldn't help being drunk when the burglars came."

"'Ush! Miss Francie," said Smith, "the Master says I've got to."

Francie put a hand into his.

"Dear Smith!"

Smith's round face grew almost long.

"It's my fault, Miss; I *was* tipsy, there's no denyin'."

"But how could you tell the burglars were coming?"

"I couldn't, Miss Francie, and that's a fact."

"Well, then!"

"If I 'adn't been tipsy," said Smith with sudden violence, "*I'd* 'ave given 'em what for!" And he worked his arm up to the angle which best displayed his formidable biceps.

"Oh! Smith," said Francie, "you *are* strong! Feel; *I* haven't got *any!*" And she angled her arm, thin, like a stick. Then the thought coming to her that soon there would be no Smith to show her lack of muscle to, the water started into her eyes.

"You're *not* to go," she cried again. "Here's Eustace, he'll say so too."

The youngest but one of the five young Rogers was now eleven, dark-haired and thin-faced like his sister, and, like her, grey-eyed, but of a calm which contrasted forcibly with Francie's fervour. He was recovering from the mumps, which had conveniently delayed his return to school.

"Have you really got to go, Smiff?" he said. "I wouldn't, if I were you. I should just stay."

Smith smiled. His smile was that of the sun at noonday.

"Faver'll forget," added Eustace.

Smith closed an eye, a practice which beyond all things endeared him to children.

"Will'e, Master Eustace? I don't fink."

"I do fink," said Eustace. "The best way wiv Faver is to take no notice. He can't birch *you;* look at your muscle."

Again Smith crooked his arm to the proper position. He never spent ten minutes with the children without having to do this at least once.

"Smith," said Francie, "we'll come with you and speak to Father."

Smith shook his head.

"I expect he hasn't seen your muscle," said Eustace.

Smith smiled. Like all powerful, good-tempered, easy-going men, he was unable to say "No."

"That's settled then," said Francie; "when Father comes in, Eustace and I will come for you. Come along, Eustace."

She turned at the door. "You shan't go—*dear* Smith!"

Smith in the centre of his pantry, slowly shook his rounded head.

He was still in undetermined mood when visited by the constable whom Roger had set in motion. Now the temperament of Smith was pre-eminently suited to the police. Sunk in humility, without edge, and highly human, it appealed to authority as cream to a cat. The constable, who had come to carp and question, remained to chat and quaff. He quaffed Roger's beer, and said:

"S'far as I can see, 'twas accidental like; a man may sleep so sound, no burglar'd wake 'im. That was your trouble, mate. You'd 'ad a nightcap no doubt. I'll do me best with your governor."

Upstairs in the dining-room Mrs. Roger was staring at the bronze clock and rehearsing a sentence which began:

"Roger, I wish you would reconsider your decision about Smith; there are many reasons why——" and then nothing would come but: "it will be out of the frying-pan into the fire," which she could not feel to be quite dignified.

Unaware of these forces being marshalled against him, Roger, alert, and with an eye on a new board announcing the sale of a house by auction, returned from the police station where he had been rendering a just and faithful account of his silver, and entered his hall with the latchkey which he had been one of the first householders to have made. As he divested himself of his overcoat a light, thin, ghostly shape flitted from the darkness under the stairs into the smell of mutton rising from the basement; another shape at the top of the stairs bestrode the banisters, waited till Roger had entered the dining-room, slid down with a run, and vanished also.

Startled by her husband's entry, Mrs. Roger took the stopper out of the cut glass bottle of pickled walnuts on the sideboard, and said:

"Oh! Roger, I wish—I wish——"

"What do you wish?" said Roger. "Some nonsense. Don't let that smell out; I can't bear a vinegary smell."

"It's Smith," murmured Mrs. Roger. "I wish you——"

"That'll do," said Roger; "he's got to go."

Mrs. Roger stoppered the bottle.

"Oh! very well, dear; only where we shall get——"

"Plenty of good fish in the sea," said Roger. "Where's that policeman they sent around?"

"He's still in the basement, I fancy."

"He would be. They're no good! What's this?"

Through the doorway was coming a procession led by Francie. It took up a position on the far side of the mahogany—from left to right, Francie, Smith, Eustace, and the policeman.

"How's this, Smith?" said Roger, caressing his left whisker. "I told you to be off. Have you got something to say?"

"Yes," said Francie, her voice shrill: "Smith's not going."

"What!" cried Roger.

"All wight, Faver!" said Eustace quietly.

"All right? What d'you mean by that, you impudent young shaver?"

"Seems as 'ow your butler was asleep, Sir," said the constable impressively.

"Of course he was asleep. He was drunk."

"Well, Sir, I'd 'ardly call it that," said the constable. "Not up to snuff at the moment, as you might say."

"If you've any excuse to make, Smith," said Roger, "make it before you pack off."

Smith shook his head. "None, Sir, I'm sure."

On one side and the other Francie and Eustace tugged at his sleeves, as if inciting him to show his muscle.

"Very well then," said Roger, "you can go. I'll talk to you in a moment, constable. You children run off, and don't let me catch you———"

"If Smith goes," said Francie, loudly, "we're going too."

Roger stared. It was his first experience of revolt.

"Go to my study, you two," he said, "and wait till I come. Mary, take them out."

But over Mrs. Roger a spell seemed to have been cast; she did not move. Crimson shame had covered Smith's face; the constable stood stolid. Roger's spare figure stiffened. He made but half of either Smith or the constable, but the expression on his face, sharp, firm and sour, redressed the balance.

"Go along," he said to Smith.

Smith moved towards the door, but the two children had placed their backs against it. Roger's very whiskers seemed to go red.

"This is too much of a good thing," burst from his tightened lips.

At this moment of exquisite deadlock the sense of duty which dominated a sober Smith came to the rescue. With a deep sigh he took a child by the belt with each hand, lifted them bodily from the door, set them down, and went out.

"Go to my study, you two," said Roger again.

The two children went out into the hall.

"Are you going to the study, Fwancie?"

"He'll birch us."

"He shan't," said Eustace. "Let's arm ourselves with knives."

"No," said Francie; "let's go away with Smith."

"Smiff will only bwing us back," said Eustace; "let's go by ourselves."

"All right," said Francie.

"We'll take Faver's umbwella and our money-box."

"We shan't be able to open it."

"No, but we can sell it to someone; it wattles."

"All right, quick!"

With their father's umbrella and the locked money-box, the two children opened the front door and, running across Kensington Road, were soon in Hyde Park, the money-box rattling all the way."

"How much is there in it?" said Eustace.

"Four shillings and elevenpence."

"Let's sell it for five shillings, then. The box cost a shilling."

"Who to?"

"We'll find an old gentleman."

They walked along the Row under the umbrella, for it was raining. Francie had neither hat nor coat, Eustace his school cap, black with a red stripe.

"Look!" said Francie. "There's one!"

They approached a bench whereon sat a tall, bulky figure, who had placed his hands on the handle of his stick with a view to rising. He had a grey goatee beard, a grey beaver hat, and a long watch-chain looped on his brown velvet waistcoat.

Francie, who carried the money-box, held it out.

"Hullo!" said the old gentleman: "what have you got there?"

"It's our money-box," said Francie; "we want to sell it. It's got four and elevenpence in coppers."

"But it's worf more," said Eustace.

"The deuce it is!" said the old gentleman. His voice rumbled, and his eyes, grey and rather bloodshot, twinkled. "Why do you want to sell it?"

"Because we haven't got the key," said Francie.

"So we can't get the money out," added Eustace. "It belongs to us and we shall want it out, you see."

"What d'you want it out for?" said the old gentleman.

"To buy our dinner."

"You're a rum couple," said the old gentleman. "What's your name?"

"Will you buy the box?" said Eustace: "then we'll tell you."

"What should I do with the box, heh?"

"You could carry it in one of your big pockets?"

"Well," said the old gentleman, "here's five bob. Hand it over. Now, what's your name?"

"Forsyte," said Francie. "I'm Francie, and this is Eustace."

"Forsyte?" grunted the old gentleman. "The deuce it is! Where d'you live?"

"Are you to be twusted?" asked Eustice, tilting the umbrella backwards.

The old gentleman uttered a guffaw.

"What do you want to trust me for?"

"Well, you see," said Eustace cautiously, "we're wunning away for the pwesent."

"Oh!" said the old gentleman, and rumbled.

"We had to," said Francie, "because of Smith. It's a long story."

"Well," said the old gentleman, rising, "come and have

your dinner with me, and tell me all about it. What's your father's Christian name?"

"Roger."

"Oh! Ah!" said the old gentleman. "Well, I know your uncles Jolyon and Swithin, and your cousin Jo. My name's Nicholas Treffry. Ever heard it?"

"No," said Eustace.

"I have," cried Francie. "Father says you're notorious. What does that mean?"

The 'notorious' Mr. Treffry chuckled.

"My carriage is out there at the Gate. Come along and I'll show you why he calls me notorious."

The two children looked at each other, then Eustace whispered:

"All wight, he's wespectable."

"The deuce, he is!" said Mr. Treffry unexpectedly. "Come along, young shavers."

The two children accompanied him silently to the Gate. Outside stood a pair of fine horses harnessed to a phaeton with the hood up. A tiger stood at their heads.

"Up you get!" said Mr. Treffry.

Francie mounted with alacrity. Eustace hung back.

"Where are you going to take us?"

"The Albany—know it?"

"Yes," said Eustace, "George went there once."

"Respectable enough for you, heh?"

"Yes," said Eustace, and furling the umbrella, mounted beside his sister.

Mr. Treffry clambered heavily to his driver's seat alongside.

"Let go, Tim."

The horses sprang forward, the tiger let go, and, running, caught on behind.

The carriage swung from side to side; Francie's eyes danced.

"I—I like it," she said.

"Your father'd have a fit, if he saw us," chuckled Mr. Treffry. "He lives in Prince's Gate, doesn't he?"

Eustace looked round at him, and in imitation of Smith, closed his left eye.

"You're a cool young man," said Mr. Treffry.

The pavements of those days not being precisely smooth, they made but a rough passage to the Albany, where, after they had been made clean and comfortable under the auspices of the valet, the children repaired to a low panelled room with pictures of dogs and horses on the walls, a case of guns in one corner, and some black Chinese tea chests, embossed with figures and flowers in coloured lacquer.

"Now," said Mr. Treffry, "let's have some prog."

The prog consisted of grouse and pancakes and spiky artichokes, and each child was given a glass of wine.

"Well," said Mr. Treffry, "what was it all about, heh?"

Francie related the story of Smith.

"H'm!" Mr. Treffry rumbled. "So your father lost his spoons?"

"And we've got his umbwella," said Eustace.

"Well, I'll see you're not birched, though I daresay you deserve it. Your mother must be in a pretty stew. Green, have the phaeton round again."

They made an even rougher passage back to Prince's Gate.

"Here's your money-box," said Mr. Treffry.

"But you bought it!"

"Tut! Here! My dear! Take my card to your master."

Francie caught the maid by the sleeve.

"Has Smith gone, Annie?"

"Not yet, Miss. We've all been in a state about you."

"Hooray! D'you hear, Eustace? Smith hasn't gone."

"All wight, don't make a wow!"

Roger, Mrs. Roger, three maids and Smith all seemed to have gathered from nowhere in particular.

"How are you?" said Mr. Treffry, advancing in front of the children. "I thought you'd be in a stew. I'm your brother Jolyon's partner—Nicholas Treffry. These young shavers ran out to cool their heads. I've given 'em their dinner and brought 'em back none the worse."

"H'm!" said Roger profoundly.

"They ought to be birched, no doubt," continued Mr. Treffry, looking bigger and bigger; "but I promised they shouldn't be. You," he added, pointing to Smith, "the chap who got drunk?"

"Yes, sir."

"H'm! Let him off this time. Here's your umbrella."

Roger took the umbrella.

"Well," he said, "I don't know what's coming to things." He held out his hand to Mr. Treffry. "My brother's always talking about you. He says you'll break your neck one of these days."

"H'm! He's a careful chap, Jo. Glad you've got 'em back. Good-bye to you, Ma'am. Good-bye, young shavers."

And, rumbling, Mr. Treffry passed out.

There was a silence.

"Well," said Roger at last, while a little smile twitched between his whiskers and vanished into them, "don't let me hear a word more about anything from any of you." And he withdrew into the dining-room.

Francie rushed at Smith, and mechanically felt his muscle.

"Dear Smith!"

"Muvver," said Eustace, "we had gwouse, pancakes, and spiky artichokes, and we dwove like Jehu."

So ended the revolt at Roger's, which, together perhaps with the Franco-German war in that same year, laid the foundations of a looser philosophy.

JUNE'S FIRST LAME DUCK

1876

JUNE'S FIRST LAME DUCK

THE life of little June Forsyte until the age of nearly
eight had been spent in superintending the existence of
her dolls. Not until the autumn of 1876 did she find a
human being whose destiny she could control.

It happened thus: The stables of her grandfather old
Jolyon Forsyte's house in Stanhope Gate where June and,
incidentally, her mother resided with her grandparents,
were round the corner. They consisted of two stalls and a
loose box occupied by the carriage horses Brownie and Betty
and by her pony Bruce. Above were the three rooms of the
coachman Betters, his wife, and little daughter, the groom
living God knew more precisely where.

One October noon, in her long blue habit, with her spirit
and her eyes looking up out of her flaming hair, June was
lifted from her pony at the stable door.

"That pony's artful, Miss June; don't you give him
more than two carrots, or 'e'll think he can do what 'e likes
with you."

"Darling!" said June in a voice strangely deep for a
small child. Having given the pony four carrots she remained standing beside it in the stall, fervently stroking its
nose. In the next stall the groom was hissing while he
wisped down Betty, preferred by Betters as a mount to
Brownie—"an 'oss that did that throw you up."

"George, which do you think is the most beautiful,
Brownie or Betty?"

The groom jerked his head at the loose box.

"That 'oss is the best-lookin', Miss June."

"Then I shall give Brownie one carrot and Betty two—
it isn't her fault, is it, poor darling?"

Having given the carrots and had her capped head
nuzzled, she went out and stood in the yard. Betters had
disappeared up the stairway to his rooms, whence a smell
of onions indicated that Mrs. Betters, a small pale puckered
woman, was cooking steak.

The yard was deserted but for a pigeon, towards which
June ran so that the pigeon at once left for the roof. Hurt
in her feelings June had gathered up her tail, and was
moving towards the house when round the corner came a
little girl blubbering into her sleeve.

"Susie Betters, what are you crying for?"

The little girl, who was plain and thin, blubbered the
louder.

"They pinched me; they said I was a thief 'cos I only
took the top what belonged to me." She displayed some
pinch marks on her arms and some mud stains on her frock.

"Who pinched you?"

"The boys and girls I go to school with."

"Did you pinch them back?"

"Nao."

"Then I will. Horrid little children. Don't cry, Susie.
I'll protect you."

Susie looked down half a head and her mouth opened.

"We'll go and look for them. I've got my whip. They
won't dare touch you again. You aren't brave, are you?"

"Nao," said Susie.

June swished the whip, which had the thickness of the
top joint of a fishing rod. "Come on!"

They went round the corner, followed by June's tail.

There was no sign of any children.

"We'll go and tell the teacher."

"Nao."

"Why not?"

"They'll larrup me proper, if we do."

"Why don't they like you, Susie? Is it because you're ugly?" Susie wailed again. "Don't cry! It's not your fault that you're ugly."

Susie wailed the louder.

Two small boys and a girl had suddenly appeared and stood pointing in a somewhat vulgar manner. June raised her whip.

The children nudged each other.

"Ill-bred little children!" said June, quoting from her governess.

One of the boys emitted a piercing whistle.

"Did you pinch little Susie Betters?"

The children laughed in a still more vulgar manner.

"You're dirty little morkins," cried June; "and I'm going to larrup you."

The children gave before the onslaught, skipping sideways with uncouth noises; one of the boys shoved June so that she tripped over her tail, and sprawled, a small blue figure, on the ground. The children, then, pinching Susie warmly, yelled in unison, and vanished.

June rose, her habit dirty, her whip gone, her cheeks crimson. Susie was wailing as she had not yet wailed.

"Don't! It's babyish to cry."

"They pinched me again."

"Where?"

"On my ba-ase."

"Come with me, and show my Gran," said June. "He'll soon astonish their weak nerves. You shall have my pudding, too. Come on!" And she dragged the reluctant Susie to the mansion of old Jolyon.

"François," said June to the Swiss servant, "this is Susie Betters; she's been pinched, and she's to have my pudding. She isn't brave, so she's not to be frightened. I want my Gran to see her pinches. Come on, Susie!"

Still tugging Susie, she passed into the dining-room.

Old Jolyon, who never went to the City on Saturdays, was in his armchair by the fire, reading *The Times* and waiting for lunch to be announced. Across the dining table laid for five he looked at the two small figures, and his eyes twinkled.

"Well, my ducky, what have you got there?"

"Susie Betters, Gran; she's been pinched behind. I wanted you to see."

She pulled Susie round to the chair, whence old Jolyon looked shrewdly at his coachman's daughter.

"H'm!" he said: "you're a thin little toad."

"Yes; she's going to have my pudding. She's too thin altogether, and she's too pale. Her face is dirty, too, but it isn't her fault."

"What's come to your habit?" said old Jolyon. "Did you fall off?"

"Oh! no; I just sat down in the street while I was larruping those morkins and they took my whip and ran away."

"H'm! Pretty pair of shoes altogether!"

He stretched out and rang the bell.

"Take this little girl downstairs, François, and have her face washed, and give her a good dinner; and tell that page chap to run over and let Betters know she's here. You go and get brushed," he added to June, "before your mother sees you, and don't say anything about it."

The two children went out. In the hall June said:

"I want to see her face washed, François."

"Veree well, Mees June."

During lunch June fidgeted, with difficulty prevented by old Jolyon's eyes from telling her story.

When her mother and her governess had withdrawn, she approached her grandfather, who had lighted his after-lunch cigar, and stood between his knees.

"I'm going to be Susie Betters' friend, Gran."

"Oh!" said old Jolyon. "Mite like you—picking up lame ducks."

"Is Susie a lame duck?"

Old Jolyon nodded. "Shouldn't be surprised if they pinched her more than ever now. She looks to me a poor thing."

"Well, I'm going to protect her."

"How?" said old Jolyon, twinkling.

"I shall dare them to pinch her."

"First catch your hare——"

"I know," said June, suddenly. "She can do lessons with *me*, Gran, instead of going to school."

Old Jolyon shook his head.

"That cock won't fight. Coming to the Zoo?"

June clapped her hands, then said at once:

"No. I must look after Susie."

Old Jolyon stared. It was his first introduction to the real nature of his little grand-daughter.

"She's a poor timid little stick," he said; "and you'll never make anything of her."

When June had gone, he sat contemplating the ash of his cigar. Children! What things they thought of! She would learn some day that you couldn't go 'protecting' everything you came across. Sooner the better, perhaps! Generous little thing—though; giving up the Zoo. Lessons! What would her mother say to that? She was such a good woman that you never knew. And old Jolyon sighed.

If his son hadn't married such a good woman, it might all have turned out very different; and Jo—— Well, well! A nap! Just forty winks. And, crushing out his cigar, he leaned back with eyes fixed on 'Dutch Fishing Boats at Sunset'; and his thin hand with pointed nails depending over the arm of his old chair. A warm-hearted little thing! Lame ducks! . . .

In spite of the misgivings of the good woman afraid of the effect on her accent, and the opposition of her governess, too deep for words, June had her way. Susie Betters, almost unnecessarily clean, sat every morning at the school-room table shedding tears over her vowels and aitches. Delivered from pinches, and advanced in all material things, soap, pudding, and frocks, she seemed at first to exude as much water per day as ever, for June frequently protected her from the governess.

"You oughtn't to make Susie cry, Miss Pearson, just because she speaks commonly. She doesn't know any better. You can't help being common, can you, Susie?"

This protection, indeed, produced as much water as any educational exhortations. Out of school hours she taught Susie every game she knew and some she didn't; instructed her in dressing and undressing dolls; delivered her from the Italian greyhound; helped her to burn her cheeks cooking cocoanut ice and toffee; and prick her fingers sewing at dolls' nightgowns. When Susie was put in the corner, June had invariably to be put in the opposite corner—so loyal was she to her 'lame duck.' The 'good woman' watched the experiment with equanimity—it would help June not to be selfish. Old Jolyon, with innate sagacity, waited for its inevitable end; he had no belief in 'lame ducks.'

The end came stealthily with every ounce of weight that

Susie Betters put on from the dinners and teas she ate, and every deepening of the contempt which familiarity slowly bred in her. She had ceased to exude water, her cheeks were becoming pink, and she wore a sky blue ribbon in hair no longer unwashed. In fact she had come to be 'twice the child'; and she no longer excited June's compassion. The habit of protection, however, lasted till the middle of November. It vanished in one day.

Susie had a doll, given her by June, which, following the law of compensation—advocated by the then fashionable philosopher Mr. Emerson—she treated in the manner in which she herself was treated, possessing its soul, placing its body in corners, and harassing it over her knee for its own good. With the increase of adipose, her treatment of the doll became more and more protective, if not arbitrary. It was not long before this treatment excited June's concern, and the doll began to seem to her a 'lame duck.'

One Saturday morning when the doll had been whipped and put first in one corner and then in another, her feelings became too much for her.

"You oughtn't to treat poor Amy like that, Susie, it's a shame!"

Susie answered:

"Why not? She's my doll!"

"Well, you shan't!" said June. "So there!"

"I will," said Susie, and promptly turned up the doll's petticoats.

June's eyes grew very blue, her hair seemed to shine.

"If you whip her," she said, "I'll whip you."

"Will you?" said Susie. "I'm bigger than you."

She laid the doll over her knee.

"Stop!" said June.

"I won't!" said Susie.

June rushed at her. The doll fell to the floor, and the two children struggled. Susie had so far profited by six weeks of good feeding that she was the stronger; but she had not June's spirit. The combat, short and sharp, ended with June sitting on her chest. Susie sobbed, wriggled and scratched. June sat tighter.

"Promise not to whip her any more."

"Shan't!"

"Then I shall sit here till you do."

Susie began to scream. June covered her mouth with a hand. Susie bit it.

The screams had attracted old Jolyon, who was in his dressing-room. The sight when he entered the room was precisely that which he had been expecting for some time.

"That'll do," he said. "Get up, June! Now, what's it all about?"

June, who had picked up the doll, stood crimson and defiant, Susie stood whimpering and overawed.

"What's that mark on your hand?" said old Jolyon to his grand-daughter.

"She shan't whip Amy," said June; "I won't have it!"

"Did you bite her?" said old Jolyon to Susie.

Susie sobbed.

The instinct to protect Susie caused June to say automatically:

"I began it, because she's not to whip Amy."

Susie blurted:

"I wasn't going to until she told me not."

"That'll do," said old Jolyon. "Give me the doll. Go and get your hand bathed, June. And you," he added to Susie, "go home for dinner."

The children went; Susie, sniffing, June, very red.

Old Jolyon was left with the doll, a furbelowed affair in

wax—which is indeed more inviting to chastisement than china—whose round blue eyes expressed nothing but indifference. Rum little toads, children! Fancy getting into a fantod over a bit of wax! Well, well——! Another lame duck, he supposed. He rearranged the doll's petticoats, and his eyes twinkled. There was the end of Susie Betters! And just as well!

Placing the doll on the table he descended slowly to the dining-room, pondering on the rumness of little toads.

June came to lunch with her hand bound up. She would not eat her pudding, and could be heard whispering to François that it was to be saved for Susie.

When told later that Susie was not to come any more, but to go to school again, she was silent; and nobody could tell what she was feeling. It was the impression of old Jolyon, however, that she was not unhappy. He had always known how it would be.

The last state of Susie Betters was worse than the first. Wild animals that are captured and regain their liberty receive but a poor welcome from their fellows. So with June's past lame duck. She was soon as thin, pinched and tearful as ever; but, as June never saw her, she remained in memory pink and plump, with a sky blue ribbon, no longer worthy of compassion. Besides, June had found a new lame duck, an organ-grinder's wife with a baby in her arms.

DOG AT TIMOTHY'S
1878

DOG AT TIMOTHY'S

MRS. SEPTIMUS SMALL, known in the Forsyte family as Aunt Juley, returning from service at St. Barnabas', Bayswater, on a Sunday morning in the Spring of 1878, took by force of habit the path which led her into the then somewhat undeveloped gardens of Kensington. The Reverend Thomas Scoles had been wittier than usual, and she had the longing to stretch her legs, which was the almost invariable effect of his 'nice' sermons. While she walked, in violet silk under a black mantle, with very short steps—skirts being extremely narrow in that year of grace —she was thinking of dear Hester and what a pity it was that she always had such a headache on Sunday mornings— the sermon would have done her so much good! For now that dear Ann was unable to stand the fatigue of service, she did feel that Hester ought to make a point of being well enough to go to church. What dear Mr. Scoles had said had been so helpful—about the lilies of the fields never attempting to improve their figures, and yet, about ladies of fashion in all their glory never being attired like one of them. He had undoubtedly meant 'bustles'—so witty— and Hester would have enjoyed hearing it, because only yesterday, when they had been talking about the Grecian bend, Emily had come in with dear James and said that the revival of crinolines was only a question of time and that she personally intended to be in the fashion the moment there was any sign of it. Dear Ann had been rather severe with her; and James had said he didn't know what was the use of them. Of course, crinolines did take up a great deal

129

of room, and a 'bustle,' though it was warmer, did not.
But Hester had said they were both such a bore, she didn't
see why they were wanted; and now Mr. Scoles had said it
too. She must really think about it, if Mr. Scoles thought
they were bad for the soul; he always said something that
one had to think about afterwards. He would be *so* good
for Hester! And she stood a minute looking out over the
grass.

Dear, dear! That little white dog was running about a
great deal. Was it lost? Backwards and forwards, round
and round! What they called—she believed—a Pomeranian, quite a new kind of dog. And, seeing a bench, Mrs.
Septimus Small bent, with a little backward heave to save
her 'bustle,' and sat down to watch what was the matter
with the white dog. The sun, flaring out between two
Spring clouds, fell on her face, transfiguring the pouting
puffs of flesh, which seemed trying to burst their way
through the network of her veil. Her eyes, of a Forsyte
grey, lingered on the dog with the greater pertinacity in that
of late—owing to poor Tommy's (their cat's) disappear-
ance, very mysterious—she suspected the sweep—there had
been nothing but 'Polly' at Timothy's to lavish her affection
on. This dog was draggled and dirty, as if it had been out
all night, but it had a dear little pointed nose. She thought,
too, that it seemed to be noticing her, and at once had a
swelling-up sensation underneath her corsets. Almost as if
aware of this, the dog came sidling, and sat down on its
haunches in the grass, as though trying to make up its mind
about her. Aunt Juley pursed her lips in the endeavour to
emit a whistle. The veil prevented this, but she held out her
gloved hand. "Come, little dog—nice little dog!" It
seemed to her dear heart that the little dog sighed as it sat
there, as if relieved that at last someone had taken notice of

it. But it did not approach. The tip of its bushy tail quivered, however, and Aunt Juley redoubled the suavity of her voice: "Nice little fellow—come then!"

The little dog slithered forward, humbly wagging its entire body, just out of reach. Aunt Juley saw that it had no collar. Really, its nose and eyes were sweet!

"Pom!" she said. "Dear little Pom!"

The dog looked as if it would let her love it, and sensation increased beneath her corsets.

"Come, pretty!"

Not, of course, that he was pretty, all dirty like that; but his ears were pricked, and his eyes looked at her, bright, and rather round their corners—most intelligent! Lost—and in London! It was like that sad little book of Mrs.—What *was* her name—not the authoress of *Jessica's First Prayer?*—dear, dear! Now, fancy forgetting that! The dog made a sudden advance, and curved like a C, all fluttering, was now almost within reach of her gloved fingers, at which it sniffed. Aunt Juley emitted a purring noise. Pride was filling her heart that out of all the people it *might* have taken notice of, she should be the only one. It had put out its tongue now, and was panting in the agony of indecision. Poor little thing! It clearly didn't know whether it dared try another master—not, of course, that she could possibly take it home, with all the carpets, and dear Ann so particular about everything being nice, and—Timothy! Timothy would be horrified! And yet——! Well, they couldn't prevent her stroking its little nose. And she too panted slightly behind her veil. It *was* agitating! And then, without either of them knowing how, her fingers and the nose were in contact. The dog's tail was now perfectly still; its body trembled. Aunt Juley had a sudden feeling of shame at being so formidable; and with instinct inherited rather than acquired, for she had no knowledge of dogs, she slid one finger round an ear and scratched. It *was* to be hoped he hadn't fleas! And then! The little dog leaped on her lap. It crouched there just as it had sprung, with its bright eyes upturned to her face. A strange dog— her dress—her Sunday best! It *was* an event! The little dog stretched up, and licked her chin. Almost mechanically Aunt Juley rose. And the little dog slipped off. Really she didn't know—it took such liberties! Oh! dear—it *was* thin, fluttering round her feet! What would Mr. Scoles say? Perhaps if she walked on! She turned towards home, and the dog followed her skirt at a distance of six inches. The thought that she was going to eat roast beef, Yorkshire pudding, and mincepies, was almost unbearable to Aunt Juley, seeing it gaze up as if saying: "Some for me! Some for me!" Thoughts warred within her: must she 'shoo' and threaten it with her parasol? Or should she——? Oh! This would never do! Dogs could be *so* —she had heard? And then—the responsibility! And fleas! Timothy couldn't endure fleas! And it might not know how to behave in a house! Oh, no! She really couldn't! The little dog suddenly raised one paw. Tt, tt! Look at its little face! And a fearful boldness attacked Aunt Juley. Turning resolutely towards the Gate of the Gardens, she said in a weak voice: "Come along, then!" And the little dog came. It was dreadful!

While she was trying to cross the Bayswater Road, two or three of those dangerous hansom cabs came dashing past —so reckless!—and in the very middle of the street a 'growler' turned round, so that she had to stand quite still. And, of course, there was 'no policeman.' The traffic was really getting beyond bounds. If only she didn't meet Timothy coming in from his constitutional, and could get a word with Smither—a capable girl—and have the little dog fed and washed before anybody saw it. And then? Perhaps it could be kept in the basement till somebody came to claim it. But how could people come to claim it if they didn't know it was there? If only there was someone to consult! Perhaps Smither would know a policeman—only she hoped not—policemen were rather dangerous for a nice-looking girl like Smither, with her colour, and such a figure, for her age. Then, suddenly, realising that she had reached home, she was seized by panic from head to heel. There was the bell—it was not the epoch of latchkeys; and there the smell of dinner—yes, and the little dog had smelt it! It was now or never. Aunt Juley pointed her parasol at the dog and said very feebly: "Shoo!" But it only crouched. She couldn't drive it away! And with an immense daring she rang the bell. While she stood waiting for the door to be opened, she almost enjoyed a sensation of defiance. She was doing a dreadful thing, but she didn't care! Then, the doorway yawned, and her heart sank slowly towards her high and buttoned boots.

"Oh, Smither! This poor little dog has followed me. Nothing has ever followed me before. It must be lost. And it looks so thin and dirty. What *shall* we do?"

The tail of the dog, edging into the home of that rich smell, fluttered.

"Aoh!" said Smither—she was young! "Paw little thing! Shall I get cook to give it some scraps, Ma'am!" At the word "scraps" the dog's eyes seemed to glow.

"Well," said Aunt Juley, "you do it on your own responsibility, Smither. Take it downstairs quickly."

She stood breathless while the dog, following Smither and its nose, glided through the little hall and down the kitchen stairs. The pit-pat of its feet roused in Aunt Juley the most mingled sensations she had experienced since the death of Septimus Small.

She went up to her room, and took off her veil and bonnet. What *was* she going to say? She went downstairs without knowing.

In the drawing-room, which had just had new pampas grass, Ann, sitting on the sofa, was putting down her prayer-book; she always read the Service to herself. Her mouth and chin looked very square, and there was an expression in her old grey eyes as if she were in pain. She wanted her lunch, of course—they were trying hard to call it lunch, because, according to Emily, no one with any pretension to be fashionable called it dinner now, even on Sundays. Hester, in her corner by the hearth, was passing the tip of her tongue over her lips; she had always been so fond of mincepies, and these would be the first of the season. Aunt Juley said:

"Mr. Scoles was delightful this morning—a beautiful sermon. I walked in the Gardens."

Something warned her to say no more, and they waited in silence for the gong; they had just got a gong—Emily had said it was 'the thing.'

It sounded. Dear, dear! What a noise—bom—bom! Timothy would never—Smither must take lessons. At dear James' in Park Lane the butler made it sound almost cosy.

In the doorway of the dining-room, Smither said:

"It's ate it all, Ma'am—it was *that* hungry."

" 'Shhh!"

A heavy footstep sounded in the hall; Timothy was coming from his study, square in his frock-coat, his face all brown and red—he had such delicate health. He took his seat with his back to the window, where the light was not too strong.

Timothy, of course, did not go to church—it was too tiring for him—but he always asked the amount of the offertory, and would sometimes add that he didn't know what they wanted all that for, as if Mr. Scoles ever wasted it. Just now he was getting new hassocks, and when they came she had thought perhaps dear Timothy and Hester would come too. Timothy, however, had said:

"Hassocks! They only get in the way and spoil your trousers."

Aunt Ann, who could not kneel now, had smiled indulgently:

"One should kneel in church, dear."

They were all seated now with beef before them, and Timothy was saying:

"Mustard! And tell cook the potatoes aren't browned enough; do you hear, Smither?"

Smither, blushing above him, answered: "Yes, sir."

Within Aunt Juley, what with the dog and her mind and the difficulty of assimilating Yorkshire pudding, indigestion had begun.

"I had such a pleasant walk in the Gardens," she said painfully, "after church."

"You oughtn't to walk there alone in these days; you don't know what you may be picking up with."

Aunt Juley took a sip of brown sherry—her heart was beating so! Aunt Hester—she was such a reader—murmured that she had read how Mr. Gladstone walked there sometimes.

"That shows you!" said Timothy.

Aunt Ann believed that Mr. Gladstone had high principles, and they must not judge him.

"Judge him!" said Timothy: "I'd hang him!"

"That's not quite a nice thing to say on Sunday, dear."

"Better the day, better the deed," muttered Timothy; and Aunt Juley trembled. He was in one of his moods. And, suddenly, she held her breath. A yapping had impinged on her ears, as if the white dog were taking liberties with Cook. Her eyes sought Smither's face.

"What's that?" said Timothy. "A dog?"

"There's a dog just round the corner, at No. 9," murmured Aunt Juley; and, at the roundness of Smither's eyes, knew she had prevaricated. What dreadful things happened if one was not quite frank from the beginning! The yapping broke into a sharp yelp, as if Cook had taken a liberty in turn.

"That's not round the corner," said Timothy; "it's downstairs. What's all this?"

All eyes were turned on Smither, in a dead silence. A sound broke it—the girl had creaked.

"Please, Miss, it's the little dog that followed Madam in."

"Oh!" said Aunt Juley, in haste; "*that* little dog!"

"What's that?" said Timothy. "Followed her in?"

"It was so thin!" said Aunt Juley's faint voice.

"Smither," said Aunt Ann, "hand me the pulled bread; and tell Cook I want to see her when she's finished her dinner."

Into Aunt Juley's pouting face rose a flush.

"I take the entire responsibility," she said. "The little dog was lost. It was hungry and Cook has given it some scraps."

"A strange dog," muttered Timothy, "bringing in fleas like that!"

"Oh! I don't think," murmured Aunt Juley, "it's a well-bred little dog."

"How do *you* know? You don't know a dog from a door-mat."

The flush deepened over Aunt Juley's pouts.

"It was a Christian act," she said, looking Timothy in the eye. "If you had been to church, you wouldn't talk like that."

It was perhaps the first time she had openly bearded her delicate brother. The result was complete. Timothy ate his mincepie hurriedly.

"Well, don't let *me* see it," he muttered.

"Put the wine and walnuts on the table and go down, Smither," said Aunt Ann, "and see what Cook is doing about it."

When she had gone there was silence. It was felt that Juley had forgotten herself.

Aunt Ann put her wineglass to her lips; it contained two thimblefuls of brown sherry—a present from dear Jolyon—he had such a palate! Aunt Hester, who during the excitement had thoughtfully finished a second mincepie, was smiling. Aunt Juley had her eyes fixed on Timothy; she had tasted of defiance and it was sweet.

Smither returned.

"Well, Smither?"

"Cook's washing of it, Miss."

"What's she doing that for?" said Timothy.

"Because it's dirty," said Aunt Juley.

"There you are!"

And the voice of Aunt Ann was heard, saying grace. When she had finished, the three sisters rose.

"We'll leave you to your wine, dear. Smither, my shawl, please."

Upstairs in the drawing-room there was grave silence. Aunt Juley was trying to still her fluttering nerves; Aunt

Hester trying to pretend that nothing had happened; Aunt Ann, upright and a little grim, trying to compress the Riot Act with her thin and bloodless lips. She was not thinking of herself, but of the immutable order of things, so seriously compromised.

Aunt Juley repeated, suddenly: "He followed me, Ann."

"Without an intro—— Without your inviting him?"

"I spoke to him, because he was lost."

"You should think before you speak. Dogs take advantage."

Aunt Juley's face mutinied. "Well, I'm glad," she said, "and that's flat. Such a how-de-do!"

Aunt Ann looked pained. A considerable time passed. Aunt Juley began playing solitaire—she played without presence of mind, so that extraordinary things happened on the board. Aunt Ann sat upright, with her eyes closed; and Aunt Hester, after watching them for some minutes to see if they would open, took from under her cushion a library volume, and hiding it behind a firescreen, began to read—it was volume two and she did not yet know 'Lady Audley's' secret: of course it *was* a novel, but, as Timothy had said, 'Better the day, better the deed.'

The clock struck three. Aunt Ann opened her eyes, Aunt Hester shut her book. Aunt Juley crumpled the solitaire balls together with a clatter. There was a knock on the door, for not belonging to the upper regions, like Smither, Cook always knocked.

"Come in!"

Still in her pink print frock, Cook entered, and behind her entered the dog, snowy white, with its coat all brushed and bushy, its manner and its tail now cocky and now deprecating. It *was* a moment! Cook spoke:

"I've brought it up, miss; it's had its dinner, and it's

been washed. It's a nice little dear, and taken quite a fancy to me."

The three Aunts sat silent with their eyes now on the dog, now on the legs of the furniture.

" 'Twould 'ave done your 'eart good to see it eat, miss. And it answers to the name of Pommy."

"Fancy!" said Aunt Hester, with an effort. She did so hate things to be awkward.

Aunt Ann leaned forward; her voice rose firm, if rather quavery.

"It doesn't belong to us, Cook; and your master would never permit it. Smither shall go with it to the Police Station."

As if struck by the words, the dog emerged from Cook's skirt and approached the voice. It stood in a curve and began to oscillate its tail very slightly; its eyes, like bits of jet, gazed up. Aunt Ann looked down at it; her thin veined hands, as if detached from her firmness, moved nervously over her glacé skirt. From within Aunt Juley emotion was emerging in one large pout. Aunt Hester was smiling spasmodically.

"Them Police Stations!" said Cook. "I'm sure it's not been accustomed. It's not as if it had a collar, miss."

"Pommy!" said Aunt Juley.

The dog turned at the sound, sniffed her knees, and instantly returned to its contemplation of Aunt Ann, as though it recognised where power was seated.

"It's really rather sweet!" murmured Aunt Hester, and not only the dog looked at Aunt Ann. But at this moment the door was again opened.

"Mr. Swithin Forsyte, miss," said the voice of Smither.

Aunts Juley and Hester rose to greet their brother; Aunt Ann, privileged by seventy-eight years, remained seated. The family always went to Aunt Ann, not Aunt Ann to the family. There was a general feeling that dear Swithin had come providentially, knowing as he did all about horses.

"You can leave the little dog for the moment, Cook. Mr. Swithin will tell us what to do."

Swithin, who had taken his time on the stairs which were narrow, made an entry. Tall, with his chest thrown forward, his square face puffy pale, his eyes light and round, the tiny grey imperial below his moustached lips gave to him the allure of a master of ceremonies, and the white dog, retreating to a corner, yapped loudly.

"What's this?" said Swithin. "A dog?"

So might one entering a more modern drawing-room, have said: "What's this—a camel?"

Repairing hastily to the corner, Aunt Juley admonished the dog with her finger. It shivered slightly and was silent. Aunt Ann said:

"Give dear Swithin his chair, Hester; we want your advice, Swithin. This little dog followed Juley home this morning—he was lost."

Swithin seated himself with his knees apart, thus preserving the deportment of his body and the uncreased beauty of his waitscoat. His Wellington boots showed stiff beneath his almost light blue trousers. He said:

"Has Timothy had a fit?"

Dear Swithin—he was so droll!

"Not yet," said Aunt Hester, who was sometimes almost naughty.

"Well, he will. Here, Juley, don't stand there stuck. Bring the dog out, and let's have a look at it. Dog! Why, it's a bitch!"

This curiously male word, though spoken with distinc-

tion, caused a sensation such as would have accompanied a
heavy fall of soot. The dog had been assumed by all to
be of the politer sex, because of course one didn't notice
such things. Aunt Juley, indeed, whom past association with
Septimus Small had rendered more susceptible, had conceived her doubts, but she had continued to be on the polite
side.

"A bitch," repeated Swithin; "you'll have no end of
trouble with it."

"That is what we fear," said Aunt Ann, "though I
don't think you should call it that in a drawing-room,
dear."

"Stuff and nonsense!" said Swithin. "Come here, little
tyke!"

And he stretched out a ringed hand smelling of dogskin
—he had driven himself round in his phaeton.

Encouraged by Aunt Juley, the little dog approached,
and sat cowering under the hand. Swithin lifted it by the
ruff round its neck.

"Well-bred," he said, putting it down.

"We can't keep it," said Aunt Ann, firmly. "The carpets—we thought—the Police Station."

"If I were you," said Swithin, "I'd put a notice in *The
Times:* 'Found, white Pomeranian bitch. Apply, The Nook,
Bayswater Road.' You might get a reward. Let's look at
its teeth."

The little dog, who seemed in a manner fascinated by
the smell of Swithin's hand and the stare of his round
china-blue eyes, put no obstacle in the way of fingers that
raised its upper and depressed its lower lip.

"It's a puppy," said Swithin. "Loo, loo, little tyke!"

This terrible incentive caused the dog to behave in a
singular manner; depressing its tail so far as was possible, it

jumped sideways and scurried round Aunt Hester's chair, then crouched with its chin on the ground, its hindquarters and tail in the air, looking up at Swithin with eyes black as boot-buttons.

"I shouldn't be surprised," said Swithin, "if it was worth money. Loo, loo!"

This time the little dog scurried round the entire room, avoiding the legs of chairs by a series of miracles, then, halting by a marqueterie stand, it stood on its hind legs and began to eat the pampas grass.

"Ring, Hester!" said Aunt Ann. "Ring for Smither. Juley, stop it!"

Swithin, whose imperial was jutting in a fixed smile, said:

"Where's Timothy? I should like to see it bite his legs."

Aunt Juley, moved by maternal spasms, bent down and picked the dog up in her arms. She stood, pouting over its sharp nose and soft warm body, like the very figure of daring with the smell of soft soap in its nostrils.

"I will take it downstairs myself," she said; "it shan't be teased. Come, Pommy!"

The dog, who had no say whatever in the matter, put out a pink strip of tongue and licked her nose. Aunt Juley had the exquisite sensation of being loved; and, hastily, to conceal her feelings, bore it lolling over her arm away. She bore it upstairs, instead of down, to her room which was at the back of dear Ann's, and stood, surrounded by mahogany, with the dog still in her arms. Every hand was against her and the poor dog, and she squeezed it tighter. It was panting, and every now and then with its slip of a tongue it licked her cheek, as if to assure itself of reality. Since the departure of Septimus Small ten years ago, she had never been properly loved, and now that something was ready to love her, they wanted to take it away. She sat down on her bed, still holding the dog, while below, they would be talking of how to send Pommy to the Police Station or put her into the papers! Then, noticing that white hairs were coming off on to her, she put the dog down. It sidled round the room, sniffing, till it came to the washstand, where it stood looking at her and panting. What *did* it want? Wild thoughts passed through Aunt Juley's mind, till suddenly the dog stood on its hind legs and licked the air. Why, it was thirsty! Disregarding the niceties of existence, Aunt Juley lifted the jug, and set it on the floor. For some minutes there was no sound but lapping. Could it really hold all that? The little dog looked up at her, moved its tail twice, then trotted away to inspect the room more closely. Having inspected everything except Aunt Juley, concerning whom its mind was apparently made up, it lay down under the valance of the dressing table, with its head and forepaws visible, and uttered a series of short spasmodic barks. Aunt Juley understood them to mean: 'Come and play with me!' And taking her sponge-bag, she dangled it. Seizing it—So unexpected!—the little dog shook it violently. Aunt Juley was at once charmed and horrified. It was evidently feeling quite at home; but her poor bag! Oh! its little teeth *were* sharp and strong! Aunt Juley swelled. It was as if she didn't care what happened to the bag so long as the little dog were having a good time. The bag came to an end; and gathering up the pieces, she thought defiantly: 'Well, it's not as if I ever went to Brighton now!' But she said severely:

"You see what you've done!" And, together, they examined the pieces, while Aunt Juley's heart took a resolu-

tion. They might talk as they liked: Finding was keeping;
and if Timothy didn't like it, he could lump it! The
sensation was terrific. Someone, however, was knocking on
the door.

"Oh! Smither," said Aunt Juley, "you see what the
little dog has done?" And she held up the sponge-bag defiantly.

"Aoh!" said Smither; "its teeth *are* sharp. Would you
go down, ma'am? Mr. and Mrs. James Forsyte are in
the drawing-room. Shall I take the little dog now? I
daresay it'd like a run."

"Not to the Police Station, Smither. I found it, and I'm
going to keep it."

"I'm sure, Ma'am. It'll be company for me and Cook,
now that Tommy's gone. It's took quite a fancy to us."

With a pang of jealousy Aunt Juley said: "I take all
the responsibility. Go with Smither, Pommy!"

Caught up in her arms, the little dog lolled its head over
the edge of Smither and gazed back sentimentally as it was
borne away. And, again, all that was maternal in Aunt
Juley swelled, beneath the dark violet of her bosom sprin-
kled with white hairs.

"Say I am coming down." And she began plucking off
the white hairs.

Outside the drawing-room door she passed; then went
in, weak at the knees. Between his Dundreary whiskers
James was telling a story. His long legs projected so that
she had to go round; his long lips stopped to say:

"How are you, Juley? They tell me you've found a
dog," and resumed the story. It was all about a man who
had been bitten and had insisted on being cauterised until
he couldn't sit down, and the dog hadn't been mad after
all, so that it was all wasted, and that was what came of

dogs. He didn't know what use they were except to make a mess.

Emily said: "Pomeranians are all the rage. They look so amusing in a carriage."

Aunt Hester murmured that Jolyon had an Italian greyhound at Stanhope Gate.

"That snippetty whippet!" said Swithin—perhaps the first use of the term: "There's no body in *them*."

"You're not going to *keep* this dog?" said James. "You don't know what it might have."

Very red, Aunt Juley said sharply: "Fiddle-de-dee, James!"

"Well, you might have an action brought against you. They tell me there's a Home for Lost Dogs. Your proper course is to turn it out."

"Turn out your grandmother!" snapped Aunt Juley; she was not afraid of James.

"Well, it's not your property. You'll be getting up against the Law."

"Fiddle the Law!"

This epoch-making remark was received in silence. Nobody knew what had come to Juley.

"Well," said James, with finality, "don't say I didn't tell you. What does Timothy say—he'll have a fit."

"If he wants to have a fit, he must," said Aunt Juley. "*I* shan't stop him."

"What are you going to do with the puppies?" said Swithin: "Ten to one she'll have puppies."

"You see, Juley," said Aunt Ann.

Aunt Juley's agitation was such that she took up a fan from the little curio table beside her, and began to wave it before her flushed face.

"You're all against me," she said: "Puppies, indeed! A little thing like that!"

Swithin rose. "Good-bye to you all. I'm going to see Nicholas. Good-bye, Juley. You come for a drive with me some day. I'll take you to the Lost Dogs' Home." Throwing out his chest, he manœuvred to the door, and could be heard descending the stairs to the accompaniment of the drawing-room bell.

James said mechanically: "He's a funny fellow, Swithin!"

It was as much his permanent impression of his twin brother as was Swithin's: "He's a poor stick, James!"

Emily, who was bored, began talking to Aunt Hester about the new fashion of eating oysters before the soup. Of course it was very foreign, but they said the Prince was doing it; James wouldn't have it; but personally she thought it rather elegant. She should see! James had begun to tell Aunt Ann how Soames would be out of his articles in January—he was a steady chap. He told her at some length. Aunt Juley sat pouting behind her moving fan. She had a longing for dear Jolyon. Partly because he had always been her favourite and her eldest brother, who had never allowed anyone else to bully her; partly because he was the only one who had a dog, and partly because even Ann was a little afraid of him. She sat longing to hear him say: "You're a parcel of old woman; of course Juley can keep what she found." Because, that was it! The dog had followed her of its own free will. It was not as if it had been a precious stone or a purse—which, of course, would have been different. Sometimes Jolyon did come on Sundays—though generally he took little June to the Zoo; and the moment he came James would be sure to go away, for fear of having his knuckles rapped; and that, she felt

sure, would be so nice, since James had been horrid about
it all!

"I think," she said, suddenly, "I shall go round to Stanhope Gate, and ask dear Jolyon."

"What do you want to do that for?" said James, taking
hold of a whisker. "He'll send you away with a flea in
your ear."

Whether or no this possibility deterred her, Aunt Juley
did not rise, but she ceased fanning herself and sat with the
expression on her face which had given rise to the family
saying: 'Oh! So-and-so's a regular Juley!'

But James had now exhausted his weekly budget. "Well,
Emily," he said, "you'll be wanting to get home. We can't
keep the horses any longer."

The accuracy of this formula had never been put to the
proof, for Emily always rose at once with the words:

"Good-bye, dears. Give our love to Timothy." She
had pecked their cheeks and gone out of the room before
James could remember what—as he would tell her in the
carriage—he had specially gone there to ask them.

When they had departed, Aunt Hester, having looked
from one to the other of her sisters, muffled 'Lady Audley's
Secret' in her shawl and tiptoed away. She knew what
was coming. Aunt Juley took the solitaire board with hands
that trembled. The moment had arrived! And she waited,
making an occasional move with oozing fingers, and stealing glances at that upright figure in black silk with jet
trappings and cameo brooch. On no account did she mean
to be the first to speak; and she said, suddenly:

"There you sit, Ann!"

Aunt Ann, countering her glance with those grey eyes of
hers that saw quite well at a distance, spoke:

"You heard what Swithin and James said, Juley."

"I will *not* turn the dog out," said Aunt Juley. "I will not, and that's flat." The blood beat in her temples and she tapped a foot on the floor.

"If it were a really nice little dog, it would not have run away and got lost. Little dogs of that sex are not to be trusted. You ought to know that, at your age, Juley; now that we're alone, I can talk to you plainly. It will have followers, of course."

Aunt Juley put a finger into her mouth, sucked it, took it out, and said:

"I'm tired of being treated like a little girl."

Aunt Ann answered calmly:

"I think you should take some calomel—getting into fantods like this! We have never had a dog."

"I don't want you to have one now," said Aunt Juley; "I want it for myself. I—I—" She could not bring herself to express what was in her heart about being loved—it would be—would be gushing!

"It's not right to keep what's not your own," said Aunt Ann. "You know that perfectly well."

"I will put an advertisement in the paper; if the owner comes, I'll give it up. But it followed me of its own accord. And it can live downstairs. Timothy need never see it."

"It will spoil the carpets," said Aunt Ann, "and bark at night; we shall have no peace."

"I'm sick of peace," said Aunt Juley, rattling the board. "I'm sick of peace, and I'm sick of taking care of things till they—till you—till one belongs to them."

Aunt Ann lifted her hands, spidery and pale.

"You don't know what you're talking about. If one can't take care of one's things, one is not fit to have them."

"Care—care—I'm sick of care! I want something human—I want this dog. And if I can't have it, I will go away and take it with me; and that's flat."

It was, perhaps, the wildest thing that had ever been said at Timothy's. Aunt Ann said very quietly:

"You know you can't go away, Juley, you haven't the money; so it's no good talking like that."

"Jolyon will give me the money; he will never let you bully me."

An expression of real pain centred itself between Aunt Ann's old eyes.

"I do not think I bully," she said; "you forget yourself."

For a full minute Aunt Juley said nothing, looking to and fro from her twisting fingers to the wrinkled ivory pale face of her eldest sister. Tears of compunction had welled up in her eyes. Dear Ann was very old, and the doctor was always saying——! And quickly she got out her handkerchief.

"I—I'm upset.—I—I didn't mean—dear Ann—I—" the words bubbled out: "b-b-but I d-do so w-want the little d-d-dog."

There was silence, broken by her sniffing. Then rose the voice of Aunt Ann, calm, a little tremulous:

"Very well, dear; it will be a sacrifice, but if it makes you happier——"

"Oh!" sobbed Aunt Juley: "Oh!"

A large tear splashed on the solitaire board, and with the small handkerchief she wiped it off.

MIDSUMMER MADNESS
1880

MIDSUMMER MADNESS

GEORGE, second son to Roger Forsyte of Prince's gate, was in the year 1880 twenty-four years of age, and supposed to be a farmer. That is to say he had failed for the Army, and had definitely refused to enter any indoor profession. This was why he spent the inside of his weeks in any country pursuit which was not farming, and the outside of his weeks in or about the Club in Piccadilly which he had nicknamed 'The Iseeum.' Nominally resident at Plumtree Park in Bedfordshire, where a gentleman farmer eked out his losses with the premiums paid by the fathers of his pupils, George Forsyte's wit, of which he had a good deal, enabled him to spend most of his time with neighbouring landowners, who let him ride their horses or shoot their pheasants and rabbits. In the summer, when horses were turned out, pheasants turned in, and even rabbits were breeding, George would sometimes look at other people shearing sheep, and cheer them with his jests; but as a general thing he would be found studying the conformation of the horse on Newmarket Heath, or the conformation of chorus girls on the stage of the Liberty Theatre. But in this particular summer of 1880, as will sometimes happen with men of the world, he had fallen in love. The object of his affection was a very pretty woman with dark dove-like eyes, who was somewhat naturally the wife of a man he knew called Basset, a neighbouring landowner and Major in the Militia. It may come as a shock to those who fifty years later have claimed for themselves the abolition of morals to learn that George already had none. It was with a mere glow that he discovered himself to be in love with a married woman. Flora Basset, like most people with dove-like eyes, was what was then known as a 'flirt'; and since she lived in the country to please her husband, when she would rather have lived in London, she considered herself entitled to such amusement as came her way. George was very amusing.

He began at Easter time by normal admiration of Flora's eyes and conformation, and a normal hankering to make her his own; but as summer came, he found these feelings gradually complicated by a sensation which he had never before known, but which other people had called jealousy. In other words it became distasteful to think of Flora as Mrs. Basset. George was not of those who examine and label their feelings, or he would perhaps have understood that desire was becoming passion.

June arriving, and the weather turning hot, Major Basset, "that poopstick" as George now called him in thought, went into camp with his Militia. George experienced a feeling, not merely of increased hope, but of relief, for, when not in the presence of his Flora, he had begun to ache. But he was soon to discover that his Flora had an excellent head, and knew how to keep it. She had no intention of being compromised. George, of course, was well aware that if he did compromise her, or rather himself, his position, dependent on his father, a man of maturer years and the morals of an old Forsyte, would become impossible; as likely as not, cut off with a shilling, he would be obliged to live on racing debts. But this was not enough to make him thankful that his Flora would not let him compromise her. On the contrary her discretion drove him nearly mad.

And the weather grew hotter; the trees, the flowers, the grasses exuded more scent; the cuckoo's note became a little querulous; the wood-pigeons emitted the ritornelles of love. With the increasing temperature more and more of his Flora became visible, and George played croquet with her, and sat listening to her singing the songs of opera bouffe, and now and again was permitted to stay to dinner, and dismissed at nine o'clock; and his wit shrivelled within him in the heat of his feelings; and half the month of June was gone.

Now in George was something dogged and tenacious; nor did he lack hardihood. He ceased not in his resolve; with heroism he fought against the shrivelling of his wit, and like the unhappy clowns of Kings in the old days, who must be merry whatever the conditions of their hearts, continued to jest in the presence of his beloved, and to subdue the smoulder in his bull-like eyes. 'Plain but pleasant'— as he called himself—to cease being pleasant must lose him the game. But dry were the lips with which he jested; and small was his knowledge of his Flora's heart. What her feelings were for the 'poopstick' who in a week's time would be returning he never dared to ask. And he suffered, he suffered as much as moralists could wish; but he continued to jest, because it was—jest or lose; and his Flora continued to smile on him with her dark and dove-like eyes, to laugh little half-shocked laughs, to press his hand faintly; to smell sweet and look enticing. And the last week passed.

Hotter and hotter, the sun flamed all day, and it was good to sit in the shade. Now, alongside the croquet lawn in front of the Bassets' house, was a shrubbery of rhododendrons, and beyond this a clump of lilacs and within it a summer house and beyond this again an orchard of plum and pear trees.

And George took from his Flora's hand the croquet mallet, and, holding it out, said with a grin:

"Who's for a cooler?   Let's go and sit in the shade with this between us."

His Flora laughed:

"George, how naughty you are!"

"Naughty but nice!" said George, and took her hand with the tips of his fingers, walking delicately, for all his heaviness, as if leading her to a minuet. And, while he walked, he thought: 'The last day—this is hell!'

They came to the summer-house.

"What?" said George; "no earwigs! Forward, the Buffs!"

They entered, sat down; George placed the mallet between them. And silence fell—for the life of him he could no longer jest.

From across the mallet, Flora was gazing, cool and sweet against the wooden wall, a little smile on her lips. It was too much! George took the mallet in both hands; his fleshy face had gone a dusky red, his full thick-lidded eyes gazed lowering in front of him, veins stood out on his forehead beneath his neatly parted hair; the muscles in his arms below the rolled-up sleeves swelled in ridges. He laid the mallet down on his other side noiselessly as if it had been a feather.

"Flora!" he said, and seized the sweet and unresisting creature.

So was accomplished his desire, with no words spoken.

He stood, presently, and watched her go, a finger to her lips and her eyes still smiling; then through the orchard himself went away, dumb and grateful for pleasure as the beasts that perish, and drunk with triumph like a god. The day had changed and darkened with the heat. The sky had an airless brooding aspect; flies buzzed viciously and clung

about him. He sat down on the bank of a stream and
lighted a cigar. He held it between lips that never ceased
to smile, and watched the smoke annoying the flies and
midges. He listened, without hearing, to their hum, and to
the cooing of the wood-pigeons; he watched, without seeing, the extreme stillness of the heat-darkened day. Thus,
he spent two hours lost in a few past minutes. He got up
with a sigh, the scent of nettles, burdock and the carted
hay deep in his nostrils. He would not go home, but
walked to the Inn. He ate bread and cheese and drank
porter. And then began again the longing to see and touch
her that had for so short time been appeased; and smoking
a village clay he ached, watching all light out of the sky;
so heavy and hot the air, that he sweated, sitting there. And
he thought: 'The last night! She might let me in—she
might!'

He rose and went out into the breathless dark, retracing
his steps to the stream, and through the blinded orchard to
the summer-house. He groped and found the mallet and
took it with him, stealing along past the lilacs, to the edge
of the rhododendron clump bordering the lawn. Dark!
It was more than dark, but he could just see the house.
And, squatting on the grass, dry as tinder, he gazed up.
Two first floor windows alone were lighted, open but cur-
tained—hers—so well he knew the windows he had longed
to enter! And he thought: 'By Gad! I'll have a shot!'
and going on his knees he searched for tiny pebbles in the
shrubbery. Then drawing deep breaths to still the pound-
ing of his heart he moved towards the house along the
rhododendrons. But then he stopped as if he had been
shot, and dropped to his knees on the grass. A curtain had
been pulled aside; in the lighted window-space stood the
figure of a half-dressed man. He was leaning there, in-

haling the heavy night! he turned and spoke into the room. George saw his profile—Basset! Their voices carried to him in the stillness—his voice and hers. He saw a shimmer of white—flesh, drapery—pass across behind; saw the man's arm go round it. And George pressed his face to the dry grass, stifling a groan. He heard a woman's low laugh, the window shut down, and furious pain jerked him to his knees. To take the mallet—to climb up—to brain him—her—to—to——! He fell forward again, with arms outstretched. The smell of parched grass mixed itself with his agony, for how long—how long—till the night was rent with a blinding flash and thunder rolled round and round him. He staggered to his feet, ran into the dark; and stumbled among the orchard trees. Lightning flashed all round, he wanted it to strike. He wanted it to strike him, but he knew it wouldn't. Then the rain fell—fell in a sheet, drenched him in a minute; fell and fell, and cooled him even to the heart. Like a drowned rat he came to where he lived, and let himself in. He went up to his bedroom, and tearing off his clothes, flung himself into bed. And behind and through the crashing of the thunder he heard that low soft laugh, and the window being shut down. He fell asleep at last.

When he woke the sun was shining in at his window; it shone across the room on to his boots—fourteen pairs of boots and shoes, treed, in triple rows, on the top of his chest-of-drawers. Boots and shoes of every kind—riding boots, shooting boots, town boots, tennis boots, pumps. George looked at them, with fish-like eyes. In those well-worn and polished boots, treed against decay, was life—his life—and in his heart, dragged from its drowned sleep, was death. That laugh! No! To hell with women! Boots! And, lying there, he ground his teeth and grinned.

THE HONDEKOETER
1880

THE HONDEKOETER

ENCOUNTERING his old friend Traquair opposite the Horse Guards, in the summer of 1880, James Forsyte, who had taken an afternoon off from the City, proceeded alongside with the words:

"I'm not well."

His friend answered: "You look bobbish enough. Going to the Club?"

"No," said James. "I'm going to Jobson's. They're selling Smelter's pictures. Don't suppose there's anything, but I thought I'd look in."

"Smelter? Selling his 'Cupid and Pish,' as he used to call it? He never could speak the Queen's English."

"I'm sure I don't know what made him die," said James; "he wasn't seventy. His '47 was good."

"Ah! And his brown sherry."

James shook his head.

"Liverish stuff. I've been walking from the Temple; got a touch of liver now."

"You ought to go to Carlsbad; that's the new place, they say."

"Homburg," said James, mechanically. "Emily likes it—too fashionable for me. I don't know—I'm sixty-nine." He pointed his umbrella at a lion.

"That chap Landseer must ha' made a pretty penny," he muttered: "They say Dizzy's very shaky. *He* won't last long."

"M'm! That old fool Gladstone'll set us all by the ears yet. Going to bid at Jobson's?"

"Bid? Haven't got the money to throw away. My family's growing up."

"Ah! How's your married daughter—Winifred?"

The furrow between James' brows increased in depth.

"She never tells me. But I know that chap Dartie she married makes the money fly."

"What is he?"

"An outside broker," said James, gloomily: "But so far as I can see, he does nothing but gallivant about to races and that. He'll do no good with himself."

He halted at the pavement edge, where a crossing had been swept, for it had rained; and extracting a penny from his trouser pocket, gave it to the crossing-sweeper, who looked up at his long figure with a round and knowing eye.

"Well, good-bye, James. I'm going to the Club. Remember me to Emily."

James Forsyte nodded, and moved, stork-like, on to the narrow crossing. Andy Traquair! He still looked very spry! Gingery chap! But that wife of his—fancy marrying again at his age! Well, no fool like an old one. And, incommoded by a passing four-wheeler, he instinctively raised his umbrella—they never looked where they were going.

Traversing St. James' Square, he reflected gloomily that these new Clubs were thundering great places; and this asphalt pavement that was coming in—he didn't know! London wasn't what it used to be, with horses slipping about all over the place. He turned into Jobson's. Three o'clock! They'd be just starting. Smelter must have cut up quite well.

Ascending the steps, he passed through the lobbies into the sale-room. Auction was in progress, but they had not yet reached the 'property of William Smelter Esq.'

Putting on his tortoiseshell pince-nez, James studied the catalogue. Since his purchase of a Turner—some said 'not a Turner'—all cordage and drowning men, he had not bought a picture, and he had a blank space on the stairs. It was a large space in a poor light; he often thought it looked very bare. If there were anything going at a bargain, he might think of it. H'm! There was the Bronzino: 'Cupid and Pish' that Smelter had been so proud of —a nude; he didn't want nudes in Park Lane. His eye ran down the catalogue: "Claud Lorraine," "Bosboem," "Cornelis van Vos," "Snyders"—"Snyders"—m'm! still life—all ducks and geese, hares, artichokes, onions, platters, oysters, grapes, turkeys, pears, and starved-looking greyhounds asleep under them. No. 17, "M. Hondekoeter." Fowls. 11 foot by 6. What a whopping great thing! He took three mental steps into the middle of the picture and three steps out again. "Hondekoeter." His brother Jolyon had one in the billiard room at Stanhope Gate—lot of fowls; not so big as that. "Snyders!" "Ary Scheffer"— bloodless-looking affair, he'd be bound! "Rosa Bonheur." "Snyders."

He took a seat at the side of the room, and fell into a reverie—with James a serious matter, indissolubly connected with investments. Soames—in partnership now—was shaping well; bringing in a lot of business. That house in Bryanston Square—the tenancy would be up in September —he ought to get another hundred on a re-let, with the improvements the tenant had put in. He'd have a couple of thousand to invest next Quarter Day. There was Cape Copper, but he didn't know; Nicholas was always telling him to buy 'Midland.' That fellow Dartie, too, kept worrying him about Argentines—he wouldn't touch them with a pair of tongs. And, leaning forward with his hands

crossed on the handle of his umbrella, he gazed fixedly up
at the skylight, as if seeing some annunciation or other,
while his shaven lips, between his grey Dundrearys, filled
sensually as though savouring a dividend.

"The collection of William Smelter, Esquire, of Rus-
sell Square."

Now for the usual poppycock! "This well-known col-
lector," "masterpieces of the Dutch and French Schools";
"rare opportunity"; "Connoisseur"; all me eye and Betty
Martin! Smelter used to buy 'em by the yard.

"No. 1. Cupid and Psyche: Bronzino. Ladies and Gentlemen: what shall I start in at—this beautiful picture, an
undoubted masterpiece of the Italian School?"

James sniggered. Connoisseur—with his 'Cupid and
Pish'!

To his astonishment there was some brisk bidding; and
James' upper lip began to lengthen, as ever at any dispute
about values. The picture was knocked down and a 'Snyders' put up. James sat watching picture after picture disposed of. It was hot in the room and he felt sleepy—he
didn't know why he had come; he might have been having
a nap at the Club, or driving with Emily.

"What—no bid for the Hondekoeter? This large masterpiece."

James gazed at the enormous picture on the easel, supported at either end by an attendant. The huge affair was
full of poultry and feathers floating in a bit of water and
a large white rooster looking as if it were about to take a
bath. It was a dark painting, save for the rooster, with a
yellowish tone.

"Come, gentlemen? By a celebrated painter of domestic
poultry. May I say fifty? Forty? Who'll give me forty
pounds? It's giving it away. Well, thirty to start it? Look

at the rooster! Masterly painting! Come now! I'll take
any bid."

"Five pounds!" said James, covering the words so that
no one but the auctioneer should see where they came from.

"Five pounds for this genuine work by a master of domestic poultry! Ten pounds did you say, Sir? Ten pounds
bid."

"Fifteen," muttered James.

"Twenty."

"Twenty-five," said James; he was not going above
thirty.

"Twenty-five—why, the frame's worth it. Who says
thirty?"

No one said thirty; and the picture was knocked down
to James, whose mouth had opened slightly. He hadn't
meant to buy it; but the thing was a bargain—the size had
frightened them; Jolyon had paid one hundred and forty
for his Hondekoeter. Well, it would cover that blank on
the stairs. He waited till two more pictures had been sold;
then, leaving his card with directions for the despatch of
the Hondekoeter, made his way up St. James' Street and on
towards home.

He found Emily just starting out with Rachel and Cicely
in the barouche, but refused to accompany them—a little
afraid of being asked what he had been doing. Entering
his deserted house, he told Warmson that he felt liverish;
he would have a cup of tea and a muffin, nothing more;
then passing on to the stairs, he stood looking at the blank
space. When the picture was hung, it wouldn't be there.
What would Soames say to it, though—the boy had begun
to interest himself in pictures since his run abroad? Still,
the price he had paid was not the market value; and, passing on up to the drawing-room, he drank his China tea,

strong, with cream, and ate two muffins. If he didn't feel better to-morrow, he should have Dash look at him.

The following morning, starting for the office, he said to Warmson:

"There'll be a picture come to-day. You'd better get Hunt and Thomas to help you hang it. It's to go in the middle of that space on the stairs. You'd better have it done when your mistress is out. Let 'em bring it in the back way—it's eleven foot by six; and mind the paint."

When he returned, rather late, the Hondekoeter was hung. It covered the space admirably, but the light being poor and the picture dark, it was not possible to see what it was about. It looked quite well. Emily was in the drawing-room when he went in.

"What on earth is that great picture on the stairs, James?"

"That?" said James. "A Hondekoeter; picked it up, a bargain, at Smelter's sale. Jolyon's got one at Stanhope Gate."

"I never saw such a lumbering great thing."

"What?" said James. "It covers up that space well. It's not as if you could see anything on the stairs. There's some good poultry in it."

"It makes the stairs darker than they were before. I don't know what Soames will say. Really, James, you oughtn't to go about alone, buying things like that."

"I can do what I like with my money, I suppose," said James. "It's a well-known name."

"Well," said Emily, "for a man of your age—Never mind! Don't fuss! Sit down and drink your tea."

James sat down, muttering. Women—always unjust, and no more sense of values than an old tom-cat!

Emily said no more, ever mistress of her suave and fashionable self.

Winifred, with Montague Dartie, came in later, so that all the family were assembled for dinner; Cicely having her hair down, Rachel her hair up—she had 'come out' this season; Soames, who had just parted with the little whiskers of the late 'seventies, looking pale and flatter-cheeked than usual. Winifred, beginning to be 'interesting,' owing to the approach of a little Dartie, kept her eyes somewhat watchfully on 'Monty,' square and oiled, with a 'handsome' look on his sallow face, and a big diamond stud in his shining shirt-front.

It was she who broached the Hondekoeter.

"Pater dear, what made you buy that enormous picture?"

James looked up, and mumbled through his mutton:

"Enormous! It's the right size for that space on the stairs." It seemed to him at the moment that his family had very peculiar faces.

"It's very fine and large!" Dartie was speaking! 'Um!' thought James: 'What does *he* want—money?'

"It's so yellow," said Rachel, plaintively.

"What do *you* know about a picture?"

"I know what I like, Pater."

James stole a glance at his son, but Soames was looking down his nose.

"It's very good value," said James, suddenly. "There's some first-rate feather painting in it."

Nothing more was said at the moment, nobody wanting to hurt the Pater's feelings, but, upstairs, in the drawing-room after Emily and her three daughters had again traversed the length of the Hondekoeter, a lively conversation broke out.

Really—the Pater! Rococo was not the word for pictures that size! And chickens—who wanted to look at chickens, even if you could see them? But, of course, Pater thought a bargain excused everything.

Emily said:

"Don't be disrespectful, Cicely."

"Well, Mater, he does, you know. All the old Forsytes do."

Emily, who secretly agreed, said: "H'ssh!"

She was always loyal to James, in his absence. They all were, indeed, except among themselves.

"Soames thinks it dreadful," said Rachel. "I hope he'll tell the Pater so."

"Soames will do nothing of the sort," said Emily. "Really your father can do what he likes in his own house —you children are getting very uppish."

"Well, Mater, you know jolly well it's awfully out of date."

"I wish you would not say 'awfully' and 'jolly,' Cicely."

"Why not? Everybody does, at school."

Winifred cut in:

"They really are the latest words, Mother."

Emily was silent; nothing took the wind out of her sails like the word 'latest,' for, though a woman of much character, she could not bear to be behindhand.

"Listen!" said Rachel, who had opened the door.

A certain noise could be heard; it was James, extolling the Hondekoeter, on the stairs.

"That rooster," he was saying, "is a fine bird; and look at those feathers floating. Think they could paint those nowadays? Your Uncle Jolyon gave a hundred an' forty for his Hondekoeter, and I picked this up for twenty-five."

"What did I say?" whispered Cicely. "A bargain. I hate bargains; they lumber up everything. That Turner was another!"

" 'Shh!" said Winifred, who was not so young, and wished that Monty had more sense of a bargain than he had as yet displayed. "I like a bargain myself; you know you've got something for your money."

"I'd rather have my money," said Cicely.

"Don't be silly, Cicely," said Emily; "go and play your piece. Your father likes it."

James and Dartie now entered, Soames having passed on up to his room where he worked at night.

Cicely began her piece. She was at home owing to an outbreak of mumps at her school on Ham Common; and her piece, which contained a number of runs up and down the piano, was one which she was perfecting for the school concert at the end of term. James, who made a point of asking for it, partly because it was good for Cicely, and partly because it was good for his digestion, took his seat by the hearth between his whiskers, averting his eyes from animated objects. Unfortunately, he never could sleep after dinner, and thoughts buzzed in his head. Soames had said there was no demand now for large pictures, and very little for the Dutch school—he had admitted, however, that the Hondekoeter was a bargain as values went; the name alone was worth the money. Cicely commenced her 'piece'; James brooded on. He really didn't know whether he was glad he had bought the thing or not. Everyone of them had disapproved, except Dartie; the only one whose disapproval he would have welcomed. To say that James was conscious of a change in the mental outlook of his day would be to credit him with a philosophic sensibility unsuited to his breeding and his age; but he was uncomfortably conscious that a bargain was not what it had been. And while Cicely's fingers ran up and down—he didn't know, he couldn't say.

"D'you mean to tell me," he said, when Cicely shut the piano, "that you don't like those Dresden vases?"

Nobody knew whom he was addressing or why, so no one replied.

"I bought 'em at Jobson's in '67, and they're worth three times what I gave for them."

It was Rachel who responded.

"Well, Pater, do you like them yourself?"

"Like them? What's that got to do with it? They're genuine, and worth a lot of money."

"I wish you'd sell them, then, James," said Emily. "They're not the fashion now."

"Fashion! They'll be worth a lot more before I die."

"A bargain," muttered Cicely, below her breath.

"What's that?" said James, whose hearing was some-times unexpectedly sharp.

"I said: 'A bargain,' Pater; weren't they?"

"Of course they were"; and it could be heard from his tone that if they hadn't been, he wouldn't have bought them. "You young people know nothing about money, ex-cept how to spend it"; and he looked at his son-in-law, who was sedulously concerned with his finger-nails.

Emily, partly to smooth James, whom she could see was ruffled, and partly because she had a passion for the game, told Cicely to get out the card table, and said with cheery composure:

"Come along, James, we'll play Nap."

They sat around the green board for a considerable time playing for farthings, with every now and then a little burst of laughter, when James said: "I'll go Nap!" At this particular game, indeed, James was always visited by a sort of recklessness. At farthing points he could be a devil of a fellow for very little money. He had soon lost thirteen shillings, and was as dashing as ever.

He rose at last, in excellent humour, pretending to be bankrupt.

"Well, I don't know," he said, "I always lose *my* money."

The Hondekoeter, and the misgivings it had given rise to, had faded from his mind.

Winifred and Dartie departing, without the latter having touched on finance, he went up to bed with Emily in an almost cheerful condition; and, having turned his back on her, was soon snoring lightly.

He was awakened by a crash and bumping rumble, as it might be thunder, on the right.

"What on earth's that, James?" said Emily's startled voice.

"What?" said James: "Where? Here, where are my slippers?"

"It must be a thunderbolt. Be careful, James."

For James, in his nightgown, was already standing by the bedside—in the radiance of a night-light, long as a stork. He sniffed loudly.

"D'you smell burning?"

"No," said Emily.

"Here, give me the candle."

"Put on this shawl, James. It can't be burglars; they wouldn't make such a noise."

"I don't know," muttered James, "I was asleep." He took the candle from Emily, and shuffled to the door.

"What's all this?" he said on the landing. By confused candle- and night-light he could see a number of white-clothed figures—Rachel, Cicely, and the maid Fifine, in their nightgowns. Soames in his nightshirt, at the head of the stairs, and down below, that fellow Warmson.

The voice of Soames, flat and calm, said:

"It's the Hondekoeter."

There, in fact, enormous, at the bottom of the stairs, was the Hondekoeter, fallen on its face. James, holding up his candle, stalked down and stood gazing at it. No one spoke, except Fifine, who said: "La, la!"

Cicely, seized with a fit of giggles, vanished.

Then Soames spoke into the dark well below him, illumined faintly by James' candle.

"It's all right, Pater; it won't be hurt; there was no glass."

James did not answer, but holding his candle low, returned up the stairs, and without a word went back into his bedroom.

"What was it, James?" said Emily, who had not risen.

"That picture came down with a run—comes of not looking after things yourself. That fellow Warmson! Where's the eau-de-Cologne?"

He anointed himself, got back into bed, and lay on his back, waiting for Emily to improve the occasion. But all she said was:

"I hope it hasn't made your head ache, James."

"No," said James; and, for some time after she was asleep, he lay with his eyes on the night-light, as if waiting for the Hondekoeter to play him another trick—after he had bought the thing and given it a good home, too!

Next morning, going down to breakfast he passed the picture, which had been lifted, so that it stood slanting, with its back to the stair wall. The white rooster seemed just as much on the point of taking a bath as ever. The feathers floated on their backs, curved like shallops. He passed on into the dining-room.

They were all there, eating eggs and bacon, suspiciously silent.

James helped himself and sat down.

"What are you going to do with it now, James?" said Emily.

"Do with it? Hang it again, of course!"

"Not really, Pater!" said Rachel. "It gave me fits last night."

"That wall won't stand it," said Soames.

"What! It's a good wall!"

"It really is too big," said Emily.

"And we none of us like it, Pater," put in Cicely, "it's such a monster, and so yellow!"

"Monster, indeed!" said James, and was silent, till suddenly he spluttered:

"What would you have me do with it, then?"

"Send it back; sell it again."

"I shouldn't get anything for it."

"But you said it was a bargain, Pater," said Cicely.

"So it was!"

There was another silence. James looked sidelong at his son; there was a certain pathos in that glance, as if it were seeking help, but Soames was concentrated above his plate.

"Have it put up in the lumber-room, James," said Emily, quietly.

James reddened between his whiskers, and his mouth opened; he looked again at his son, but Soames ate on. James turned to his teacup. And there went on within him that which he could not express. It was as if they had asked him: "When is a bargain not a bargain?" and he didn't know the answer, but they did. A change of epoch, something new-fangled in the air. A man could no longer buy a thing because it was worth more! It was—it was the end of everything. And, suddenly, he mumbled: "Well, have it your own way, then. Throwing money away, I call it!"

After he had gone to the office, the Hondekoeter was conducted to the lumber-room by Warmson, Hunt, and Thomas. There, covered by a dust-sheet to preserve the varnish, it rested twenty-one years, till the death of James in 1901, when it went forth and again came under the hammer. It fetched five pounds, and was bought by a designer of posters, working for a poultry-breeding firm.

CRY OF PEACOCK
1883

CRY OF PEACOCK

THE Ball was over. Soames decided to walk. In the cloak-room, whence he retrieved coat and opera hat, a mirror showed him a white-waistcoated figure still trim, but a half-melted collar, and a brown edging to the gardenia in his button-hole. Hot with a vengeance it had been! And taking a silk handkerchief from his cuff he passed it over his face before putting on his hat.

Down the broad red-carpeted steps where Chinese lanterns had burned out, he passed into the Inner Temple and the dawn. A faint air from the river freshened his face. Half-past three!

Perhaps he had never danced so often as that night—so often and so long. Six times with Irene! Six times with girls of whom he now remembered nothing. Had he danced well?—dancing with *her* he had been conscious only of her closeness and her scent; and, dancing with those others, only of her circling apart, out of his reach.

Only fourteen days and fourteen nights—until her closeness and her scent should be for ever his! She should be nearly home by now, with that stepmother of hers, in the hansom cab wherein he had placed them. How Irene detested that woman, and no wonder! For Soames knew well enough that to 'that woman's' wish to get her step-daughter married, so that she might marry again herself, he had owed his own chances these past eighteen months.

From the hall, bright with colour and dark gleaming wood, he moved slowly into half-lit stillness haunted by the drawl of a waltz fading as he went. And, inhaling long breaths of air grass-scented by the Temple Gardens,

Soames stripped off his gloves, thin, black-stitched, of lavender hue.

Irene loved dancing! It would not be good form to
dance with one's wife. Would that prevent him? No, by
Jove!

By a rambler rose-bush in a tub and a Chinese lantern
still alight—last splash of colour in the grey of dawn—he
turned, past one dim lamp at the corner of Middle Temple
Lane, down to the Embankment, and Cleopatra's Needle.
Cleopatra! A bad lot! If she'd been alive now, they'd
have cut her in Rotten Row, and run her in for suicide;
and there was her needle and herself a great figure of
romance—like those other bad lots, Helen of Troy, Semi-
ramis, Mary Queen of Scots—because—because she had
felt in her veins what he felt now! Grand passion, no
grander than his own! Well, they would never make *him*
a figure of romance! And Soames grinned.

He walked half-conscious, a sensation about his ribs, as
though his soul were bathing in a scent of sweet briar. All
was empty of sound—no footsteps, and no wheels—empty,
foliaged, broad, the grey river coming to colour as the sun
trembled to the horizon. All waiting for the one idea of
the whole world—heat. And Soames, with his one idea,
walked fast. Her window! Surely the light in that window would not yet be out! If, for a moment of fresh air,
she drew aside the blind, he might still see her, unseen himself, behind some lamp-post, in some doorway—see her as
he had never seen her yet, as soon he would see her every
night and every morning. And with that thought racing
through him he almost ran past each paling lamp, past Big
Ben and the Abbey, slowly creeping to colossal life from its
roof down, into Victoria Street, past his own rooms to the
corner of the street where she was staying. There he

stopped, his heart beating. He must take care! She mustn't
see him. She was strange, she was fitful—she mightn't like
it—she wouldn't like it. He edged along the far side of
the empty street. Dared he go further? Surely she could
not mind if he walked swiftly past. Fourth house now—
first window on the second floor? And by a lamp-post he
halted peering up. Open—yes—and the curtains half
drawn back to cool the room before she slept! Dared he?
Suppose she saw him stealing by, stealing on her when she
thought herself alone, unseen? Yet, if she saw him, would
it not prove to her once more how that she was his one
thought, one prize, and one desire? Could she mind that?
In truth—he did not know, and he stood there, waiting.
She must come to close the curtains against the brightening
daylight. If only she had for him the feeling he had for
her, then, indeed, she could not mind—she would be glad,
and their gaze would cling together across this empty London street, eerie in its silence with not a cat to mark the
meeting of their eyes. Blotted against the lamp-post he
stayed unmoving, aching for a sight of her. With his coat
he blotted the whiteness of his shirt-front, took off his hat
and crushed it to him. Now he was any stray early idler
with cheek against lamp-post and no face visible, any returning reveller. But his eye close to the lamp-post's iron
moved not from that blank oblong where the curtain stirred
feebly in the dawn breeze. And, then he trembled. A
white arm from the elbow up had slid into his view, and
on the hand of it he saw her face resting, looking straight
up over the roof opposite at the brightening sky. With a
sort of passion he screwed his eyes to slits that he might see
the expression on her face. But he could not—too far, far
as she always was, as she must not, should not always be.
Of what was she thinking? Of him? Of those little fleecy

clouds passing from the west? Of the cooling air? O
herself? Of what? Joined with the lamp-post he stood
still as the dead, for if she caught sight of its thickened base
she would vanish. Her neck, her hair looped back were
mixed into the folds of curtain—just the arm round and
white he saw, just the oval of her lifted face, so still that he
held his breath there, a hundred feet away. And then—the
sparrows cheeped, all the sky brightened. He saw her rise;
for a second saw her nightgowned figure, her hands reach
up, the long white arms, and the screening curtains close.
A sensation as of madness stirred in his limbs, he sprang
away, and, muffling his footsteps, fled back to Victoria
Street. There he turned not towards his rooms, but away
from them: Paradise deferred! He could not sleep. He
walked at a great rate. A policeman stared at him, an early
dust-cart passed, the thick horse clop-clopping out the only
sound in all the town. Soames turned up towards Hyde
Park. This early world of silent streets was to him un-
accustomed, as he himself, under this obsession, would be
to all who knew and saw him daily, self-contained, diligent,
a flat citizen. In Knightsbridge a belated hansom, with a
dim couple, fled jingling by, another and another. Soames
walked west to where the house, which he with her would
inhabit, stood bright with its fresh paint, and a board with a
builder's name. In the garnishing thereof he and she had
been more conjoined than ever yet, and he gazed at the little
house with gratitude, and a sort of awe. Twelve hours ago
he had paid the decorator's bill. And in that house he would
live with *her*—incredible! It looked like a dream in this
early light—that whole small long square of houses like a
dream of his future, her future, strange and unlived.

And superstitious dread came to the unsuperstitious
Soames; he turned his eyes away lest he should stare the little

house into real unreality. He walked, past the barracks to
the Park rails, still moving west, afraid of turning home-
wards till he was tired out. Past four o'clock, and still an
empty town, empty of all that made it a living hive, and yet
this very emptiness gave it intense meaning. He felt that
he would always remember a town so different from that
he saw every day; and himself he would remember—walking thus, unseen and solitary with his desire.

He went past Prince's Gate and turned. After all he had
his work—ten-thirty at the office! Road and Park and
houses stared at him now in the full light of earliest morning. He turned from them into the Park and crossed to
the Row side. Funny to see the Row with no horses tearing up and down, or trapesing past like cats on hot bricks,
no stream of carriages, no rows of sitting people, nothing
but trees and the tan track. The trees and grass, though no
dew had fallen, breathed on him; and he stretched himself
at full length along a bench, his hands behind his head, his
hat crushed on his chest, his eyes fixed on the leaves pat-
terned against the still brightening sky. The air stole faint
and fresh about his cheeks and lips, and the backs of his
hands. The first sunlight came stealing flat from trunk to
trunk, birds did not sing but talked, a wood pigeon back
among the trees was cooing. Soames closed his eyes, and
instantly imagination began to paint, for the eyes deep down
within him, pictures of her. Picture of her—standing passive in her frock flounced to the gleaming floor, while he
wrote his initials on her card. Picture of her adjusting
with long gloved fingers a camellia come loose in her cor-
sage; turning for him to put her cloak on—pictures, countless pictures, and ever strange, of her face sparkling for
moments, or brooding, or averse; of her cheek inclined for
his kiss, of her lips turned from his lips, of her eyes looking

at him with a question that seemed to have no answer; of her eyes, dark and soft over a grey cat purring in her arms; picture of her auburn hair flowing as he had not seen it yet. Ah! but soon—but soon! And as if answering the call of his imagination a cry—long, not shrill, not harsh exactly, but so poignant—jerked the blood to his heart. From back over there it came trailing, again and again, passionate— the lost soul's cry of peacock in early morning; and with it there uprose from the spaces of his inner being the vision that was for ever haunting there, of her with hair unbound, of her all white and lost, yielding to his arms. It seared him with delight, swooned in him, and was gone. He opened his eyes; an early water-cart was nearing down the Row. Soames rose and walking fast beneath the trees sought sanity.

FRANCIE'S FOURPENNY FOREIGNER
1888

FRANCIE'S FOURPENNY FOREIGNER

IN the latest 'eighties there was that still in the appearance of Francie Forsyte which made people refer to her on Forsyte 'Change as 'Keltic' looking. The expression had not long been discovered, and, though no one had any knowledge of what a Kelt looked like, it was felt to be good.

If she did not precisely suggest the Keltic twilight, she had dark hair and large grey eyes, composed music, wrote stories and poems, and played on the violin. For all these reasons she was allowed a certain license by the family, who did not take her too seriously, and the limit of the license granted is here recorded.

Thin, rather tall, intense and expressive, Francie had a certain charm, together with the power, engrained in a daughter of Roger, of marketing her wares, and at the age of thirty she had secured a measure of independence. She still slept at Prince's Gate, but had a studio in the purlieus of Chelsea. For the period she was advanced, even to the point of inviting to tea there her editors, fellow writers, musicians, and even those young men with whom she danced in Kensington, generically christened 'Francie's lovers' by her brother George.

At Timothy's in the Bayswater Road, they would say to her at times:

"Do you think it's quite nice, dear, to have young men to tea with you?"

And Francie would answer:

"Why not?" which always stopped further enquiry, for the aunts felt that it would be even less nice to put a finer

point on it, and, after all, dear Francie was musical.   It was
believed in the family, rather than known, that she was
always in love with someone, but that seemed natural in
one of her appearance, and was taken to be spiritual rather
than bodily. And this diagnosis was perfectly correct, such
was the essential shrewdness underlying the verbal niceties
on Forsyte 'Change.

It was shortly after she had at last succeeded in getting
her violin sonata—so much the most serious item of her
music—published, that she met the individual soon to be
known as "Francie's Fourpenny Foreigner."   The word
'Dago' not having then come to the surface, the anti-
pathetic contempt felt by Anglo-Saxons for everything
male, on two legs, deriving from below the latitude of
Geneva, had no verbal outlet.   From above the latitude of
Geneva a foreigner was, if not respected, at least human,
but a foreigner from below was undoubtedly 'fourpenny,'
if not less.

This young man, whose surname, Racazy, had a catch in
it which caught every Forsyte, but whose Christian name
was Guido, had come, if Francie was to be believed, from
a place called Ragusa to conquer London with his violin.
He had been introduced to her by the publisher who had
brought forth her sonata, as essentially the right interpreter
of that considerable production; partly, no doubt, because
at this stage of his career he would interpret anything for
nothing, and partly because Francie, free at the moment
from any spiritual entanglement, had noticed his hair, like
that of Rafael's best young men, and asked for the introduction.

Within a week he was playing the sonata in her studio
for the first and last time. The fact that he never even of-
fered to play it again ought to have warned Francie, but

with a strange mixture of loyalty to what she admired at the moment and a Forsytean perception that the more famous he became the more famous would she become, she installed him the 'lover' of the year, and proceeded to make his name. No one can deny that her psychology was at fault from the first; she gauged wrongly Guido, her family, and herself; but such misconceptions are slow to make themselves felt, and the license she enjoyed had invested Francie with a kind of bravura. She had the habit of her own way, and no tactical sense of the dividing line between major and minor operations. After trying him out at the Studio on an editor, two girl friends, and a 'lover' so out of date that he could be relied on, she began serious work by inviting the young man to dinner at Prince's Gate. He came in his hair, undressed, with a large bow tie 'flopping about on his chest,' as Eustace put it in his remonstrance after the event. It was a somewhat gruesome evening, complicated by the arrival of George, while the men were still at wine, to 'touch his father for a monkey.' His Ascot had been lamentable, and he sat, silently staring at the violinist as though he were the monkey.

Roger, in his capacity of host, alone attempted to put the young man at his ease.

"I hear you play the fiddle," he said. "Can you make your living at that?"

"But yes, I maka ver' good living."

"What do you call good?" said Roger, ever practical.

"I maka quite a 'undred pound a year."

"H'm!" said Roger: "Do you like the climate here?"

The young man shook his hair.

"No! Rain he rain; no sun to shina."

"Ha!" said Roger. "What's your own part of the world?"

"Ragusa."

"Eh! In the Balkans, um?"

"I am ze 'alf Italiano."

At this moment Eustace, obeying a wink from George's brooding eyes, rose, and said:

"Shall we go up and have some—er—music?"

Roger and George were left; nor was either of them seen again that evening.

In the drawing-room Mrs. Roger, placid by now to the point of torpor, had said to Francie:

"Of course, my dear, he is striking in a way, but he doesn't look very clean, does he?"

"That's only his skin, Mother."

"But how do you know, dear?"

"Oh! Well, he comes from Ragusa."

"I wonder," said Mrs. Roger, "if that is where 'ragouts' originally came from. I felt that he didn't care very much for the dinner to-night."

"He's all spirit," said Francie. "Everybody here thinks so much about food."

"Yes," sighed Mrs. Roger, "if it weren't for your father, I shouldn't think nearly as much about food as I have to. I sometimes wish I could go where sheep and oxen are unknown, and there are no seasons."

"Food is a terrible bore," said Francie.

Her mother looked at her intently.

"I'm sure you had nothing but a bun for lunch."

"A bath bun, dear."

"It's not enough, Francie."

"I never have more if I can help it."

"Your independence will ruin you one of these days. I'm certain your father won't like you seeing much of *that* young man."

"Father's hopeless," said Francie. "He ought to be stuffed."

A faint smile appeared on Mrs. Roger's face, as if she were thinking: 'Perhaps he is,' but she said:

"Don't be disrespectful, dear."

At this moment they came, Eustace exceptionally dandified as though to counterbalance his associate. Francie seated her 'foreigner' on the sofa, dark and sulky, and herself beside him. Eustace and his mother played piquet. The sound of George leaving (without his monkey) and soon thereafter of Roger going up to bed, brought a somewhat painful evening to its end.

In their bedroom, after holding forth on a son like George, Roger said abruptly:

"And as to Francie, what does she want to pick up with a fourpenny foreigner for! That girl will get herself into a mess."

Mrs. Roger having exhausted her powers of palliation over George, did not reply.

"A fiddler, too," added Roger.

"She can't help being musical, dear," said Mrs. Roger.

"No good ever came of music," said Roger. "Wake me if I snore; it gives me a sore throat . . ."

Undeterred by the wintry nature of that evening, Francie continued to promote the fortunes of her 'lover.' She even took him to Timothy's. It was at a period when the whole family was still slightly in mourning, over that "dreadful business of Soames, Irene and young Bosinney, my dear," which had so nearly got into the papers. Extraordinary sensitiveness prevailed, and anything manifestly un-Forsytean was scrutinised as with the eyes of parrots.

What Francie was doing with a young man whose hair stood out round him like a tea-tray, whose complexion was olive and whose eyes were almost black, was an insoluble problem which all did their utmost to solve, shaking the head and wagging the tongue. Aunt Juley alone ventured the opinion that he was romantic-looking, and was stigmatised by Swithin as a 'sentimental old fool.'

"The fellow ought to be jumping about on a barrel organ in a red cap," he added: "Romantic!"

It was, indeed, the damning of faint praise among a family who felt that romance was the last thing they wanted to hear of for a very long time to come. The visit to Aunts Hester and Juley, at which only Swithin and Euphemia were present, lasted but twenty minutes and was 'carried off' by Francie's bravura. She took her foreigner away in a bus and soothed him with broken Italian all the way home to her studio. Her protective feeling and something slightly rapturous had been roused in her by the sight of Swithin, block-like and portentous above his waistcoats, in a light blue chair. Guido was so delightfully unlike that! Her main energies were now concentrated on securing a concert for him. There was little she did not dare to this end. It took place just as the season closed in a small hall newly opened by a firm of piano-makers.

Among many others, the whole Forsyte family were sent cards of invitation written by Francie. Even Swithin received one at his Club. This was probably the first time he had ever been invited to a concert and he announced his intention of going and seeing what it was all about. In his opinion the girl was spending a pretty penny on this fourpenny foreigner (Roger's phrase having become current). From uneasy curiosity, in fact, rather than from love of music, a considerable number of the clan attended. Swithin found himself situated between his niece Winifred Dartie, whom he always found personable, and his niece

Euphemia, who was too thin and squeaked. He slept heavily during the second number and woke just in time, with a snore so loud that it elicited from Euphemia one of the most outstanding squeaks that even she had ever let escape. During the applause which followed, he turned to her, so far, indeed, as he was able, and enquired: 'What on earth she had made that noise for?' To which Euphemia replied:

"Oh! Uncle Swithin, you'll kill me!" She had a great, if inconvenient, sense of humour.

During the third number Swithin remained awake, staring, pop-eyed, at the young man's agility and wishing he had remembered to put cotton-wool in his ears. In the interval which followed he manœuvred himself out of his seat, and not waiting for his carriage, took a four-wheeled cab to his Club, where he lit a cigar and instantly fell asleep. It was his opinion, afterwards recorded, that the fellow had made a lot of noise—a capering chap!

The concert, which produced the sum of thirteen pounds, three shillings and sixpence, cost Francie practically all her savings. Far more serious, however, was its spiritual effect. The notices were bad. Francie was furious. Guido, who had borne one bad notice beautifully with a curl of his lip, broke into imprecations at the second, tore at his hair after the third, and dissolved into tears with the fourth. Greatly moved, Francie took his head between her hands and kissed him above the tears. And with that kiss was born in her a serious feeling, not exactly bodily, but as if he belonged to her, and must be sustained through thick and thin. A fortnight later—a fortnight spent in storm and shine, during which she gave him a pair of silver-backed brushes, some special hair shampoo, some new ties, and an umbrella—she announced to her mother by note that she and Guido were engaged. She added that she was going to sleep at the Studio till father had got over the fit he would certainly have.

There again she went wrong in her psychology, incapable, like all the young Forsytes, of appreciating exactly the quality which had made the fortunes of all the old Forsytes. In a word, they had fits over small matters, but never over large. When stark reality stared them in the face they met it with the stare of a still starker reality.

Beyond the words: "The girl's mad," Roger, to the infinite relief of Mrs. Roger, said absolutely nothing. His face acquired a sudden dusky-red rigidity, and he left the dining-room. He went into his sanctum—the room where he had thought out the future of countless pieces of house property—took up a paper-knife and sat down in an arm-chair. He sat there for fully half an hour without a sound except the dull click of the paper-knife against his lower teeth still firm as rocks. Francie was his only daughter, and in his peculiar way (not for nothing was Roger considered eccentric in the family) he was fond of her; fonder than of his mere sons Roger, George, Eustace, and Thomas; and he sat, not fuming—the matter was too serious. Presently he arose and returned to the dining-room where Mrs. Roger was in distraction over the composition of a letter to her daughter.

"Do you know where that young fellow lives?" he said.

"Yes, Roger, at 5, Glendower Mews, Kensington."

"Write a note asking him to lunch here with Francie to-day week. Do the same to Francie. Where's *The Times?*"

Mrs. Roger produced *The Times*, and faltered out:

"What are you going to do, Roger?"

"Ask no questions and you'll be told no lies; don't get into a fantod, leave it to me!"

He took *The Times* to his sanctum, scanned a page carefully, looked at his calendar, and wrote a note. Then he got up and stood with his square back to the fireplace and his head bent forward. His full, rather bumpy forehead was flushed. He alone of the old Forsytes had become entirely clean-shaven—another sign of eccentricity at that period—and his rather full lips were compressed into a straight line. The die he was going to cast was momentous even for one who had been bidding at auctions all his life. Ten minutes to ten! Taking up his cheque book, he signed a cheque form, tore it out, put his cheque book into his pocket and rang the bell.

The broad and cheerful butler stood within the doorway.

"Yes, Sir?"

"Come in, Smith, and shut the door. I want you to do a job for me. Take this note down in a cab at once, get what I've asked for, pay for it with this cheque—you can fill in the right amount; then bring it straight to me at 5, Glendower Mews. I'll expect you soon after eleven. Look sharp, and take your toothbrush; you may be away for the night."

"Yes, Sir."

When the butler had removed his smile Roger stood at the window looking at the day. It was fine.

"I'll take no chances," he said, and went out into the hall. There he took down a grey top hat—the only one then in the family, extracted his umbrella from the stand, and went out. It was the Friday before August Bank Holiday, and he was only in town because a house that he intended to buy was coming up to auction on the Tuesday.

He walked slowly, taking care not to get hot. The young fellow—a fiddler and a foreigner—would not be up before eleven, but he had no intention of missing him, and he arrived at Glendower Place about half-past ten. He knew it well enough, for he owned a house there. The Mews was round the corner. Noting that it had but one entrance, he went on patrol. Beyond cats and caretakers no one took any interest in him, and he spent thus a good half-hour. As a neighbouring clock struck eleven a hansom cab drew up and Smith alighted. He handed Roger a large envelope. Having perused its contents, Roger nodded. "Wait here," he said to the cabman. "Now, Smith, follow me." At Number 5 he raised his umbrella and knocked. The door was opened by the very pattern of a coachman's wife.

"I want to see the young foreign gentleman who lodges here—Mr. Guido Ratcatski." The strains of a bow being scraped up and down a violin were audible. "Up these stairs, I suppose?"

The coachman's wife, with her eyes on Roger's hat, replied:

"Yes, Sir, and mind the little step at the top."

Roger ascended, followed by the smiling Smith.

"Stay here," said Roger, at the little step; and, raising his umbrella, tapped. The door was opened.

"Good morning," said Roger, removing his hat and walking in. "Good place for practising you have here. Sit down, I want to talk to you."

The young man, who was in his hair and shirt-sleeves, put down his violin, and, frowning darkly, leaned against the window-sill, crossing his arms.

Roger surveyed the room. It was, in his view, exceptionally sordid, containing a yellow chest of drawers, an iron bedstead, a round washstand, some clothes littered about, and little else. It was hot, too, had a sloping roof, and smelled of stables. "Phew!" he said.

Behind the young foreigner's glowering gaze, his shrewd grey eyes had not failed to remark a certain panic.

"Well, young man, I take it you're ambitious."

"Ambeetious? Vot is dat?"

"Want to get on in your profession."

"Yees."

"That's right—quite right, and so you will! Now, about this affair with my daughter?"

"Vell!"

Roger looked straight into his eyes.

"It won't do, you know. You can't afford to marry a girl who'll have nothing. I won't beat about the bush. She's got no money of her own, and if she marries you, she won't get a penny from me."

"Money!" said the young man, violently: "Money! It ees all money!"

"Yes," said Roger, "all money. And I repeat, she won't get a penny from me. How old are you?"

"Tventee-fife."

"She was bottled in fifty-eight. She's thirty if a day. You told me you made a hundred a year. With her stories she makes fifty if she's lucky. A hundred and fifty a year between you? Are you going to support babies on that, at the beginning of your career?"

"Ve lof each oder," said the young man, sullenly.

Roger shook his head.

"No such thing as love on a hundred and fifty a year. Now listen to me."

"I vill not listen—I vill not listen."

Roger slowly raised his umbrella, as if taking a lunar of the young man's capacity.

"This is a passing fancy of my daughter's," he said; "she has one every year—you're the last. Now you're not getting on in London, your concert was a failure, the climate doesn't suit you. I make you an offer." He drew the envelope and his cheque book from his breast pocket. "Here's a first-class passage to New York by the boat to-morrow morning from Liverpool." He tapped his cheque book: "And three hundred pounds if you'll go straight off now, without saying good-bye to her."

He paused, steadily regarding the unfortunate young man, who broke into a violent perspiration, writhed on the window-sill, thrust his hands into his hair, and uttered a curious hissing. Roger made out the words:

"It ees dishonourable. She lof' me."

"Nonsense!" he said. "However, I'll make it four hundred, and you can cash it on the way to the station. Now be sensible. My butler's outside. He'll see you comfortably off at Liverpool. With four hundred pounds you can make your name. With a wife and babies you'll starve in a kennel. Give me a pen and ink."

The young man's face was 'a study,' his hair stood up, he stammered incomprehensible words, while his eyes made desperate efforts to avoid the cheque book. Roger waited, holding it open. It was like bidding at an auction.

"I'll throw you in another fifty to start you fair. Don't be a fool and condemn my daughter and yourself to wretchedness. I mean what I said—not one penny will she have from me. Now be a man and save her."

The young man clapped his hand to the breast of his pink striped shirt.

"I feel it 'ere," he said. "I cannot go like that."

"Save her!" repeated Roger. "Come! Where's the ink?"

The young man pointed. Roger saw on the mantelpiece

a penny bottle of ink, and suddenly his nerves twittered. It was as if he had seen the brink on which his daughter was standing.

"Five hundred!" he said, sharply.

The young man threw up his hands. "I save her!" he cried.

Roger wrote the cheque.

"Smith! Take Mr. Ratcatski to Euston and catch the next train to Liverpool. Go to a good hotel, see he has everything he wants, and put him on board the boat for New York in the morning. He is called there on important business. On the way to the station go to my bank and get this cheque cashed, and give him the notes and his ticket, when he's on board and *not before*. He's a foreigner, and might get imposed on." Then, turning to the young man, who was staring dreadfully, he added: "There's a cab waiting. Smith will put your things together."

Francie's foreigner remained rooted to the window-sill, his hands embedded in his hair. Suddenly he came to life, and, seizing his violin, clasped it to his pink striped chest.

"Dees is my vife," he said.

A feeling that the young man was at the moment perfectly sincere quarrelled violently in Roger with the desire to kick him.

"That's right!" he said.

In the doorway he heard Smith murmur: "He'll not get away from me, Sir, if I 'ave to 'old 'im by the slack of his breeches. I'll get 'im off all right."

Roger nodded. "Mum's the word! And if he writes any letters, collar them."

Out in the Mews, he wiped his forehead. Hot work! Passing the cab, he stopped at the corner to watch. He didn't trust that young beggar a yard. In a few minutes, however, he saw him coming hugging his violin and followed by Smith carrying a large bag. They got into the cab and drove off. Roger uttered a sigh of such relief that a passer stopped to look at him; his knees had suddenly given way, and but for the man's arm he would have fallen.

" 'Allo, Sir!" said the man. "Took ill?"

Roger shook off his arm.

"No," he said, testily.

He moved away a few steps to assert his independence, but was obliged to stand still again. After all, he was seventy-five, the day was hot, and he had been bidding for the life of his only daughter. To think that a four-penny foreigner had cost him five hundred odd pounds! Yes, and he'd only got him by pure bluff. *He* knew—if that young beggar didn't—that no Forsyte would be capable of watching his own daughter in actual want. If the fellow had held out and refused to budge, the fat would have been in the fire. Sooner or later he would have had to make them an allowance to keep the wolf from the door. A narrow shave! A regular squeak! And seeing a hansom in the distance, he hailed it.

At home, under the strict seal of secrecy, he retailed the matter to Mrs. Roger. She listened in a turmoil of admiration and dismay. "Poor Francie!" she said, tremulously.

"Poor fiddlesticks! A fourpenny foreign adventurer! she ought to thank me on her knees. But there it is, I never get thanked for anything."

"Oh! Roger, I'm sure we're all very grateful; but—er —poor dear Francie!"

"If you ever tell her," said Roger, "I'll cut you off with a shilling."

"Of course I shan't tell her, Roger. But why did you make me ask them to lunch next week?"

"To put her off the scent, of course! What did you think? But women never think. Here! Give me one of those powders. I've got a headache."

Smith returned the following afternoon. He had seen 'Mr. Ragcatchy' off. The young man had seemed low-spirited but had counted the notes twice. So far as he—Smith—knew, he had written no letter. As the ship moved out, Smith from the dock below had noticed that he was like a bear on hot bricks, and had caught hold of his hair.

"Hope he pulled some out," said Roger. "I shall raise your wages for this."

"Thank you, Sir," said Smith, "but it was a reel pleasure to me, I do assure you. 'E wouldn' never 'ave done for Miss Francie, if I may say so, Sir."

And Francie! What she suffered, what she suspected, what she knew, no one ever heard. She wrote to her mother after four days saying that there had been a mistake and Guido had gone away. A week later she returned to Prince's Gate, paler, thinner, more Keltic-looking than ever. She left town for Ilfracombe on the following day. In the autumn she took another 'lover.' No one ever heard her allude again to her "fourpenny foreigner." In Roger's mind alone did he remain enshrined as the most expensive fourpennyworth ever known.

FOUR-IN-HAND FORSYTE

1890

FOUR-IN-HAND FORSYTE

SUCH historians as record the tides of social manners and morals, have neglected the bicycle. Yet would it be difficult to deny that this 'invention of the devil,' as Swithin Forsyte always called it because 'a penny-farthing' had startled his greys at Brighton in 1874—has been responsible for more movement in manners and morals than anything since Charles the Second. At its bone-shaking inception innocent, because of its extraordinary discomfort, in its 'penny-farthing' stage harmless, because only dangerous to the lives and limbs of the male sex, it began to be a dissolvent of the most powerful type when accessible to the fair in its present form. Under its influence, wholly or in part, have wilted chaperons, long and narrow skirts, tight corsets, hair that would come down, black stockings, thick ankles, large hats, prudery and fear of the dark; under its influence, wholly or in part, have bloomed weekends, strong nerves, strong legs, strong language, knickers, knowledge of make and shape, knowledge of woods and pastures, equality of sex, good digestion and professional occupation—in four words, the emancipation of woman. But to Swithin, and possibly for that reason, it remained what it had been in the beginning, an invention of the devil. For, apart from that upset to his greys, having lived his first sixteen years with 'Prinny' in the offing, and formed himself under Lord Melbourne, the Cider Cellars and the Pavilion at Brighton, he remained to the end in taste and deportment a Buck of the Regency, unable to divest himself of a love for waistcoats and jewellery, or the conviction that women were perquisites to whom elegance and—ah—charm were of the first necessity.

These are the considerations which must be borne in mind when we come to the recital of an episode current on Forsyte 'Change in the year 1890.

Swithin had spent the early months at Brighton and was undoubtedly feeling his liver by April. The last three years had tried him severely and for some time past he had parted with his phaeton, confining his carriage exercise to a double brougham, in which, drawn by his greys, he passed every afternoon up and down the front from the end of Hove to the beginning of Kemptown. What he thought of during these excursions has never been disclosed. Possibly of nothing. And why not? For so entirely lonely an old man, provocation towards thought was conspicuous by its absence; and though there was always himself to think about, a man cannot for ever be bothered by that. The return to his hotel would be achieved by four o'clock. He would be assisted to alight by his valet, and would walk into the hotel unaided, Alphonse following with the specially strong air-cushion on which he always sat, and his knee rug of a Highland plaid. In the hall Swithin would stand for perhaps a minute, settling his chin more firmly, rounding his heavy eyelids more carefully over his gouty eyes. He would then hold out his gold-headed malacca cane to be taken from him, and slightly spread his hands, gloved in bright wash-leather, to indicate that his coat, blue, lined with squirrel and collared with astrakhan, should be removed. This having been done and his gloves and black felt hat with somewhat square top taken off, he would touch the tuft on his lower lip, as if to assure himself that its distinction was still with him.

At this hour he was used to take a certain seat in a certain draughtless corner and smoke half a cigar before ascending in the lift to the sitting-room of his suite. He sat there so motionless and was known to be so deaf, that no one spoke to him; but it seemed to him that in this way he saw more life and maintained the out-lived reputation of 'Four-in-Hand' Forsyte. Wedged forward by cushions, as though still in his brougham, with his thick legs slightly apart, he would apply the cigar to his ear; having heard it carefully in its defence, he would hold it a minute between puffy thumb and puffier forefinger of that yellowish-white which betokens the gouty subject, then place it in his mouth and wait for it to be lighted. With chest pouted, under a black satin stock and diamond pin, so that he appeared to be of one thickness from neck down, he would sit, contemplating that which was not yet called the Lounge from under drooped puffy lids, as might some Buddah from the corner of a temple. His square old face, perfectly pale, of one long withdrawn from privilege of open air, would be held so still that people would glance at it as they might have at a clock. The little white moustaches and tuft on the lower lip, the tufts above the eyes, and hair still stylish on the forehead, accentuated perhaps its resemblance to a dial. Once in a way someone whose father or uncle had known him in old days, would halt in passing, as though about to set his watch by him and say: "How d'you do, Mr. Forsyte?" Then would an expression as of a cat purring spread on Swithin's face, and he would murmur in a voice fat and distinguished: "Ah! How de do? Haven't seen your father lately." And as the father was almost always dead, this would end the conversation. But Swithin would sit the squarer because he had been spoken to.

When his cigar was about half smoked a change would

come. The hand holding it would loll over the arm of the chair, trembling a little. The chin would slip slowly down between the wide apart point of the stiff white collar; the puffy rounding of the eyelids would become complete; a slight twitching would possess the lips, a faint steady puffing take its place—Swithin would be asleep. And those who passed would look at him with cold amusement, a kind of impatience, possibly a touch of compassion, for, on these occasions, as if mindful of past glories, Swithin did not snore. And then, of course, would come the moment of awakening. The chin would jerk up, the lips part, all breath would seem to be expelled from him in a long sigh; the eyes coming ungummed would emit a glassy stare; the tongue would move over the roof of the mouth and the lips; and an expression as of a cross baby would appear on the old face. Pettishly he would raise the half-smoked cigar, look at it as if it owed him something which it was not going to pay, and let it slip between finger and thumb into a spittoon. Then he would sit the same, yet not the same, waiting for some servant to come near enough for him to say: "Hi! Tell my valet to come, will you?" and when Alphonse appeared: "Oh! There you are! I nodded off. I'll go up now."

Assisted from the chair, he would stand fully a minute feeling giddy, then square but bearing heavily on the cane and one leg, would move towards the lift, followed by Alphonse and the special cushions. And someone perhaps would mutter as he passed: "There goes old Forsyte. Funny old boy, isn't he?"

But such was not the order of events on that particular April afternoon reported on Forsyte 'Change. For when, divested of hat and overcoat, he was about to walk to his accustomed corner, he was observed to raise his cane with the words: "Here! There's a lady sitting in my chair!"

A figure, indeed, in rather a short skirt, occupied that sacred spot.

"I'll go up!" said Swithin, pettishly. But as he moved, she rose and came towards him.

"God bless me!" said Swithin, for he had recognised his niece Euphemia.

Now the youngest child of his bother Nicholas was in some respects Swithin's pet aversion. She was, in his view, too thin, and always saying the wrong thing; besides, she squeaked. He had not seen her since, to his discomfort, he had sat next her at the concert of Francie's fourpenny foreigner.

"How are you, Uncle? I thought I *must* look you up, while I was down."

"I've got gout," said Swithin. "How's your father?"

"Oh! just as usual. He says he's bad, but he isn't." And she squeaked slightly.

Swithin fixed her with his stare. Upset already by her occupation of his chair, he was on the point of saying: 'Your father's worth twenty of you,' but, remembering in time the exigencies of deportment, he murmured more gallantly: "Where have you sprung from?"

"My bicycle."

"What!" said Swithin. "You ride one of those things!"

Again Euphemia squeaked.

"Oh! Uncle! One of those things!"

"Well," said Swithin, "what else are they—invention of the devil. Have some tea?"

"Thank you, Uncle, but you must be tired after your drive."

"Tired! Why should I be tired? Waiter! Bring some tea over there—to my chair."

Having thus conveyed to her the *faux pas* she had committed by sitting in his chair, he motioned her towards it and followed.

On reaching the chair there was an ominous moment.

"Sit down," said Swithin.

For a moment Euphemia hovered on its edge, then with a slight squeak said: "But it's your chair, Uncle."

"Alphonse," said Swithin, "bring another."

When the other chair had been brought, the cushions placed for Swithin in his own, and they were seated, Euphemia said:

"Didn't you know that women were beginning to ride bicycles, Uncle?"

The hairs on Swithin's underlip stood out.

"Women," he said. "You may well say women. Fancy a lady riding a thing like that!"

Euphemia squeaked more notably.

"But, Uncle, why *like that?*"

"With a leg on each side, disturbing the traffic," and glancing at Euphemia's skirt, he added: "Showing their legs."

Euphemia gave way to silent laughter.

"Oh! Uncle," she said, at last, in a strangled voice, "you'll kill me!"

But at this moment came tea.

"Help yourself," said Swithin, shortly; "I don't drink it." And, taking from the waiter a light for his cigar, he sat staring with pale eyes at his niece. Not till after her second cup did she break that silence.

"Uncle Swithin, do tell me why they called you 'Four-in-Hand Forsyte,' I've always wanted to know."

Swithin's stare grew rounder.

"Why shouldn't they?"

" 'Four-in-hand'; but you never drove more than a pair, did you?"

Swithin preened his neck. "Certainly not! It was just a compliment to my—er—style."

"Style!" repeated Euphemia. "Oh, Uncle!" and she grew so crimson that he thought she had swallowed a crumb.

Then slowly but surely it dawned on him that he was the cause of her emotion. Into his cheeks a faint pink crept; something moved in his throat, something that might choke him if he were not careful. He did not stir.

Euphemia rose.

"I *must* be going, Uncle. I *have* enjoyed seeing you, you're looking so well. Don't get up, please, and thank you ever so for the tea." She bent above him, pecked at his forehead, and showing her legs, walked towards the door. Her face was still very red and as she went, Swithin seemed to hear her squeak.

He stayed unmoving for a second, then struggled to get up. He had no stick to help him, no time to give to the process, and he struggled. He got on his feet, stood a moment to recover, and then, without his cane, walked, he knew not how, to the window of the hall that looked out on to the parade. There she was—that niece of his, that squeaker, mounting her bicycle, moving it, mounting it, riding it away. Into the traffic she went, pedalling, showing her ankles; not an ounce of grace, of elegance, of anything! There she went! And Swithin stood, drumming a puffy forefinger against the pane, as if denouncing what he saw. Style! Style! She—she had been laughing at him. Not a doubt of it! If he *had* only driven a pair, it had been the finest in the kingdom! He stood with that distressing pink still staining the pallor of his cheeks—ruffled to the bottom of his soul. Was he conscious of the full sting in his niece's laughter? Conscious of how the soubriquet 'Four-in-hand Forsyte' epitomised the feeling Society had ever held of him; the feeling that with his craving for distinction he had puffed himself out into the double of what he really was? Was he conscious of that grievous sneer? Only, perhaps, sub-conscious, but it was enough; a crabbed wrath possessed him to the soles of the patent leather boots still worn, in public, on his painful feet.

So she rode one of 'those things,' and laughed at him, did she? He would show her. He left the window and went to the writing table. And there, his eyes round and yellow, his hand trembling, he took paper and began to write. In a shaky travesty of what had once been almost copperplate, he traced these lines:

"This is a codicil to the last Will of me Swithin Forsyte. To mark my disapproval of the manners and habits of my niece Euphemia, the daughter of my brother Nicholas Forsyte and Elizabeth his wife, I hereby revoke the bequest of the share of my property left to her in my said Will. I leave her nothing whatever."

He paused and read it through. That would teach her! Faithful to the ladies, the half of his property he had left to his three sisters in equal shares; the other half to his eight nieces in equal shares. Well, there would only be seven now! And he sounded the bell.

"Boy, fetch my valet and tell the hall porter to come here."

When they arrived he was adding the words: "Signed in the presence of——"

"Here!" he said. "This is a codicil to my Will. I want you to witness it. Write your names and occupations here."

When they had done so, and he had blotted the whole, he addressed an envelope, wrote:

"DEAR JAMES,

"This is a codicil. Put it with my Will, and let me know you've had it. "Your affectionate brother,

"SWITHIN FORSYTE."

and sealed the envelope with the 'pheasant proper' obtained from the College of Arms in 1850 at some expense.

"Take that," he said to Alphonse, "and post it. Here, help me back to my chair."

When he was settled in again, and Alphonse had gone, his eyes moved restlessly.

Style! His old cronies—all gone! No one came in here now who had known him in the palmy days of style! Days when there was elegance. Bicycles, forsooth! Well, that young lady had had an expensive ride, an expensive laugh. Cost her a matter of six or seven thousand pounds. They laughed best who laughed last! And with the feeling that he had struck a blow for elegance, for manners, for—for style, Swithin regained his pallor, his eyes grew less yellow, his eyelids rounder over them, and the expression in those eyes became almost wistful. This damned East wind—if he didn't take care he'd have no appetite for dinner.

Four-in-hand Forsyte! Why not—why not? He could have driven four-in-hand if he'd liked, any day. Four-in-ha——! His chin dropped slightly. Four-in——! His eyes closed; his lips puffed; he slept, his hand still resting on his cane.

Into the hall strolled two young men on a week-end from town. Hatted, high-collared, with their canes swinging, they passed not far from Swithin's chair.

"Look at that old buck," said one in a low voice. And they halted, staring at him sideways.

"Hallo! It's old Uncle Swithin, Giles."

"By George! So it is. I say, Jesse, look at his rings, and his pin, and the shine on his hair and his boots. Fancy the old josser keeping it up like that!"

"By jove! Hope *I'll* never be old. Come on Giles!"

"Stout old boy!"

And 'the Dromios,' as they were called, swung on, their lean hungry faces bravely held above their collars.

But the old pale lips of Swithin, between the little white moustaches and the little white tuft, puffed and filled, puffed and filled. He had not heard.

THE SORROWS OF TWEETYMAN

1895

THE SORROWS OF TWEETYMAN

WHEN Marian, daughter of Nicholas Forsyte, married Edward Tweetyman in 1882, Nicholas was heard to say: "That chap'll never make money, she'd better have married his brother." The remark, repeated on Forsyte 'Change, invited the family's dispassionate consideration of two individuals as far apart in character and appearance as is permitted by the laws of consanguinity and partnership. The two Tweetymans were engineers by profession, and regrettably, it was felt, pump manufacturers in practice, having their business premises in King William Street. Albert, the elder, was square and stocky in build, red and fleshy in face, with an early smile, and Georgian eyes that reminded one of a bull concerned with Europa. He it was who took the orders, directed the operations, and made the money. Edward, the younger, was a little taller and a great deal thinner, with a refined white face and hollowed temple bones; his weak hair waved faintly on his white forehead, his weak and fair moustache drooped like twin wisps of hay above a selfless smile, and his pale blue eyes looked wistfully forth with the saintlike fervour of an inventor. He invented the pumps, or at least understood how they worked, had a passion for truth, and lived as it were at the bottom of the wells for which they were both designed. Incidentally he received what his brother didn't. It was not much. But being of a loyal and unassuming nature he was not conscious of the discrepancy. Albert had the force of one born to rake in, Edward the charm of one born to give out. The family soon perceived how just had been the remark of Nicholas. But it is not improbable that in this conclusion Marian had been before them. She had, for a daughter of Nicholas, a somewhat sweetened disposition, redeemed by a distinctly having tendency; a good-looking, well-built young woman with an instinctive knowledge of how to dress any shop window. In marrying Edward Tweetyman she had perhaps overlooked the fact that before you can dress a shop window there must be one to dress. The fellow had none. His frontage, as it were, was of stained glass, and she could set nothing in it. With the real shrewdness which she inherited from her father, she had accepted the fact before her honeymoon was over, and had decided to exhibit him unvarnished and ungarnished for what he was worth. This was extraordinarily little in a monetary sense—say four hundred a year and possibilities. She herself had the three hundred and fifty which Nicholas, with a perfect equity, gave to all his children when he threw them out of the nest in Ladbroke Grove. But even in the 'eighties, seven hundred and fifty a year was not the income of a Forsyte with a collecting propensity and fashionable proclivities, so that it was not surprising that Marian banked on the 'possibilities.' Difficult indeed to live with Edward Tweetyman without noticing how illumined by ideas he was: as from one of those wells to which he was always fitting his pumps, they bubbled from him by day and even by night. But with her more practical nature Marian soon grasped the fact that Edward's mind never pursued those ideas to the pitch of profit; his mind stopped at the discovery—the invented machine; what would come of it he left to "my brother." So left, they were not possibilities; Albert, in the words of the prophet, or rather of her cousin George Forsyte, would always 'nobble the lot.' It was not long before she was saying on Forsyte 'Change that Edward was 'a genius and a saint'; which in the terms of family common-sense equalled 'unpractical and rarefied in his conjugal attentions.' And every sympathy was felt with Marian's obvious intention to fill the silk purse she had acquired. It was thought, however, that she might have trouble, bounded on the West by Nicholas, and on the East by Edward's brother. She herself recognised these limitations, for her first attempt was to break towards the South and ally her Tweetyman with one Charles Podmore of North Street, Westminster. He it was who, not long before, had eaten the cherries of Rachel and Cicely, on the Lake of Lucerne, to show them that maggots were harmless when taken in any quantity, and had been a friend of the family ever since. Meeting him at a dance given by her Aunt, Mrs. Roger Forsyte, at Prince's Gate, Marian soon discovered in him a fanatical devotee of ice cream. He had, in advance of science, expressed the opinion that there was nothing more nourishing and wholesome, a very daring view at a period when what gave sensual pleasure was still almost universally regarded as harmful. "Everybody," he said, "ought to eat it; it only wants a really good machine." She had introduced him and his idea to Edward in a corridor, certain that something would come of it. The acquaintanceship ripened at Hurlingham on tickets furnished by Podmore, a man of independent means, who desired them to see him shooting pigeons; for this was in the full blush of that desirable practice, when a robuster community still connected the expression pigeon-shooting with the expression sport. The afternoon, however, furnished Marian with a fresh instance of her Edward's impracticability and plunged her into a certain gloom. For as Podmore was about to destroy his seventh pigeon running, Tweetyman, who had hitherto been occupied by an idea for helping the seat of his chair to turn itself up on a spring, said loudly: "Look out, bird!" and Podmore missed. Marian took him away almost immediately. "How on earth, Edward," she said, in the hansom cab, "you expect ever to get on if you are so absentminded, I can't think." Edward smiled, and looking forth with his pale fervour, said: "Pigeon's wings are hinged like this," moving a bluish white forefinger in front of Marian's eyes. "Quite!" she answered drily—perhaps the first use of this expression—"but are you going to do anything about that ice cream machine? Charles Podmore is set on it, and he has lots of money." He had pressed her hand. "The Romans," he said, "knew how to make ice cream better than we do"; and then began nodding his head, from which she understood that an idea had come to him. She had lived on hopefully and abstained from bothering him with questions, for she had a horror of fussing, till one day, going almost mechanically through his pockets, she came on a beautiful little drawing of an ice cream machine in a catalogue connected with the pumps of A. & E. Tweetyman, and realised that it had been finished and had passed into the keeping of his brother. She was really angry. The incident raised so acutely the whole question of his brother in relation to his possibilities. Something must be done! And she did it! She invited his brother to dinner, and on the principle of Greek cut Armenian, exerted all her wiles to get her father to meet him. It was seldom indeed that Nicholas would budge from his fireside, his papers, and his evening journal, except for those public functions at which he invariably made the best speech of the evening. But, though he had no declared preferences among his children, Marian was secretly his favourite; and he came. The evening was one long battle for the soul, or rather the possibilities, of

Tweetyman, and he remained completely unconscious of the fact. The whole difficulty with the man, indeed, arose from the impossibility of making him realise his own sorrows. Here he was, with his real gifts, wholly at the beck and call of that despoiler his brother, and incapable of resenting it. Here, if the battle went against his brother, he would be—as Marian realised before the night was out—wholly at the beck and call of Nicholas's Companies, and incapable of profiting by it. For a side of her father's character which she had never yet realised, was revealed to Marian that evening: If he secured and employed Edward, it would be as a servant to his Companies and not as a son-in-law—no nepotism for *him!* In other words Edward the inventor would jump out of one sorrow into another just as deep, and do it without a sigh. Marian had seldom been more disillusioned. The net result of the affair was that Nicholas left the house with an added respect for Albert, and less respect for Edward. When Marian got her husband to bed, she did not blow out the candle, but lay on his side and looked at him. He was lying on his back, with his temple bones extremely hollowed, and a slight smile under the wisps of his moustache. Something Nicholas had said in connection with the watering of engines on his railway had started his inventivity, and he was already halfway towards an improvement. In that dim light he looked almost too saint-like, above his flannel nightgown. Marian was moved; there was charm in the man in spite of the sorrows of which he was so unconscious, and after all she had married him for love. A long time she looked at him with a faint greed in her eyes, and a faint flush on her cheeks.

"Edward," she said at last, "you seem very far away. After all, I *am* your wife."

The lever which at the moment was engaging his attention, dropped.

"Certainly, my dear!" he said, and turned towards her.

She took full advantage of the movement. After all, he had other possibilities, and the evening need not be entirely wasted.

The result, Patricia, was in 1895 already twelve years old, and to her father one of his best inventions. The years had contracted his girth and increased that of his brother, now an Alderman. The aspirations of Marian had remained unfulfilled. True, Nicholas now allowed his children £500 a year apiece, and Edward was drawing £700 a year from his brother, but what was this to a comely and fashionable young matron? The sorrows of her Tweety-man seemed to her more, and to him, if anything, less noticeable than ever. For he was engaged on what he regarded as, so far, his prime invention, a species of pump for the evacuation of goods from Cross Channel and other steamers. He was almost blue-white now and perfectly happy. His cheeks were even more hollow than his temple bones, and Marian had almost despaired of his possibilities. So much so, that her old feeling against his brother had changed to a sort of regard for his possessive genius. That she had remained entirely faithful to her man of sorrows says much for his charm, and the sterling qualities of a Forsyte.

The year of 1895 will long be remembered for its weather. After opening with a frost of some two months' duration, it broke into a passion of warmth and life which lingered on into the late autumn. A bone-shaking automobile rattled people around at the South Kensington Exhibition, bicycles were all the rage, the river Thames was covered with punts; young matrons went astray. That Marian felt the temper of the year cannot be denied, but to say that she had anything but the most domestic intentions in what has now to be related, would not be true. As Edward approached the finish of his momentous invention, she approached her Waterloo. It was surely now or never, if his possibilities were ever to be capitalised, and his sorrows abated! And she conceived a plan which for daring and realism was indeed worthy of a daughter of Nicholas. To snatch her Edward out of the jaws of sorrow she proceeded to lay deliberate siege to Albert. Though an Alderman, he was still a bachelor, a man of full habit and much red blood, in every respect the reverse of her poor Edward. She besieged him with little dinners, after which she would place him with his cigar in a very easy chair; and send Edward up to his invention. Sitting well within Albert's view in an evening dress admirably cut to display her charms, she would soothe and incite him with conversation bordering on sex: the scandal of the year (that year fortunately very considerable), the latest dancer, this novel, that play. From this it was easy to pass to the playing of piquet, a game during which the knees of opponents can with a little care be made to touch. Nor was it many days before she perceived with a well-simulated surprise that the virile Albert was smouldering. Her duty was then plain. She threw with circumspection just enough cold water on him; performed just sufficiently the function of the wet blanket; watched him fume and then begin to go out; and lit him again with her eyes and knees. After many evenings of this careful preparation she felt that to whatever lead she gave, he would respond adequately; and her only fear was that he would respond before she gave it. This, though it might not be altogether unpleasant, would defeat the truly domestic object she had in view, namely, that Edward should discover her in his arms. She wished to synchronise this discovery by Edward so far as possible with the actual completion of his invention. For she reasoned thus: Unless he had finished it he might be so upset that he would never finish it; whereas if he had finished it she would beg him to take her right away from this man, his brother, to have nothing more to do with him, and to go straight into Featherstone's firm on his own terms with his new invention. It was essential to get Edward to realise that Albert was violently in love with her, and that he would never believe unless he saw it for himself. She had already prepared Featherstone's firm, which was indeed monetarily composed of Charles Podmore; and she had prepared Albert. It now remained to prepare Edward. This caused her much reflection. The room where Edward wrestled with his inventive fancy was at the top of the house, and the problem was how to get him down to the drawing-room so that he could surprise her in the arms of Albert, without going up to fetch him. It was some time before she hit on the solution—simple when thought of, like all great solutions: She would hide the model. She calculated that it would take him two minutes to get upstairs and moon around, finding that it was gone. Another three minutes to search and return to the drawing-room to ask her what could have happened to it. If then she lighted Albert up four minutes after Edward went upstairs she would be fairly safe.

It was not till the morning of the longest day that Edward, singing like a wren in his bath, announced to her that he had completed the model of his invention. Looking at his emaciated form, she said drily: "And high time too." After breakfast she wired to Albert (telephones were not yet installed) to come and dine that evening. Having carefully ordered a heating meal she awaited the crisis with a fluttering heart. All went well during dinner, even to the touching of her foot by Albert, to which she did not respond, so that his eyes became more than ever like the bull's in connection with Europa. She brought up the subject of the new invention, and suggested to Edward that after dinner he should go up and bring the model down. Sitting there, opposite her, his face, though hollow and almost blue, had the shining happiness of one about to enter heaven; and a certain compunction seized on her for the shock she was going to give him. 'It's for his good,' she thought, and passed the tip of her toe across Albert's instep. Dear Edward, how blind he was! When, in the drawing-room, they had partaken of coffee, she said: "Now, Edward!" and looked at the clock. As Edward left the room, she left the sofa, and moved towards the clock. It was of ormolu, a wedding present from her Uncle Roger, and stood on the mantelpiece.

"Albert!" she said, "come here! I want your opinion on this clock."

The Alderman rose. Through her lashes she could see the added flush on his fleshy face, and his quivering lips that almost seemed to slobber. He stood beside her, and with her eyes on the clock Marian pointed out its period. When exactly four minutes had elapsed her straining ears caught a sound on the stairs, and she moved awkwardly, so that her white shoulder came in contact with his chest. The rest was automatic; she found herself face to face with him, his arms round her waist and his lips inclining for her lips. She reined back and his mouth came forward, reaching for her neck. All was as it should be. Then the door opened, and there stood Patricia in her dressing-gown.

"Mummy!" came her treble cry, "Daddy's lost his—

Oh!" She vanished: and with a sensation as of vertigo Marian heard her shriller:

"Daddy, Daddy! Quick! Uncle Albert's biting Mummy's neck!"

Then it was that Marian showed her breeding. With inimitable presence of mind she lost it and fell on the sofa in one of those dead faints which are so difficult to see through. Edward, attended by the scared Patricia, found her with Albert standing by and running his fingers through his somewhat scant but well-pomatumed hair.

"Here, I say!" he said, "she's fainted"; and with a certain aplomb, added: "It's the heat."

They revived her with some difficulty, and on Edward's arm she went up to bed. Albert departed.

"If Albert hadn't caught me," she said on the stairs, "I should have fallen badly; it's lucky he's so strong. Patricia, Daddy's model is in the top cupboard. I put it there for safety, and forgot to tell him."

Three days later the model was patented by A. & E. Tweetyman. Edward had seen nothing. Patricia, who had seen everything, was young and easily gulled; but for some days Marian's manner to her offspring, who had spoiled it all, was somewhat sharp. Her defeat had been so signal that, like the sensible woman she was, she accepted it completely. Edward was hopeless! She gave him up. A man of sorrows, who, until he died of it, would never know what manner of man he was. As for Albert, she gave him up too. With difficulty Edward noticed that his brother was never asked to dinner again.

It was in a mood of Forsytean humour, one day, that Marian told the story of her defeat to her sister Euphemia, whose squeaks on the occasion were notable; and through this source it became current on Forsyte 'Change.

THE DROMIOS

1900

THE DROMIOS

WHEN the Boer war had been in progress for some time and things were going badly, Giles and Jesse Hayman—commonly known in the Forsyte family as 'the Dromios'—decided to enlist in the Imperial Yeomanry. Their decision, a corporate one—for they never acted apart —was made without unnecessary verbal expenditure. Giles, the elder by one year and of the stronger build, withdrew his pipe from between his teeth, turned a fox-terrier off his lap, and, pointing to the words 'Black week' in the *Daily Mail* said:

"Those beggarly Boers!"

Jesse, in an armchair on the other side of the hearth, took the fox-terrier on his lap, tapped out his pipe, and answered:

"Brutes!"

There was again silence. Then Giles said:

"What price the Yeomanry? Are you on?"

Jesse put his empty pipe between his teeth and nodded. The matter had been concluded. They then remained a considerable time with their high-booted legs outstretched towards the fire, their grey thrusting eyes fixed on the flames, and no expression whatever on their lean red-brown faces.

Being almost majestically without occupations except riding, shooting and games of various kinds, they dwelt in a small timbered manor-house close to some racing stables on the Hampshire Downs. Each had five hundred a year and no parents; their mother—Susan, the married Forsyte sister—having followed Hayman to his rest at Woking in

1895. Neither of them had married or even dreamed of it, neither of them had a mistress; but periodically they went up to London.

Having thus decided to enlist, the first step was naturally to have a night out; and they took train to the Metropolis. They put up at their usual quarters—a hostelry called 'Malcolm's,' of a somewhat sporting character in the neighbourhood of Covent Garden; and, after dressing themselves, went to dine at the 'Cri.' There they ate in silence, despatching the preliminaries of a 'night out'—oysters, devilled kidneys, a partridge, a welsh rabbit, 'a bottle of the boy,' and a glass of old port, with only two lapses into conversation, the first when Jesse said:

"Those Johnny birds, the Boers, are getting above themselves!"

To which Giles replied:

"You bet."

And the second when Giles said:

"Buller'll stay the course."

To which Jesse replied:

"Good old Buller."

Having finished, placed cigars in their mouths, secured their coats, and put on their Opera hats, they went out into a mild night, to walk to the 'Pandemonium.'

In old days when they were living in the Hayman house on Campden Hill and reading for examinations which, by some curious fatality not connected with brains, they never passed, so that they had been compelled to remain without professions, there had been few evenings when they could not be observed leaning over the balustrade of the Promenade at that establishment. Thence had they watched the acrobats, ventriloquists, conjurers, ballad singers, comedians, and ballet dancers of the period, never manifesting approbation, but not infrequently with a sort of smile bitten in on their faces. Generally they left as much with each other as they arrived, occasionally they left without each other, but with somebody else. It was not known even to each other whether they ever spoke to those others with whom they left.

Having been out of London since the Boer war broke out they had not yet heard 'Tommy Atkins' sung; and when this inevitable item was reached the effect on Giles was observed by Jesse to be as noticeable as the effect on Jesse observed by Giles. After a certain resistance to words and tune due to the need for maintaining 'form' their heads began almost imperceptibly to move in time to the refrain, and, a line or so behind the rest of the audience, their mouths began in a muffled manner to take up the chorus. The effect on them, in fact, was distinctly emotional, which to some extent explains what happened afterwards. The song was scarcely over and a ventriloquist had taken his seat on the stage with a midshipman on his knee when Jesse's attention was diverted by smothered voices behind him. His hearing, trained by listening in coverts for the music of hounds or the flushing of birds, was sharp, and he distinctly heard the following conversation:

"If you don't get me ten pounds to-night it'll be the worse for you."

"Ten pounds? How can I?"

"Well, don't you come home without it."

"Oh! You are a brute!"

"All right, my girl!"

Jesse turned round. He saw, moving away, a hulking fellow of an unpleasant type, and a young woman, rouged but rather pretty, under a big hat, looking after him.

"Hear that, Giles?"

Giles nodded. "Swine!"

Having thus registered their disapproval, they reconcentrated their attention on the stage. It was during the song of a gentleman in a kilt that Jesse felt his arm pressed, and heard a voice in his ear say:

"Oh! Beg pardon! He *is* funny, isn't he?"

The same rouged young woman in the big hat was leaning over the balustrade beside him.

She was really young; her mouth was pretty if somewhat artificial, and her eyes, which were dark, looked scared.

"Are you having a night out?" she whispered.

Jesse shrugged his shoulders. Then the strains of 'Tommy Atkins' moving within him, he said:

"I heard what that swine said to you just now."

The professional smile died off the young woman's lips. She crossed her arms on her breast, and air escaped her in a long: "Oh!" Jesse edged his arm away from hers. A minute passed; then her arm pressed his again, and out of the corner of his eye, accustomed to the observation of woodcock, he could see her glancing furtively round. The 'swine' in question was just behind again with two male friends; he was bending on the girl such a look that Jesse said with surprising suddenness:

"Send the swine to hell!"

"What?" said Giles.

"That swine behind us. Swine who live on girls!"

"Steady, old man!" said Giles.

The man and his companions moved on, muttering.

"Oh!" said the girl under her breath: "whatever made you? I'll never dare to go 'ome to-night. What shall I do?"

Jesse did not answer, having no idea. An objection to scenes, rooted in his type, caused him to resume his stare at the stage, now occupied by a male dancer with brisk and glancing legs; but he was conscious of a tear slowly trickling down the girl's cheek, making a narrow track in her rouge and powder.

"You wouldn't take me on, I suppose?" he heard her say. Jesse shook his head.

"Only up for the night. Going to the war."

"Oh!" said the girl, blankly. *"He will* wallop me."

Jesse stared.

"D'you mean to say——"

The girl nodded violently.

"Hear that, Giles?"

Giles grunted.

The girl stealthily removed the traces of emotion.

Jesse turned, and, leaning back against the balustrade, surveyed the promenaders. Giles, with mechanical conformity, had done the same. The girl continued to stare at the stage. If she had been 'kidding' him—Jesse thought—she would have turned too; besides, her face had gone a queer colour.

"I believe she's going to cat," he murmured to Giles.

They both looked at her, but she seemed to have recovered from the impulse, and was sniffing at a bottle of salts. Deciding to move away from her, Jesse had raised his hand to his hat, when he caught sight of the 'swine' among a group of men, all of whom were gazing in his direction.

"See those swine?" he said.

Giles nodded.

The group, seeing the brothers staring at them, moved on. Jesse turned to the girl.

"Look here," he said, "you go to an hotel for the night. We'll see you there. Better come now."

The girl, who still looked very queer, turned from the balustrade.

"Thank you very much," she said, "but I 'aven't any money."

"That's all right," said Jesse. "Come on!"

They crossed the promenade and went down the steps with the girl between them.

"D'you know an hotel?" said Jesse, in the Square. "They won't take you at ours—men only."

"There's Robin's Hotel, off Covent Garden."

"All right; that's on our way. Here's a fiver for you. You're looking queer."

"I feel queer," said the girl, simply. They walked a little in silence, and then she said:

"I couldn't have stood being walloped to-night—I just couldn't."

"Swine!" said Jesse. Giles growled.

Turning into Bedford Street, the girl touched Jesse's arm.

"Oh!" she said in a scared voice; "they're after us!"

About fifty yards behind, five men were strolling, keeping their distance, but quite clearly following. Instinctively the Dromios increased their pace, turning into Henrietta Street.

"If they turn down here too, we'll know," said Giles.

"I think I'm going to faint," said the girl.

"Bosh!" said Jesse. "If they follow, we'll stop them at the bottom here. You can slip on to the hotel sharp. They won't know where you are. Take her other arm, Giles."

At the Covent Garden end, he looked back; the men were just turning into Henrietta Street. He gave the girl a shove.

"Now run for it! Don't be a little fool! They shan't see where you go; we'll stop 'em here. Cut on!"

The girl caught her breath, and stammered out:

"Oh! Thank you!" Then, helped by a push from Giles, she vanished round the corner. The Dromios began walking with extreme slowness back towards the men. Giles hummed out of tune, the air of 'Tommy Atkins.' The five pursuers, who had been hurrying, slowed up, and came to a halt. Indeed, without going off the pavement, the two parties could not pass each other. 'That swine' who was the biggest of the lot, took a step forward, and raising his fist, thus addressed the Dromios.

"We want you two ——. What the —— did you mean by what you said just now? Swine indeed? Swine yourselves!"

The Dromios did not answer.

"You——have got to learn manners, and you're—— well going to."

Giles turned to Jesse. "These sportsmen," he said, "are rather a bore."

"Give 'em socks, boys!" said the 'swine.'

The proceedings which followed had elements so unsporting as to offend every instinct of the Dromios. From the point of view of 'form' the whole thing was deplorable; the only feature in good taste being the first blow, a left-hander from Giles which tapped the 'swine's claret.' He was instantly thereafter involved with three of the 'sportsmen' and Jesse with the other two. The Dromios were expert boxers, but their opponents butted, kicked, and collared below the belt, so that the brothers were unable to assume any attitude other than those in which circumstances placed them. They were, however, lean and in hard conditon, their winds were good, and they fought like tiger cats. The sight of Giles, overborne by weight, being dragged horizontally, so stimulated Jesse that, contrary to all the canons of sportsmanship, he brought his knee up against the chin of one of his opponents; springing at the other, he seized him by the throat in a manner totally unorthodox, and rammed his head against the lintel of a door, then, dashing to Giles's rescue he so socked one of the 'sportsmen' behind the ear that he fell prone. The other two let go of Giles, and the two Dromios were able to place themselves in proper postures of defence. Thereon the combat ceased as instantly as it had begun, the 'sportsmen' vanished and the Dromios were left in an empty Covent Garden. Giles had a cut on his cheekbone, a broken knee, a rent in the tail of his overcoat; Jesse a bruised jaw. Both their ties had come untied, both their Opera hats were in the gutter. In silence they retied their ties, pinned up the rent, brushed each other, recovered their hats, and walked on towards their hotel.

Going up to their bedrooms, they washed, plastered Giles's cheek, bound a handkerchief round his knee, put on smoking jackets, and went down to the billiard-room. There in a corner they sat down, ordered themselves whiskies and sodas, and lit their pipes.

"Those sportsmen!" said Giles.

"They got what for, all right!" said Jesse.

Both grinned, and for a long time, in silence, gazed before them with the same hungry expression in their thrusting grey eyes.

"Hang that Judy!" said Jesse suddenly. Giles nodded.

Soon after, they retired to bed, and completed their night out.

The next day they enlisted, and a month later 'went out' on horses.

A FORSYTE ENCOUNTERS THE PEOPLE

1917

A FORSYTE ENCOUNTERS THE PEOPLE

IN October 1917, when the air raids on London were acutely monotonous, there was a marked tendency on the part of Eustace Forsyte to take Turkish baths. The most fastidious of his family, who had carried imperturbability of demeanour to the pitch of defiance, he had perceived in the Turkish bath a gesture, as of a finger to a nose, in the face of a boring peril. As soon then as the maroons of alarm went off, he would issue from his rooms or Club and head straight for Northumberland Avenue. With his springy and slightly arched walk, as of a man spurning a pavement, he would move deliberately among the hurrying throng; and, undressing without haste, would lay his form, remarkably trim and slim for a man well over fifty, on a couch in the hottest room at about the moment when less self-contained citizens were merely sweating in their shoes. Confirmed in the tastes of a widower of somewhat self-centred character, he gave but few damns to what happened to anything—he it was who used to set his study on fire at school in order to practise being cool in moments of danger, and at college, on being dared, had jumped through a first-floor window and been picked up sensible. On his back, with his pale clean-shaven face composed to a slight superciliousness and his dark grey eyes, below the banding towel, fixed on those golden stars that tick the domed ceilings of any room with aspirations to be oriental, he would think of Maidenhead, or of Chelsea china, and now and then glance at his skin to see if it was glistening. Not a good mixer, as the saying was, he seldom

spoke to his bathing fellows, and they mostly fat. Thus
would he pass the hours of menace, and when the 'all
clear' had sounded, return to his club or to his rooms with
the slight smile of one who has perspired well. There he
would partake of a repast feeling that he had cheated the
Boche.

On a certain occasion, however, towards the end of that
invasive period, events did not run true to type. The alarm
had sounded, and Eustace had pursued his usual course, but
the raid had not matured. Cool and hungry, he emerged
from the Baths about eight o'clock and set his face towards
the Strand. He had arrived opposite Charing Cross when
a number of explosions attracted his attention; people began to run past him and a special constable cried loudly:
"Take cover, take cover!" Eustace frowned. A second
Turkish bath was out of the question, and he stood still wondering what he should do, the only person in the street not
in somewhat violent motion. Before he could make up
his mind whether to walk back to his club or on to the
restaurant where he had meant to dine, a large and burly
'special' had seized him by the shoulders and pushed him
into the entrance of the Tube Station.

"Take cover, can't you!" he said, rudely.

Eustace freed his sleeve. "I don't wish to."

"Then you—well will," replied the 'special.'

Perceiving that he could only proceed over the considerable body of this intrusive being, Eustace shrugged his
shoulders and endeavoured to stand still again, but an in-
flowing tide of his fellow-beings forced him down the slope
into the hallway and on towards the stairs. Here he made
a resolute effort to squeeze his way back towards the air. It
was totally unavailing, and he was swept on till he was
standing about halfway down the stairs among a solid mass

of men, women and children of types that seemed to him
in no way attractive. He had frequently noticed that man-
kind in the bulk is unpleasing to the eye, the ear, and the
nose; but this deduction had, as it were, been formed by his
brain. It was now reinforced by his senses in a manner, to
one purified by a Turkish bath, intensely vivid and unpleasing. The air in this rat-run, normally distasteful to Eustace,
who never took the Tube, was rapidly becoming fetid, and
he at once decided that he would rather brave all the shrapnel of all the anti-aircraft guns defending him than stay
where he was. Unfortunately the decision was rendered
nugatory by the close pressure of a stout woman with
splotches on her face, who kept saying: "We're all right in
'ere, 'Enry"; by 'Enry, a white-faced mechanician with a
rat-gnawed moustache; by their spindle-legged child, who
muttered at intervals: "I'll kill that Kaiser"; and by two
Jewish-looking youths, on whom Eustace had at once passed
the verdict 'better dead'! His back, moreover, was wedged
partly against the front of a young woman smelling of stale
powder who panted in one of his ears, and partly against the
bow window of her partner, who, judging from the breeze
that came from him, was a whisky-taster. On the slopes to
right and left, and further to the front were dozens and
dozens of other beings, none of whom had for Eustace any
fascination. It was as if Fate had designed at one stroke
to remove every vestige of the hedge which had hitherto
divided him from 'the general.'

Placing his handkerchief, well tinctured by eau-de-
Cologne, to his nose, he tried to calculate: It would probably be a couple of hours before the 'all clear' sounded.
Could he not squeeze his way very gradually to the entrance? His neighbours seemed to think that by being
where they were they had 'struck it lucky' and scored off

the by-our-lady Huns. Since they evidently had no intention of departing, it seemed to Eustace that they would prefer
his room to his company. He was startled, therefore, when
his attempt to escape was greeted by growling admonitions
not to 'go shovin',' 'to keep still, couldn't he,' and other
displeased comments. It was his first lesson in mob
psychology: what was good enough for them was good
enough for him. If he persisted, he would be considered a
traitor to the body politic, and would meet with strenuous
resistance! So he abandoned his design and endeavoured
to make himself slimmer, that the bodies round him might
be in contact with his shell rather than with his essence.
Behind his fast evaporating eau-de-Cologne he developed a
kind of preservative disdain of people who clearly preferred
this stinking ant-heap to the shrapnel and bombs of the
open. Had they no sense of smell; were they totally in-
different to heat, had they no pride, that they let the Huns
inflict on them this exquisite discomfort? Did none of them
feel, with him, that the only becoming way to treat danger
was to look down your nose at it?

On the contrary, all these people seemed to think that by
taking refuge in the bowels of the earth they had triumphed
over the enemy. Their mental pictures of being blown into
little bits, or stunned by the shrapnel, must be more vivid
than anything he could conjure up. And Eustace had a
stab of vision. Good form discouraged the imagination till
it had lost the power of painting. Like the French aristo-
crats who went unruffled to the guillotine, he felt that he
would rather be blown up, or shot down, than share this
'rat-run' triumph of his neighbours. The more he looked
at them, the more his nose twitched. Even the cheeriness
with which they were accepting their rancid situation annoyed him. The sentiment of the spindly child: "I'll kill

that Kaiser," awakened in him, for the first time since the war began, a fellow-feeling for the German Emperor; the simplification of responsibility adopted by his country-men stood out so grotesquely in the saying of this cockney infant.

"He ought to be 'ung," said a voice to his right.

"My! Ain't it hot here!" said a voice to his left. "I shall faint if it goes on much longer."

'It'll stop her panting,' thought Eustace, rubbing his ear.

"Am I standing on your foot, Sir?" asked the stout and splotchy woman.

"Thanks, not particularly."

"Shift a bit, 'Enry."

"Shift a bit?" repeated the white-faced mechanician cheerfully: "That's good, ain't it? There's not too much room, is there, Sir?"

The word 'Sir' thus repeated, or perhaps the first stirrings of a common humanity, moved Eustace to reply:

"The black hole of Calcutta's not in it."

"I'll kill that Kaiser."

"She don't like these air-raids, and that's a fact," said the stout woman: "Do yer, Milly? But don't you worry, dearie, we're all right down 'ere."

"Oh! You think so?" said Eustace.

"Ow! Yes! Everyone says the Tubes are safe."

"What a comfort!"

As if with each opening of his lips some gas of rancour had escaped, Eustace felt almost well disposed to the little family which oppressed his front.

"Wish I 'ad my girl 'ere," said one of the Jewish youths, suddenly; "this is your cuddlin' done for you, this is."

"Strike me!" said the other.

'Better dead!' thought Eustace, even more emphatically.

" 'Ow long d'you give it, Sir?" said the mechanician, turning his white face a little.

"Another hour and a half, I suppose."

"I'll kill that Kaiser."

"Stow it, Milly, you've said that before. One can 'ave too much of a good thing, can't one, Sir?"

"I was beginning to think so," murmured Eustace.

"Well, she's young to be knocked about like this. It gets on their nerves, ye know. I'll be glad to get 'er and the missis 'ome, and that's a fact."

Something in the paper whiteness of his face, something in the tone of his hollow-chested voice, and the simple altruism of his remark, affected Eustace. He smelled of sweat and sawdust, but he was jolly decent!

And time went by, the heat and odour thickening; there was almost silence now. A voice said: "They're a —— long time abaht it!" and was greeted with a sighing clamour of acquiescence. All that crowded mass of beings had become preoccupied with the shifting of their limbs, the straining of their lungs towards any faint draught of air. Eustace had given up all speculation, his mind was concentrated blankly on the words: 'Stand straight—stand straight!' The spindly child, discouraged by the fleeting nature of success, had fallen into a sort of coma against his knee; he wondered whether she had ringworm; he wondered why everybody didn't faint. The white-faced mechanician had encircled his wife's waist. His face, ghostly patient, was the one thing Eustace noticed from time to time; it emerged as if supported by no body. Suddenly with a whispering sigh the young woman, behind, fell against his shoulder, and by a sort of miracle found space to crumple down. The mechanician's white face came round:

"Poor lidy, she's gone off!"

"Ah!" boomed the whisky-taster, "and no wonder, with this 'eat." He waggled his bowler hat above her head.

"Shove 'er 'ead between her knees," said the mechanician.

Eustace pushed the head downwards, the whisky-taster applied a bunch of keys to her back. She came to with a loud sigh.

"Better for her dahn there," said the mechanician, "the 'ot air rises."

And again time went on, with a ground bass of oaths and cheerios. Then the lights went out to a sound as if souls in an underworld had expressed their feelings. Eustace felt a shuddering upheaval pass through the huddled mass. A Cockney voice cried. "Are we dahn-'earted?" And the movement subsided in a sort of dreadful calm.

Down below a woman shrieked; another and another took it up.

" 'Igh-strikes," muttered the mechanician; "cover 'er ears, Polly." The child against Eustace's knee had begun to whimper. "Milly, where was Moses when the light went out?"

Eustace greeted the sublime fatuity with a wry and wasted smile. He could feel the Jewish youths trying to elbow themselves out. "Stand still," he said, sharply.

"That's right, Sir," said the mechanician; "no good makin' 'eavy weather of it."

"Sing, you blighters—sing!" cried a voice; " 'When the fields were white wiv disies.' " And all around they howled a song which Eustace did not know; and then, abruptly as it had gone out, the light went up again. The song died in a prolonged "Aoh!" Eustace gazed around him. Tears were running down the splotchy woman's cheeks. A smile of relief was twitching at the mechanician's

mouth. "The all clear's gone! The all clear's gone! . . .
'Ip, 'ip, 'ooraay!" The cheering swelled past Eustace, and
a swinging movement half lifted him from his feet.

"Catch hold of the child," he said to the mechanician,
"I've got her other hand." Step by step they lifted her,
under incredible pressure, with maddening slowness, into
the hall. Eustace took a great breath, expanding his lungs
while the crowd debouched into the street like an exploding
shell. The white-faced mechanician had begun to cough, in
a strangled manner alarming to hear. He stopped at last
and said:

"That's cleared the pipes. I'm greatly obliged to you,
Sir; I dunno 'ow we'd 'a got Milly up. She looks queer,
that child."

The child's face, indeed, was whiter than her father's,
and her eyes were vacant.

"Do you live far?"

"Nao, just rahnd the corner, Sir."

"Come on, then."

They swung the child, whose legs continued to move
mechanically, into the open. The street was buzzing with
people emerging from shelter and making their way home.
Eustace saw a clock's face. Ten o'clock!

'Damn these people,' he thought. 'The restaurants will
be closed.'

The splotchy woman spoke as if answering his thought.

"We oughtn't to keep the gentleman, 'Enry, 'e must be
properly tired. I can ketch 'old of Milly. Don't you
bother with us, Sir, and thank you kindly."

"Not a bit," said Eustace: "it's nothing."

" 'Ere we are, Sir," said the mechanician, stopping at the
side door of some business premises; "we live in the basement. If it's not presuming, would you take a cup o' tea

with us?" And at this moment the child's legs ceased to function altogether.

" 'Ere, Milly, 'old up, dearie, we're just 'ome."

But the child's head sagged.

"She's gone off—paw little thing!"

"Lift her!" said Eustace.

"Open the door, Mother, the key's in my pocket; you go on and light the gas."

They supported the spindly child, who now seemed to weigh a ton, down stone stairs into a basement, and laid her on a small bed in a room where all three evidently slept. The mechanician pressed her head down towards her feet.

"She's comin' to. Why, Milly, you're in your bed, see! And now you'll 'ave a nice 'ot cup o' tea! There!"

"I'll kill that Kaiser," murmured the spindly child, her china-blue eyes fixed wonderingly on Eustace, her face waxy in the gaslight.

"Stir yer stumps, Mother, and get this gentleman a cup. A cup'll do you good, Sir, you must be famished. Will you come in the kitchen and have a smoke, while she's gettin' it?"

A strange fellow-feeling pattered within Eustace looking at that white-faced altruist. He stretched out his cigarette case, shining, curved, and filled with gold-tipped cigarettes. The mechanician took one, held it for a second politely as who should imply: 'Hardly my smoke, but since you are so kind.'

"Thank'ee, Sir. A smoke'll do us both a bit o' good, after that Tube. It was close in there."

Eustace greeted the miracle of understatement with a smile.

"Not exactly fresh."

"I'd 'a come and 'ad the raid comfortable at 'ome, but

the child was scared and the Tube just opposite. Well, it's all in the day's work, I suppose; but it comes 'ard on children and elderly people, to say nothing of the women. 'Ope you're feelin' better, Sir. You looked very white when you come out."

"Thanks," said Eustace, thinking: 'Not so white as you, my friend!'

"The tea won't be a minute. We got the gas 'ere, it boils a kettle a treat. You sit down, old girl, I'll get it for yer."

Eustace went to the window. The kitchen was hermetically sealed.

"Do you mind if I open the window," he said, "I'm still half suffocated from that Tube."

On the window-sill, in company with potted geraniums, he breathed the dark damp air of a London basement, and his eyes roved listlessly over walls decorated with coloured cuts from Christmas supplements, and china ornaments perched wherever was a spare flat inch. These presents from seaside municipalities aroused in him a sort of fearful sympathy.

"I see you collect china," he said, at last.

"Ah! The missis likes a bit of china," said the mechanician, turning his white face illumined by the gas ring; "reminds 'er of 'olidays. It's a cheerful thing, I think meself, though it takes a bit o' dustin'."

"You're right there," said Eustace, his soul fluttering suddenly with a feather brush above his own precious Ming. Ming and the present from Margate! The mechanician was stirring the teapot.

"Weak for me, if you don't mind," said Eustace, hastily.

The mechanician poured into three cups, one of which he brought to Eustace with a jug of milk and a basin of damp white sugar. The tea looked thick and dark and Indian, and Eustace, who partook habitually of thin pale China tea flavoured with lemon, received the cup solemnly. It was better than he hoped, however, and he drank it gratefully.

"She's drunk her tea a treat," said the splotchy woman, returning from the bedroom.

" 'Ere's yours, Mother."

" 'Aven't you 'ad a cup yerself, 'Enry?"

"Just goin' to," said the white-faced mechanician, pouring into a fourth cup and pausing to add: "Will you 'ave another, Sir? There's plenty in the pot."

Eustace shook his head. "No, thanks very much. I must be getting on directly." But he continued to sit on the window-sill, as a man on a mountain lingers in the whiffling wind before beginning his descent to earth. The mechanician was drinking his tea at last. "Sure you won't 'ave another cup, Sir?" and he poured again into his wife's cup and his own. The two seemed to expand visibly as the dark liquid passed into them.

"I always say there's nothin' like tea," said the woman.

"That's right; we could 'a done with a cup dahn there, couldn't we, Sir?"

Eustace stood up.

"I hope your little girl will be all right," he said: "and thank you very much for the tea. Here's my card. I've enjoyed meeting you."

The mechanician took the card, looking up at Eustace rather like a dog.

"I'm sure it's been a pleasure to us, and it's you we got to thank, Sir. I shall remember what you did for the child."

Eustace shook his head: "No, really. Good-night, Mrs. —er——"

"Thompson, the nyme is, Sir."

He shook her hand, subduing the slight shudder which her face still imposed on him.

"Good-night, Mr. Thompson."

The hand of the white-faced mechanician, polished on his trousers, grasped Eustace's hand with astonishing force.

"Good-night, Sir."

"I hope we shall meet again," said Eustace.

Out in the open it was a starry night, and he paused for a minute in the hooded street with his eyes fixed on those specks of far-off silver, so remarkably unlike the golden asterisks which decorated the firmament of his Turkish bath. And there came to him, so standing, a singular sensation almost as if he had enjoyed his evening, as a man will enjoy that which he has never seen before and wonders if he will ever see again.

SOAMES AND THE FLAG
1914–1918

SOAMES AND THE FLAG

I

ON that day of 1914 when the assassinations at Sera-jevo startled the world, Soames Forsyte passed in a taxi-cab up the Haymarket, supporting on his knee a picture by James Maris, which he had just bought from Dumetrius. He was pleased at the outcome of a very considerable duel. The fellow had come down to his price at the last minute, and Soames had wondered why.

The reason dawned on him that night in Green Street, while reading his evening paper: "This tragic occurrence may yet shake Europe to its foundations. Sinister possibilities implicit in such an assassination stagger the imagination." They must have staggered Dumetrius. The fellow had suddenly seen "blue." The market in objects whose "virtue" varied with the quietude of men's minds and the tourist traffic with America, was—Soames well knew—extremely sensitive. Sinister possibilities! He put the paper down and sat reflecting. No! The chap was an alarmist. What, after all, was an Archduke more or less—they were always getting into the papers, one way or another. He would see what *The Times* said about it to-morrow, but probably it would turn out a storm in a tea-cup. Soames was not in fact of a European turn of mind. 'Trouble in the Balkans' had become a proverb; and when a thing became a proverb there was nothing in it.

He read *The Times* journeying back with the James Maris to Mapledurham the following day. Editorial hands were lifted in the usual horror at assassination, but there was nothing to prevent him going out fishing.

Indeed, in the month that followed, even after the Aus-

trian ultimatum had appeared, Soames, like ninety-nine per
cent. of his fellow-countrymen, didn't know what there was
"to make such a fuss about." To suppose that England
could be involved was weak-minded. The idea, indeed,
never seriously occurred to one born just after the Crimean
war, and accustomed to look on Europe as fit to be advised,
perhaps, but nothing more. Fleur's holidays, too, were just
beginning, and he was thinking of buying her a pony: at
twelve years old it was time she learned even that rather
futile accomplishment—riding. Besides, was there not
plenty of fuss in Ireland, if they must have something to fuss
about? It was Annette who raised the first bubbles of an
immense disquiet. Beautiful creature as she was at that
period—"rising thirty-five," as George Forsyte put it—she
did not read the English papers, but she often had letters
from France. On the 28th of July she said to Soames:

"Soames, there is going to be war—those Germans are
crazy mad."

"War over a potty little affair like that? Nonsense!"
growled Soames.

"Oh! you have no imagination, Soames. Of course there
will be war, and my poor country will have to fight for
Russia; and you English—what will you do?"

"Do? Why, nothing! If you're fools enough to go to
war, we can't help it."

"We expect you to help us," said Annette; "but you
English we never can rely on. You wait always to see
which way the cat jump."

"What business is it of ours?" Soames answered testily.

"You will soon find what business when the Germans
take Calais."

"I thought you French fancied yourselves invincible."
But he got up and left the room.

And that evening it was noticed even by Fleur that he took no interest in her. All Saturday and Sunday he was fidgety. On Sunday afternoon came a rumour that Germany had declared war on Russia. Soames put it down to the papers; but he remained awake half the night, and, on reading of its confirmation in *The Times* on Monday morning, went up to Town by the first train. It was Bank holiday, and he sought his City Club as the only spot where he might possibly get City news. He found that a good many other men were there with the same object, among them one of the partners in the firm of his brokers, Messrs. Green and Greening—more familiarly known as "Grin and Grinning." To him he detailed his views on the sale of certain stocks. The fellow—it was 'Grin'—regarded him askance.

"Nothing doing, Mr. Forsyte," he said: "The Stock Exchange will be closed some days they say."

"Closed?" said Soames. "You don't mean to say they'd let business stop, even if——"

"It will *have* to stop, or prices will flop to nothing. As it is, there's panic enough——"

"Panic!" repeated Soames, staring at his broker—'a sleek beggar!' "Cancel those orders; I shan't sell anything."

Not realising that in this he had voiced more than a personal decision, he got up and went to the window. Outside was a regular fluster. Newsvendors were crying: "German ultimatum to Belgium!" Soames stood looking down at the faces in the street. It was not his custom, but he found himself doing it. One and all had a furrow between the eyes. Here was a how-de-do! Down there, on the river, he hadn't realised. And he had a sudden longing for telegraphic tape.

It was surrounded by men he did not know, and Soames,

who had a horror of doing what other people were doing, and especially of waiting to do it, moved into the smoking-room and sat down. One of the least of club-men, he literally did not know how to get into conversation with strange members, and was confined to listening to what they were saying. This was sufficiently alarming. The three or four within earshot seemed suffering only from fear that "this damned Government" wouldn't "come up to the scratch." Soames' ears stood up more and more. He was hearing more abuse of radicals and the working classes than he had ever heard in so short a space of time. The words "traitors" and "politicians" beat through the talk with a sort of rhythm. Though the general trend of the sentiments voiced might be his own, all that was reticent, measured and calculating within him was shocked. What did they think a war would be—a sort of water picnic?

"If we don't go in now," said one of the group, "we shall never hold up our heads again."

Soames sniffed audibly. How? He didn't see. Germany and Austria against France and Russia—if they chose to make such fools of themselves. Europe was always at war in the old days. And now that they had these thundering great armies, it was a wonder they hadn't come to loggerheads long since. What was the use of having no conscription and a big navy, if one wasn't going to keep out of war? Fellows like these! All they thought of was their dividends; and much good that would do them. If England lost her head now, and went in, there wouldn't *be* any dividends. War, indeed! The whole interior of one, who for all his sixty years had been at peace as a matter of course, rose against that grisly consummation. What had the Russians ever done, or the French for that matter, that they should expect England to pull the chestnuts out of the fire for them? As for the Germans—their Kaiser was a "cock-snoop" of a chap, always rattling his sabre, and talking through his hat—but they were at least more understandable than the Russians or the French; as for Austria—the idea of going to war with her was simply laughable.

"Albert has appealed to the Powers," said a voice.

Albert! That was the King of Belgium. So he'd appealed, had he? Belgium! Wasn't she guaranteed like Switzerland? The Germans would never be fools enough to—! This was a civilised age—treaties and that! He rose. It was no use listening to jingo chatter. He would go and lunch.

But he could scarcely eat—the weather was so hot. He shouldn't be a bit surprised if that had a lot to do with the state of affairs. Put these Emperors and General chaps on ice, and you'd have them piping small at once. He was drinking a glass of barleywater, when he heard the waiter at the next table say to a member: "So it says, Sir."

"Good God!" said the member, starting up.

Soames forgot his manners.

"What does it say?"

"The Germans have invaded Belgium, Sir."

Soames put down his glass.

"Who told you that?"

"It's on the tape, Sir."

Soames emitted a sound that might have come from his very boots—so deep it was. He must think. But you couldn't tell what you were thinking in this place.

"My bill," he said.

When it came, he gave the waiter a shilling against club rules and the habit of a lifetime; for he had an obscure feeling that the fellow had done something unique to him.

Then with a sudden homing instinct, he took a cab to Paddington, and all the way in the train read the evening paper, or sat staring out of the carriage window.

He said nothing when he got home—nothing whatever to anybody of what he had heard—the whole of him absorbed in a sort of silent and awful adjustment. That fellow Grey—a steady chap, best of the bunch—must be making his speech to the House by now. What was he saying? And how were they taking it? He got into his punt and sat there listening to the wood-pigeons, in the leafy peace of the bright day. He didn't want a soul near him. England! They said the fleet was ready. His mind didn't seem able to get further than that. To be on water gave him queer consolation, as if his faith in the fleet would glide with that water down to the sea whereon the pride and the protection of England lay. He put his hand down and the water flowed green-tinged through his opened fingers. By George! There went that kingfisher—hadn't seen him for weeks—flash of blue among the reeds. He wouldn't be that fellow Grey for something. They said he was a fisherman and liked birds. What was he saying to them in there under Big Ben? The chap had always been a gentleman, could he say anything but that England would stand by her word? And for the second time Soames uttered a sound which seemed to travel up from the very tips of his toes. He didn't see what was to be done except agree with that. And what then? All this green peace, every home throughout the land, and stocks and shares—falling, falling! And old Uncle Timothy—ninety-four! He would have to see that they kept it from the old chap. Luckily no newspaper had come into the "Nook" since Aunt Hester died; reading about the House of Lords in 1910 had so upset Timothy, that he had given up taking even *The Times*.

'And my pictures!' thought Soames. Yes, and Fleur's
governess—a German, Fleur having always spoken French
with her mother. Annette would want to get rid of her, he
wouldn't be surprised. And what would become of her—
nobody would want a German, if there were war. A
dragon-fly flew past. Soames watched it with an ache,
dumb and resentful, deep within him. A beautiful summer,
fine and hot, and they couldn't leave it alone, but must
kick up this devil's tattoo, all over the world. This thing
might—might come to be anything before it was over. He
got up and slowly punted himself across. From there he
could see the church. He never went to it, but he supposed
it meant something. And now all over Europe they were
going to blow each other to bits. What would the parsons
say? Nothing—he shouldn't wonder—they were a funny
lot. Seven o'clock! It must be over by now in the House
of Commons. And he punted himself slowly back. The
scent of lime blossom and of meadow-sweet, the scent of
sweetbriar and honeysuckle, yes, and the scent of grass
beginning to cool, drifted and clung. He didn't want to
leave the water, but it was getting damp.

The mothers of the boys going off to the war out there;
young chaps—conscripts—Russia and Austria, Germany
and France—and not one knowing or caring a dump about
it. A pretty how-de-do! There'd be a lot of volunteering
here—if—if—! Only he didn't know, he couldn't tell
what use England could be except at sea.

He got out of the punt and walked slowly up past the
house to his front gate. Heat was over, light paling, stars
peering through, the air smelled a little of dust. Soames
stood like some pelican awaiting it knew not what. A
motor-cycle came sputtering from the direction of Reading.
The rider, in dusty overalls, flung words at him:

"Pawlyment! We're goin' in!" and sputtered past. Soames stretched out a hand. So might a blind man have moved.

Going in? With little food inside and the stars above him, all the imaginative power, which as a rule he starved, turned active, clutched and groped. Scattered, scuttling images of war came flying across the screen of his consciousness like so many wild geese over the sand, over the sea, out of the darkness into the darkness of a layman's mind; a layman who had thought in terms of peace all his days, and his days many. What a thing to happen to one at sixty! They might have waited till he was like old Timothy. Anxiety! That was it, anxiety. Kitchener was over from Egypt, they said. That was something. A grim-looking chap, with his eyes fixed beyond you like a lion's at the Zoo; but he'd always come through. Soames remembered, suddenly, his sensations during the black week of the Boer war—potty little affair, compared with this. And there was old Roberts—too old, he supposed.

'But perhaps,' he thought, 'we shan't have to fight on land.' Besides, who knew? The Germans might come to their senses yet, when they heard England was going in. There was Russia, she had more millions than all the rest put together—Steam-roller, they called her; but had she the steam? Japan had beaten her.

'Well!' and the thought gave him the queerest feeling, proud and miserable: 'If we begin, we shall hold on.' There was something at once terrible to him and deeply satisfying about that instinctive knowledge. They'd be singing "Rule Britannia" everywhere to-night—he shouldn't wonder. People didn't *think*—a little-headed lot!

The stars burned through a sky growing blue-dark. All over Europe men and guns moving—all over the seas ships

tearing along. And this silence—this hush before the storm.
That couldn't last. No; there they were already—singing
back there along the road—drunk, he should say. Tune—
words—he didn't know them—vulgar stuff:

> "It's a long, long way to Tipperary,
> It's a long, long way to go . . .
> Good-bye, Piccadilly, Farewell, Leicester Square!
> It's a long, long way to Tipperary,
> And my heart's right there!"

What had that to do with it—he should like to know?
They were cheering now. Some beanfeast or other had got
the news—common people! But—common or not, to-
night all was England, England! Well, he must go in-
doors.

2

Silence, as of one stricken by decision, come to instinctively
rather than by will, weighed on Soames that night and all
next day. He read 'that chap Grey's' speech and, in con-
spiracy with his country, waited for what he felt would
never come: an answer to the ultimatum sent. The Germans had tasted of force, and would never go back on their
invasion of Belgium.

In the afternoon he could neither bear his own gloom nor
the excitement of Annette, and, walking to the station, he
took a train to Town. The streets seemed full and to get
fuller every minute. He sat down late, at the Connoisseurs'
Club, to dine. When he had finished a meal which seemed
to stick in his gizzard, he went downstairs. From his seat
in the window he could see St. James' Street, and the people
eddying down it towards the centre of the country's life.

He sat there practically alone. At eleven—they said—the ultimatum would expire. In this quiet room, where the furniture and wall-decorations had been accumulated for men of taste throughout a century of peace, was the reality of life as he had known it, the reality of Victorian and Edwardian England. The Boer wars, and all those other little wars, Ashanti, Afghan, Soudan, expeditionary adventures, professional affairs far away, had hardly ruffled the minds of Connoisseurs. One had walked and talked upon one's normal way, just conscious of their disagreeable necessity, and their stimulation at breakfast time, like a pinch of Glauber's salts. But this great thing—why, it had united even the politicians, so he had read in the paper that morning. And there came into his mind Lewis Carroll's rhyme:

"And then came down a monstrous crow,
      As black as a tar-barrel;
   It frightened both the heroes so
      They quite forgot their quarrel."

He got up and moved, restless, into the hall. All there was of connoisseur in the club was gathered round the tape —some half-dozen members, none of whom he knew. Soames stood a little apart. Somebody turned and spoke to him. A shrinking from his fellows, accentuated in Soames' emotional moments, sent a shiver down his spine. He couldn't stay here and have chaps babbling. Answering curtly, he got his hat and went out. In the crowd he'd be alone, and he moved with it down Pall Mall towards Whitehall. Thicker every moment, it was a curious blend of stillness and excitement. Down Cockspur Street into Whitehall he was slowly swept, till at the mouth of Downing Street the crowd became solidity itself, and there was no moving. Ten minutes to the hour! Impervious by nature and by training to mob-emotion, Soames yet was emotionalised. Here was something that was not mere mob-sensation—something made up of individual feelings stronger than mere impulse; something to which noise was but embroidery. There was plenty of noise, rumorous, and strident now and again, but it didn't seem to belong to the faces—didn't seem to suit them any more than it suited the stars that winked and waited. All sorts and conditions of men and women, and he cheek by jowl with them—like sardines in a box—and he didn't mind. Civilians, they were, peaceful folk—not a soldier or a sailor in the lot! They had begun to sing 'God save the King!' His own lips moved; he could not hear himself, and that consoled him. He fixed his eyes on Big Ben. The hands of the bright clock, halfway to the stars, crept with incredible slowness. Two minutes more and the thing would begin—the Thing! What would come of it? He couldn't tell, he didn't know. A bad business, a mad business—once in, you couldn't get out —you had to hold on—to the death—to the death! The faces were all turned one way now under the street lights, white faces, from whose open mouths still came that song; and then—Boom! The clock had struck, and cheering rose. Queer thing to cheer for! "Hoora-a-ay!" *The Thing* had started! . . .

Soames walked away. Had he cheered? He did not seem to know. A little ashamed he walked. Why couldn't he have waited down there on the river, instead of rushing up into the crowd like one of these young clerks or shop fellows? He was glad nobody would know where he had been. As if it did any good for him to get excited; as if it did any good for him to do or get anything at his age.

Sixty! He was glad he hadn't got a son. Bad enough to have three nephews. Still, Val was in South Africa and his leg wasn't sound; but Winifred's second son, Benedict— what age was he—thirty? Then there was Cicely's boy— just gone up to Cambridge. All these boys! Some of them would be rushing off to get themselves killed. A bad sad business! And all because—! Exactly! Because of what?

Walking in a sort of trance he had reached the Ritz. All was fiz-gig in the streets. Waiters stood on the pavement. Ladies of the night talked together excitedly or spoke to policemen as though they had lost their profession. Soames went on down Berkeley Square through quieter streets to his sister's house. Winifred was waiting up for him, still in that half mourning for Montague Dartie, which Soames considered superfluous. As trustee, he had been compelled to learn the true history of that French staircase, if only to keep it from the rest of the world.

"They tell me war's declared, Soames. Such a relief!"

"Relief! Pretty relief!"

"You know what I mean, dear boy. One never knows what those Radicals might have done."

"This'll cost a thousand millions," said Soames, "before it's over. Over? I don't know when it'll be over—the Germans are no joke."

"But surely, Soames, with Russia and ourselves. And they say the French are so good now."

"They'd say anything," said Soames.

"But you're glad, aren't you?"

"Glad we haven't ratted, yes. But it's ruination all round. Where's your boy Benedict?"

Winifred looked up sharply.

"Oh!" she said. "But he's not even a volunteer."

"He will be," said Soames, gloomily.

"Do you really think it's as serious as that, Soames?"

"Serious as hell," answered Soames; "you mark my words."

Winifred was silent for some minutes; on her face, so fashionably composed, was a look as though someone had half drawn up its blind. She said in a small voice:

"I'm thankful dear Val has got his leg. You don't think we shall be invaded, Soames?"

"Not if they keep their heads. All depends on the fleet. They say there's a chap called Jellicoe, but you never know. There are these Zeppelins, too—I shall send Fleur down to school in the west somewhere."

"Ought one to lay in provisions?"

"If everyone does that, there'll be a shortage, and that won't do. The less fuss the better. I shall go down home by the first train. Going to bed, now. Good-night." He kissed the forehead of a face where the blind was still half-drawn down.

He slept well, and was back at Mapledurham before noon. Fleur's greeting, and the bright peace of the river, soothed him, so that he lunched with a certain appetite. On the verandah, afterwards, his head gardener came up.

"They're puttin' off the 'orticultural show this afternoon, Sir. Looks as if the Germans had bitten off more than they can chew, don't you think, Sir?"

"Can't tell," said Soames. Everybody seemed to think it was going to be a picnic, and this annoyed him.

"It's lucky Lord Kitchener's over here," said the gardener, "he'll show them."

"This may last a year and more," said Soames; "no waste of any sort, d'you understand me?"

The gardener looked surprised.

"I thought——"

"Think what you like, but don't waste anything, and grow vegetables. See?"

"Yes, Sir. So you think it's serious, Sir?"

"I do," said Soames.

"Yes, Sir." The gardener moved away; a narrow-headed chap! That was the trouble; hearts were in the right place, but heads were narrow. They said those Germans had big round heads and no backs to them. So they had, if he remembered. He went in and took up *The Times*. To read the papers seemed the only thing one could do. While he was sitting there Annette came in. She was flushed and had a ball of wool in her hand.

"Well," he said, over the top of the paper, "are you satisfied now?"

She came across to him.

"Put your paper down, Soames, and let me kiss you."

"What for?" said Soames.

Annette removed *The Times* and sank on his knees. Placing her hands on his shoulders she bent and kissed him.

"Because you have not deserted my country. I am proud of England."

"That's new," said Soames. She was a weight, and smelled of verbena; "I don't know what we can do," he added, "except at sea."

"Oh! it is everything. We have not our backs on the wall any more; we have our backs on you."

"You certainly have," said Soames; not that it was unpleasant.

Annette rose. She stood, slightly transfigured.

"We shall beat those 'orrible Germans down. Soames, we cannot keep Fräulein, she must go."

"I thought that was coming. Why? It's not her fault."

"To have a German in the house? No!"

"Why not? She's harmless. If you send her away, what'll she do?"

"What she likes, but not in this house. Who knows if she is a spy."

"Stuff and nonsense!"

"Oh! you English are so slow—you wait always till the fat is in the fire, as you say."

"I don't see any good in hysteria," muttered Soames.

"They will talk in the neighbourhood."

"Let them!"

"*Non!* I have told her she must go. After the holiday Fleur must go to school. It is no use, Soames, I am not going to keep a German. 'A la guerre comme à la guerre!' "

Soames uttered a sound of profound disapproval. There she went on her high horse! Something deeply just within him was offended, but something sagacious knew that if he opposed her, the situation would become impossible.

"Send her to me, then," he said.

"Do not be sloppee with her," said Annette, and went away.

Sloppy! The word outraged him. Sloppy! He was still brooding over it, when he became conscious that the German governess was in the room.

She was a tall young woman, with a rather high cheekboned, high-coloured face, and candid grey eyes, and she stood without speaking, her hands folded one over the other.

"This is a bad business, Fräulein."

"Yes, Mr. Forsyte; Madame says I am to go."

Soames nodded. "The French have very strong feelings. Have you made any arrangements?"

The young woman shook her head. Soames received an impression of desolation from the gesture.

"What arrangements could I make? No one will want me, I suppose. I wish I had gone back to Germany a week ago. Will they let me now?"

"Why not? This isn't a seaside place. You'd better go up and see the authorities. I'll give you a letter to say you've been quietly down here."

"Thank you, Mr. Forsyte. That is kind."

"*I* don't want you to go," said Soames. "It's all nonsense; but one can't control these things"; and, seeing two tears glistening on her cheekbones, he added hastily: "Fleur'll miss you. Have you got money?"

"Very little. I send my salary to my old parents."

There it was! Old parents, young children, invalids, and all the rest of it. The pinch! And here he was administering it! A personable young woman, too! Nothing against her except the war! "If I were you," he said slowly, "I shouldn't waste time. I'd go up before they know where they are. There'll be a lot of hysteria. Wait a minute, I'll give you money."

He went to the old walnut bureau, which he had picked up in Reading—a fine piece with a secret drawer, and a bargain at that. He didn't know what to give her—the whole thing was so uncertain. Though she stood there so quietly, he was conscious that her tears were in motion.

"Damn it!" he said, softly, "I shall give you a term's salary and fifteen pounds in cash for your journey. If they won't let you go, let me know when you come to the end of it."

The young woman raised her clasped hands.

"I don't want to take money, Mr. Forsyte."

"Nonsense," said Soames; "you'll take what I give you. It's all against my wish. You ought to be staying, in my opinion. What's it to do with women?"

He took from the secret drawer an adequate number of notes and went towards her.

"I'll send you to the station. Go up and see the authorities this very afternoon; and while you get ready I'll write that letter."

The young woman bent and kissed his hand. Such a thing had never happened to him before, and he didn't know that he ever wanted it to happen again.

"There, there!" he said, and turning back to the bureau, wrote:

"SIR,—

"The bearer of this, Fräulein Schulz, has been governess to my daughter for the last eighteen months. I can testify to her character and attainments. She has lived quietly at my house at Mapledurham all the time with the exception of one or two holidays spent, I believe, in Wales. Fräulein Schulz wishes to return to Germany, and I trust you will afford her every facility. I enclose my card, and am, Sir,

Faithfully yours,

"SOAMES FORSYTE."

He then telephoned for a car, having refused so far to have one of his own—tearing great things, always getting out of order.

When the machine arrived, he went out into the hall to wait for the young woman to come down. Fleur and a little friend had gone off to some wood or other; Annette was in the garden and would stay there, he shouldn't wonder; he didn't want the young woman to go off without a hand to shake.

First they brought down a shiny foreign trunk, then a handbag, and a little roll with an umbrella stuck through it. The young woman came last. Her eyes were red. The whole thing suddenly seemed to Soames extraordinarily barbarous. To be thrown out at a moment's notice like this because her confounded Kaiser's military cut-throats had lost their senses! It wasn't English!

"Here's the letter. You'd better stay at that hotel near Victoria until you go. Good-bye, then; I'm very sorry, but you'll be more comfortable at home while the war's on."

He shook her gloved hand, and perceiving that his own was again in danger, withdrew it hastily.

"Give Fleur a kiss for me, please, Sir."

"I will. She'll be sorry to have missed you. Well, good-bye!" He was terrified that she would begin crying again, or attempt to thank him, and he added hastily: "You'll have a nice drive." As a fact he doubted it, for in fancy he could see her oozing into her handkerchief all the way.

The luggage was in now, and so was she. The car was making the usual noises. Soames, in the doorway, lifted his hand, twiddling it towards her turned red face.

Her lips was drooping, she wore a scared expression. He gave her a wan smile, and turned back into the house. Too bad!

3

Rumours! Soames would never have believed that people could be such fools. Rumours of naval engagements, rumours of spies, rumours of Russians. Take, for instance, his meeting with the village schoolmistress outside the school.

"Have you heard the terrible news, Mr. Forsyte?"

Soames' hair stood up under his hat.

"No; what's that?"

"Oh! there's been a dreadful battle at sea. We've lost six battleships. Isn't it awful?"

Soames' fists clenched themselves in his pockets.

"Who told you that?"

"It's all over the village. Six ships—isn't it terrible?"

"What did the Germans lose?"

"Twelve!"

Soames almost jumped.

"Twelve! Then the war's over. What do you mean—terrible—why, it's the best news we could have!"

"Oh! but six of our own ships—it's awful!"

"War is awful," said Soames. "But if this is true——"
He left her abruptly and made for the Post Office. It was not true, of course. Nothing was true. Not even his own suspicions. Take, for instance, those two square-shouldered men in straw hats whom he met walking down a lane with their feet at right angles, as Englishmen never walked. Germans, and spies into the bargain, or he was a Dutchman; especially as his telephone went out of order that very afternoon. And of course they turned out to be two Americans staying at Pangbourne on a holiday, and the wire had been affected by a thunderstorm. But what were you to think, when the newspapers were full of spy stories, and the very lightning was apparently in the German secret service. As to mirrors in daylight and matches after dark, they were in obvious communication with the German fleet in the Kiel Canal, or wherever it was. Time and again Soames would say:

"Bunkum! The whole thing's weak-minded!" Only to feel himself weak-minded the next moment. Look at those two hundred thousand Russians whom everybody was seeing in trains all over the country. They turned out to be eggs, and probably addled at that; but how could you help believing in them, especially when you wanted to! And then the authorities told you nothing; dumb as oysters; as if that were the way to treat an Englishman—it only made him fancy things. And there was Mons. They couldn't even let you know about the army, except that it was heroic, and had killed a lot of Germans, and was marching backwards in order to put the finishing touch to them. That was about all one heard, till suddenly one found it was touch and go whether Paris could be saved, and the French Government had packed their traps and gone off to Bordeaux. And all the time nothing to do but read the papers, which he couldn't believe, and listen to the click of Annette's needles. And then came the news of the battle of the Marne, and he could breathe again.

He breathed freely—he had gone weeks, it seemed to him, without taking a deep breath. People were saying it was the beginning of the end, and the Allies—he himself had always called it Allie-es—and why not?—would soon be in Germany now. He wanted to believe this so much, that he said he didn't believe a word of it, much as when, the weather looking fine, he would take his umbrella to make sure. And then, forsooth, they went and dug themselves in! This beginning of warfare which was to last four years, produced but moderate premonition in his mind. There was a certain relief in the immobility of things after the plunging excitement of Mons and the Marne. He continued to read the papers, shake his head, and invest in War Loan. His nephew Benedict was training for a commission in Kitchener's army; Cicely's boy, also, had joined up, as they called it. He supposed they had to. Annette had said several times that she wanted to go to France and be a nurse. It was all her fancy. She could do much more good by knitting and being economical.

Presently he took Fleur down to her school in the West; and not much too early, for the Zeppelins became busy soon after. In regard to their exploits, he displayed a somewhat natural perversity, for though he had taken his daughter down to a remote region to avoid them, he thought people made much too much fuss about them altogether. From a top window in his Club he was privileged to see one of them burst into flames. He said nothing and was glad of it afterwards—some of his fellow-members had shown their feelings, and those not all they should be. There was provocation, no doubt; but, after all, the crew were being burned alive. Generally speaking, while the war dragged on, the reality of it was kept from him most efficiently not only by the Government, the papers, and his age, but by a sort of barrage put up by himself from within himself. There the thing was, and what was the use of making more of it than he absolutely had to? If one ever came to the end, one might indulge one's feelings, perhaps. And always the doings at sea, the adventures and misadventures of ships, impinged on him with a poignancy absent from the events on land. Of all that happened in the early part of the war, the bombardment of Scarborough affected him, perhaps, most painfully. It was like a half-arm jab above the heart. His pride was stunned. The notion that ships had dared to come so near as to throw shells into English houses and not been sunk for doing it, was peculiarly horrible to him. What would they be doing next? He had a continual longing for something definite at sea, some sign there of British superiority, as if "Rule Britannia" had got into the composition of his blood. The sinking of the *Lusitania* gave him at first much the same shock that it gave everyone else, but when he heard people abusing the Americans for not declaring war at once, he felt that they were extravagant. The Americans were a long way off—to talk about their being in danger was as good as saying that England was go-

ing to be defeated; which, curiously, considering his constitutional apprehensiveness, Soames never could believe. He
had a sort of deep feeling, indeed, that he did not want to
be rescued by America or anybody else. But these feelings
were curiously mixed up with another feeling that if England had, like America, lost a lot of English people drowned
like that, she would have gone to war like a shot, and with
his approval, into the bargain.

Early in 1915, owing to depletion of the office staff, he
had gone back into regular harness at Cuthcott Kingson
and Forsyte's. He worked there, harder than he had ever
worked. In view of national anxieties the legal issues he
was dealing with often seemed to him "petty," but he dealt
with them conscientiously; they took his mind off, and incidentally gave him more money to invest in War Loan.
After the second battle of Ypres, he had contributed an am-
bulance, and had the exquisite discomfort of seeing his name
in the papers. When in the train, going up and down, or at
lunch time in his City Club, he listened to elderly wiseacres
discussing the conduct of the war, the nature of Germans,
politicians, Americans, and other reprehensible characters,
he would look exactly as if he were going to sniff.

'What do they know about it,' he would think, 'talking
through their hats like that—it's un-English.' There was so
much in those days that was hysterical and 'un-English';
the papers encouraged it with their "intern-the-Hun" and
other "stunts," as they called it nowadays. If ever there
were a time when mouths required shutting, it was now;
and there they were, spluttering and bawling all over the
place.

In these ways, then, nearly two years passed before in
his paper that June morning he read the first official account
of the battle of Jutland. Taking the journal in his hand so

that no one else should see it till he himself had recovered,
he passed out of the drawing-room window on to the dewy
lawn, and walked blindly towards the river. There was a
sinking sensation in the pit of his stomach. Standing there
bareheaded in the sunshine and the peace of leaves and
water, with birds all round as if nothing had happened, he
tried to get hold of himself. Almost a sense of panic he
had. A real battle at last, and all those losses! Under a
poplar tree he read the account again. The sting was in the
head of it; the tail was all right! Why couldn't they have
reversed the order and begun with the fact that the Germans had run for home? What had possessed them to make
him feel so bad? It was a victory even if we *had* lost all
those ships. A blundering lot—making the worst of it lke
that! It was like being shot by your own side. Tell the
truth—yes; but not so as to give you a stomach-ache, where
there was no need for it. He went back to breakfast with
his jaw set.

"There's been a big battle at sea," he said to Annette;
"we lost a lot of ships, but the Germans cut and ran for it.
I shouldn't be surprised if they never come out again."
Thus out of instinctive perversity did he fortell the future.

The rest of the day and the day after, further reports
confirmed his resentment with the authorities for making
him suffer like that. What on earth had they been about!
They kept all sorts of things from you, and then when they
had what really amounted to good news, blurted it out as if
it were a disaster.

The death of Kitchener a few days later, though lowering to his temperature, had not the same staggering effect.
He had done a lot for the country, and looked like a lion
in a Zoo, but in the ebb and flow of world events even his
great figure seemed small.

Towards the end of 1916 he had a curious little personal experience which affected him more than he would have admitted, so that he never mentioned it. This was in the train going up to London. From patriotic motives he was at that time travelling third, but on this particular morning, the train being full, he got into a first-class compartment, occupied by a young officer in uniform with his military kit in the rack above, and a pretty young woman whose eyes were red. From behind his paper Soames felt that if they were not married, they ought to be, for they were mutually occupied with each other's eyes and hands and lips. At stations where their occupation had to cease he observed them round his nose. The pallid desperation of the young man's face and the look in the girl's reddened eyes gave him definite discomfort. Here was a case of impending separation, with all the tragic foreboding, and utter grief of wartime partings such as were taking place millionfold all over the world. It was the first Soames had seen, close up, and far more painful than he had realised. They were locked in a desperate embrace when the tran ran in to Westbourne Park. The girl was evidently to get out here, and seemed incapable of doing so. She stood swaying with the tears running down her face. The young officer wrenched the door open and almost pushed her out. Her face, looking up from the platform, was so intensely wretched that it made Soames sore. The train moved on, the young officer flung himself back into his corner with a groan. Soames looked out of the opposite window. For a whole minute even after the train had reached Paddington, he continued to gaze in at a deserted carriage alongside. At last, grasping his umbrella, he evacuated the now empty compartment and getting into a taxi, uttered the word "Poultry" in a gruff voice. He was gruff all day. All over the world it was like that—

a shocking business! And yet, by now, people seemed more concerned about their sugar and butter rations than about the war itself. Air-raids, ships being sunk, and what they could get to eat, were all people thought about—except, of course, dancing in night clubs and making up their faces. In all his life he had never seen so many made-up faces as he saw now. In coming from the office late and passing down the Strand, every woman he met seemed like the street women he used to see in his younger days. Paint and powder, with khaki alongside!

And so 1917 went by, and Fleur was getting a big girl. He had good reports of her—she was quick at lessons and games; it was some comfort. At her school down in the West, he gathered, they heard and saw very little of the war; and in the holidays he kept her at home as much as he could. There were few signs of war at Mapledurham, though of course khaki was everywhere. When conscription came in, Soames had shaken his head. He didn't know what the newspapers were about. The thing was un-English. Once it was introduced, however, he supposed it was the only thing. All the same, he never approved of the way they bullied those conscientious objectors. He had no sympathy with the fellows' consciences, of course, but the idea of harassing your fellow-countrymen at a time like this, repelled him; all his native individualism, too, remained in secret revolt against the slave-driving which had become the everyday procedure of abominable times. He had lost two gardeners in the opening year, and now they took the other two and left him with an old man and a boy, so that he often took a spud and dug up weeds himself, while Annette killed slugs with a French mixture. In the house he had never had anything but maids, so that they couldn't take the butler he hadn't got, which was some consolation. But

if he'd had a car, they'd have taken his chauffeur. He felt
he could have lost the lot with composure, if they'd gone of
their own free will, but he would not have urged their going. Some reticent, secret belief in the sanctity of private
feelings, even feelings about the country, would have prevented him. They had a right, he supposed, to their own
ideas about things. If he, himself, had been under forty,
he supposed he would have gone—though the mere notion
gave him a pain below the ribs, so crude, so brutal, and so
empty did all this military business appear to him; but he
was not prepared to tell anybody else to go. His retention
of this kind of delicacy made him lonelier than ever in the
City, in the Club, and in trains, where most people seemed
prepared to tell anybody to do anything. Soames himself
was almost ashamed of his delicacy; you couldn't carry on
a war without ordering people about. And he tried to conduct himself so that people shouldn't suspect him of this
weakness. But on one occasion it led him into a serious
tiff with his cousin George Forsyte at the "Iseeum" Club.
George, just a year younger than himself, had, it appeared,
gone in for recruiting down in Hampshire; while spending
the week-ends in town "to enjoy the air-raids," as he put it.
Soames suspected him of enjoying something else, besides.
Catching sight of George, then, one Saturday afternoon,
sitting in the bow window of the "Iseeum," Soames had
inadvertently returned his greeting and was beckoned up.

"Have a drink?" said George: "No? Some tea, then;
you can have my sugar."

His japing, heavily-lidded eyes took Soames in from top
to toe.

"You're thin as a lathe," he said: "What are you doing
—breeding for the country?"

Soames drew up the corner of his lip.

"That's not funny," he said tartly. "What are you do-ing?"

"Getting chaps killed. You'd better take to it, too. The blighters want driving, now."

"Thank you," said Soames; "not in my line."

George grinned.

"Too squeamish?"

"If you like."

"What's your general game, then?"

"Minding my own business," said Soames.

"Making the wills, eh?"

Soames put his cup down, and took his hat up. He had never disliked George more than at that moment.

"Don't get your shirt out," said George; "somebody must make the wills. You might make mine, by the way—equal shares to Roger, Eustace and Francie. Executors yourself and Eustace. Come and do an air-raid with me one night. Did you see St. John Hayman's boy was killed? They say the Huns are preparing a big push for the spring."

Soames shrugged.

"Good-bye," he said, "I'll send you a draft of your will."

"Pitch it short," said George, "and have me roasted. No bones by request."

Soames nodded, and went out.

A big push! Would they never tire of making mince-meat of the world? He had often been tempted towards the Lansdowne attitude; but some essential bulldog within him had always stirred and growled. An end that was no end—after all this, it wouldn't do! Hold on—until! For never, even at the worst moments, had he believed that England could be beaten.

In March 1918 he had been laid up at Mapledurham with a chill and was only just out again, when the big German

"push" began. It came with a suddenness that shook him
to the marrow, and induced the usual longing to get away
somewhere by himself. He went up rather slowly on to a
bit of commonland, and sat down on his overcoat among
gorse bushes. It was peaceful and smelled of spring; a lark
was singing. And out there the Germans were breaking
through! A sort of prayer went up from him while he sat
in the utter peace of the mild day. He had heard so many
times that we were ready for it; and now we weren't, it
seemed. Always the way! Too cocksure! He sat listening,
as if—as if one could hear the guns all that way off. The
man down at the lock was reported to have heard them once.
All me eye! You couldn't! Couldn't you? Wasn't that
——? Nonsense! He lay back and put his ear to the
ground, but only the whisper of a very gentle wind came to
him, and the hum of a wild bee wending to some blossom
of the gorse. A better sound than that of guns. And then
the first chime of the village church bell tingled his ears.
There they would soon be sitting and kneeling and thinking about the break-through, and the parson would offer up
a special prayer for the destruction of Germans—he
shouldn't wonder. Well, it was destroy or be destroyed—it
all came back to that. Funny thing, life—living on life,
or rather on death! According to the latest information, all
matter was alive, and every shape lived on some other shape,
or at least on the elements of shape. The earth was nothing
but disintegrated shape, out of which came more shapes and
you ate them, and then you disintegrated and gave rise to
shapes, and somebody ate them, and so it went on. In spite
of the break-through, he could not help being glad to be
alive after a fortnight cooped up in the house. His sense of
smell, too, so long confined to eau-de-Cologne, was very
keen this morning; he could smell the gorse—a scent more

delicate than most, 'the scent of gorse far-blown from distant hill,' he'd read somewhere. And to think that out there his countrymen were struggling and dying and being blown to smithereens—young fellows, from his office, from his garden, from every English office and garden, to save England—to save the world, they said—but that was flim-flam! And, perhaps, after all these horrible four years they wouldn't save England! Drawing his thin legs under him, he sat staring down towards the river where his home lay. Yes, they would save her, if it meant putting another ten years on to the conscription age, or taking the age limit off altogether. England under a foreigner? Not for Joe! He scrabbled with his hand, brought up a fistful of earth, and mechanically put it to his nose. It smelled exactly as it should smell—of earth, and gave him ever so queer and special a sensation. English earth! H'm! Earth was earth, whether in England or in Timbuctoo! Funny to give your life for what smelled exactly like his mushroom house. You put a name to a thing and you died for it! There was a lark singing—very English bird, cheery and absent-minded, singing away without knowing a thing about anything and caring less, he supposed. The bell had ceased to toll for service. If people thought God was particularly interested in England, they were mistaken. He wouldn't do a thing about it! People had to do things for themselves, and if they didn't, that was the end. Take those submarines. Leave them to God and see what happened—one would be eating one's fantails before one could say Jack Robinson!

The mild air and a slant of March sunlight gently warmed his cheek pale from too much contact with a pillow. And—out there! If ever this thing ended, he would come up here again and see what it was like without an ache under his fifth rib. A nice spot—open and high. And now he would have to get back to the house and they would give him chicken broth, and he would have to listen to Annette saying that the English never saw an inch before their noses —which as a matter of fact they didn't—and tell her that they did. A weary business when you felt as he felt about this news. He rose. Twelve o'clock! They'd have finished praying now and got to the sermon. He pitied that parson —preaching about the Philistines, he shouldn't wonder! There were the jawbones of asses about, plenty, but not a Samson among the lot of them. The gorse—it was early— looked pretty blooming round him—when the gorse was out of bloom, kissing was out of fashion. He wondered idly what had to go out of bloom before killing was out of fashion. There was a hawk! He stood and watched it hover and swoop sideways, and the red glint of it, till again it rested hovering on the air; then slowly in the pale sunlight he wended his way down towards the river.

4

July came. The "break-through" had long been checked, the fronts repaired, the Americans had come over in great numbers, Foch was in supreme command. Soames didn't know—perhaps it was necessary, but Annette's undisguised relief was unpleasant to him, and so far as he could see, things were going on as interminably as before. It was to Winifred that he spoke the words which definitely changed the fortunes of the world.

"We shall never win," he said, "I despair of it. The men are all right, but leaders! There isn't one among the lot—I despair of it." No one had ever heard him talk like that before, or use such a final word. The morning papers on the following day were buoyant with the news that the German offensive against the French had been stopped and that the French and Americans had broken through. From that day on the Allie-es, as Soames still called them, never looked back.

Those interested in such questions will pause, perhaps to consider whether Soames—like so many other people— really won the war, or whether it was that in him some hidden sensibility received in advance of the newspapers the impact of events and put up the instantaneous contradiction natural from one so individualistic. Whichever is true, the relief he felt at having his dictum contradicted was extraordinary. For the first time in three years he spent the following Sunday afternoon in his picture gallery. The French were advancing, the English were waiting to advance; the Americans were doing well; the air-raids had ceased; the submarines were beaten. And it all seemed to have happened in two days. While he stood looking at his Goya and turning over photographs of pictures in the Prado, a notion came to him. In that painting of Goya's called "La Vendimia," the girl with the basket on her head reminded him of Fleur. There was really quite a resemblance. If the war ever stopped, he would commission an artist to make him a copy of that Goya girl—the colouring, if he remembered rightly, was very agreeable. It would remind him of pleasant things—his daughter and his visit to the Prado before he bought Lord Burlingford's 'Goya' in 1910. A notion so utterly unconnected with the war had not occurred to him for years—it was almost like a blessing, with its suggestion of life apart from battle and murder, and once more connected with Dumetrius. And ringing the bell, he ordered a jug of claret cup. He drank very little of it, but it gave him a feeling that was almost Victorian.

What had that fellow Jolyon, and Irene, done with themselves all these war years? Had they sweated in their shoes and lost weight as he had done—he hoped so! Their boy, if he remembered, would be of military age next year; for the thousandth time he was glad that Fleur had disappointed him and been a girl. That day was, on the whole, the happiest he had spent since he bought his James Maris in July 1914 . . .

He began now to put on weight slowly, for though the battles went on, anxious and bloody, the movement was always in the right direction, of which he had despaired just in time. The enemy was caving-in; the Bulgarians, the Turks, soon the Austrians would go—they said. And all the time the Americans were swarming over. Soames met their officers in London on his way to and from the City. They wore khaki with high collars and sometimes pince-nez—they must feel very uncomfortable; but they seemed in good spirits and had everything money could buy—which was the great thing. He often thought what he would do when the end came. Some men would get drunk, he supposed; others would lose their heads and probably their hats; but so far as he could see, there didn't seem to be any adequate way of expressing what he himself would feel. He thought of Brighton, and of fishing in a punt; he thought of taking train down to Fleur's school and taking train back; he thought of standing in a crowd opposite Downing Street, as he had stood when the thing began. Nothing seemed satisfactory. Then the Austrians gave up. Somehow he had never thought that he had actually been at war with the Austrians—they were an amiable lot, with too many archdukes. And now that they were down and out, and the archdukes done with, he felt quite sorry for them. People were saying it had become a question of days.

Soames didn't know. The Germans always seemed to have something up their sleeves. They had been marvellous fighters—no good saying they hadn't—in fact, they had fought too well altogether. He shouldn't be surprised if they tried to destroy London at the last minute. And with unconscious perversity he took up his quarters with Winifred in Green Street. On the ninth of November he had his sixty-fourth birthday there—fortunately no one remembered it; he never could bear receiving presents and being wished many happy returns, such nonsense! Everybody was sure now that it was all over bar the shouting. Soames, however, said: "You mark my words—they'll try a big airraid before they finish." Terms for an Armistice were being prepared; it was rumoured that they would be signed at any moment. Soames shook his head. He was sufficiently in two minds, however, not to go to the City on November 11th, and was seated in the dining-room at Green Street, when there came the sound of maroons which always preluded an air-raid. What had he told them? It would be a quarter-of-an-hour or more before the raid began. He would put his nose out, and see what they were up to. The street was empty but for an old woman—charlady she seemed to be—standing with a duster in her hand on the doorstep of the next house. Soames was struck by her face. It wore a smile such as a poet might have called ecstatic. She waved her duster at him, and then—most peculiar— began to wipe her eyes with it. Sound rolled into the street from Park Lane—cheering, gusts of it, waves of cheering. Soames saw other people rushing out of houses. One of them threw his hat down and danced on it. It couldn't be an air-raid then—no man would do that for an air-raid. Why? Why—of course—it was the Armistice. *At last!* And very quietly, trembling all over, Soames muttered:

"Thank God!" For a moment he was tempted to hurry down towards Park Lane whence the sound of cheering came. Then, suddenly, the idea seemed to him vulgar. He walked back into the house and slammed the door. Going into the dining-room, he sat down in an armchair which had its back to everything. He sat there without movement except that he breathed as if he had been running. His lips kept quivering. It was queer. And then—he never admitted it to a soul—tears ran out of his eyes and rolled on to his stiff collar. He would not have believed them possible and he let them roll. The long, long Thing—it was over. All over! Then suddenly, feeling that if he didn't take care he would have to change his collar, he took out his pocket handkerchief. This confession of his emotion acted like a charm. The moisture ceased, and removing all trace of it, he leaned back with eyes closed. For some time he stayed like that, as if at the end of a long day's work. The clamour of bells and rejoicing penetrated the closed room, but Soames sat with his head sunk on his chest, still quivering all over. It was as if age-long repression of his feelings were taking revenge in this long, relaxed, quivering immobility. Out there, they would be dancing and shouting; laughing and drinking; praying and weeping. And Soames sat and quivered.

He got up at last and going to the sideboard, helped himself to a glass of his dead father's old brown sherry. Then taking his overcoat and umbrella, he went out—he didn't know why, or whither on earth.

He walked through quiet streets towards Piccadilly. When he passed people they smiled at him, and he didn't like it—having to smile back. Some seemed to toss remarks at the air as they passed—talking to themselves, or to God, or what not. Every now and then somebody ran. He

reached Piccadilly, and didn't like it either—full of lorries
and omnibuses crowded with people all cheering and behaving like fools. He crossed it, as quickly as possible, and
went down through the Green Park, past the crowds in
front of Buckingham Palace. He walked on to the Abbey
and the Houses of Parliament—crowds there—crowds
everywhere! He skirted them and kept on along the Embankment—he didn't know why and he didn't know where.
From Blackfriars he moved up Citywards and reached
Ludgate Hill. And suddenly he knew where he was going
—St. Paul's! There stood the dome, curved massive against
the grey November sky, huge above the stir of flags and
traffic, silent in the din of cheering and of bells. He walked
up the steps and went in. He hadn't been since the war
began, and his visit now had no connection with God. He
went because it was big and old and empty, and English,
and because it reminded him. He walked up the aisle and
stood looking at the roof of the dome. Christopher Wren!
Good old English name! Good old quiet English stones
and bones; No more sudden death, no more bombs, no
more drowning ships, no more poor young devils taken
from home and killed! Peace! He stood with his hands
folded on the handle of his umbrella and his left knee
flexed as if standing at ease; on his restrained pale face upturned was a look wistful and sardonic. Rivers of blood
and tears! Why? A gleam of colour caught his eye.
Flags! They couldn't do without them even here! The
Flag! Terrible thing—sublime and terrible—the Flag!

THE END

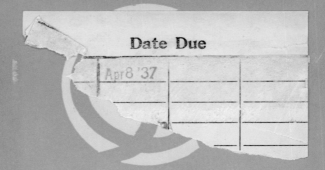

Date Due